COMMUNION:

A COLLECTION OF
MODERN IRISH STORIES

JACK SCOLTOCK

BARKING RAIN PRESS

This is a work of fiction. Names, characters, places and events described herein are products of the author's imagination or are used fictitiously. Any resemblance to actual events, locations, organizations, or persons, living or dead, is entirely coincidental.

First Communion: A Collection of Modern Irish Stories

Edited by Sheri Gormley (www.sherigormley.com)

Cover artwork by Justine Scoltock

Barking Rain Press
PO Box 822674
Vancouver, WA 98682 USA

www.BarkingRainPress.org

ISBN print: 1-935460-32-3
ISBN eBook: 1-935460-33-1

Library of Congress Control Number: 2011960938

First Edition: December 2011

Printed in the United States of America

9 7 8 1 9 3 5 4 6 0 3 2 9

DEDICATION

For Ursula, with love.

Thanks to my beautiful sister, Marie for her photograph, and thanks to my beautiful daughter, Justine, for the cover. Thanks to Sheri Gormley and the Barking Rain Press team for having faith in me.

ALSO AVAILABLE FROM JACK SCOLTOCK

The Sand Clocker

The Meltin' Pot: From Wreck to Rescue and Recovery

COMING SOON FROM JACK SCOLTOCK

The Golden Weddin' and the B.V.M.

Challenge of the Red Unicorn

WWW.JACKSCOLTOCK.COM

CONTENTS

1

WHO KILLED BAMBI?

Sean listened at the sitting room door. His heart was pounding against his chest like a lambeg drum as he eavesdropped on his parents.

"The big wan's on Wednesday night, a two hundred pounder, outside Hill's shop..."

"Shh, Kevin," hissed Sean's mother, interrupting her husband. Rising from the settee, she slipped to the door, but her son was already halfway up the stairs.

In the bedroom, Sean lay back on his bed. A Spiderman comic lay crumpled beneath his narrow shoulders. Worried, he thought again about his father and the bombings that had been happening recently. He knew his father was involved. *What odds about a United Ireland?* All he knew was his own area, Gobnascale and the Waterside. He sighed again. What if his father were caught and sent to the Kesh—jailed for his part in the bombings?

Rising from bed, he pulled back the curtains and gazed out at the moonlit hills behind the large housing estate. High above, he could just about make out the eerie shapes of cows and sheep. Suddenly a dog barked and he heard the back gate slam. His father had gone out.

"O'Hara! Are you daydreaming again, boy?"

Sean gave a start. He had been dozing and was awakened by the burly teacher's angry bellow.

Mr. McLaughlin strode quickly between the row of desks towards him. Now glaring down at Sean, he reached to place a podgy thumb and forefinger on each side of the unfortunate boy's left ear and hauled him to his feet. Yelping like a dog and on tiptoes Sean was marched to the front of the classroom.

"Now stand in that corner and pay attention, O'Hara," snapped the teacher.

Sean stared at the walls feeling both embarrassed and annoyed. He knew his pals would slag him off on the way home, but that wasn't what bothered him. Last night when he had eventually fallen asleep, he had been shocked awake by a loud explosion that had shaken the house. Twenty minutes later, he heard his father come in the back door. After that, he lay awake almost the whole night worrying.

After school, he walked home with his pals—Mickey Simpson, his next-door neighbor, was a small, ginger-haired boy whose face was covered in freckles, and Jim Moran, a stout, pimple-faced boy who was already picking his seemingly forever-filled nose.

"Pick! Pick!" yelled Sean, suddenly shoving Jim's elbow and causing Jim's forefinger to almost disappear up his broad left nostril.

"Ah, damn ye, Sean!" cried Jim. "Ye might have wrecked me nose!" He swung his schoolbag at Sean, who dodged nimbly out of the way laughing. This annoyed Jim and he began to tease Sean. "Daydreamin' again, O'Hara!" he shouted, mimicking the teacher's voice.

Feigning anger, Sean began to chase him up the road, and shortly they reached the corner of the street where Jim lived.

"Are ye really goin' lampin' the night?" Sean asked Mickey.

"Aye."

"What if the Brits see ye?"

"Ach, sure Jim and me will be over at the Whinnies. Nobody ever goes there at this time of the year."

The Whinnies, as they were known locally, were so named because of the maze of narrow paths bordered by the thick whin bushes that grew in abundance in a wide area at the foot of Corrody Hill.

"Why don't ye come with us?" asked Jim.

"Naw. Me da says I'm to stay in at night now fer a while. All the bombin's, ye know," said Sean with a shrug.

"Aye," said Mickey. "There's been a wile lot of bombin's recently. That wan last night scared the shit out of me."

"Me too," said Sean. He knew he could have slipped out this particular night and gone lamping with his pals, for he knew his father would be out late. The reason he did not want to go was he could not bear to see the small rabbits lured out of their warrens by the bright flashing lights, then beaten to death. He had been horrified by the cruelty of his pals the first and only time he had accompanied them in their savage sport, but he had said nothing at the time. Now he made up excuses not to go with them.

That evening he put down his comic then slipped out of bed to switch off the light. The bright digits of his bedside clock told him it was 10:14. Drawing back his curtains, he peered out. The moon was shining brightly above the hills, but he scanned the area until he saw two bobbing lights away up on the Whinnies. *It must be Mickey and Jim.* He watched until the lights disappeared, then got back into bed.

He fidgeted there and turned, too restless to get to sleep. After about ten minutes, he got out of bed again and went to the window. The lights were back again, bobbing about in the darkness like the terrifying eyes of some indescribable night creature. In a moment, Sean made up his mind. Quickly he dressed and slipped out onto the landing to listen outside his parent's bedroom door. Seconds later, he was slipping downstairs and out the back door.

Within minutes, he was coming up the field and scrambling up the high ditch that bordered the Whinnies. As he headed through the paths, he giggled to himself as he thought about how he would scare his pals. Maybe he could frighten them enough that they wouldn't go lampin' again.

He could see a light ahead, but as he drew nearer he heard voices—not the voices of his pals, but coarse men's voices. With a shock he recognized that one of the voices was his father's. *What's me da doin' up here? Not lampin'!* Bending low now he almost crawled to the bend in the path and squinted into the dim light to see what his father and the man with him were doing.

"There, that's the lot hidden," he heard his father say.

The other man (whose voice Sean couldn't recognize) replied, "We might need them after the big bomb on Wednesday, Kevin."

"Aye, maybe Johnny. Come on, let's head down. I have a meetin' the night to finalize plans fer Wednesday."

Relieved, Sean saw them move off but instead of heading off in the other direction, he grew curious. Looking left and right, he slipped over to where his father and his companion had been bending. Sean studied the ground. Searching around, he found a piece of broken whin branch, began to scratch hard at the ground, and soon he had exposed a piece of thick cloth. Bending, he pulled hard on it and fell back; he righted himself and looked down into the shallow hole. He was shocked by what he had unearthed; guns, bullets and what looked like bombs, along with some long rifles wrapped in oily black cloth below these.

With sweat glistening like diamonds in the moonlight on his pale brow and with his heart pounding so hard Sean thought it would burst, he looked around to make sure no one was about. *Guns and rifles? What does me da want with guns?* He glanced about again then quickly began to bury the cache, doing his best to leave the weapons as he had found them.

When he was satisfied that the ground was the way he had found it, he straightened, but his whole body was covered in sweat. Then he remembered how late it was and as he headed back the way he had come, he brushed himself down. With his thoughts still on the guns and what his father was doing with them, Sean was halfway up the ditch when he heard a strange sound. It was a high-pitched barking noise coming from close by, and the bushes shaking had him crouching lower.

Me da must still be around! Keeping still, he tried to listen above the sound of his pounding heart and this time, a soft cry and more movement of the bushes along the ditch caused him to scramble on up. At the top of the ditch, careful to avoid the sharp whins, he peered into the semi-darkness and in the shadows to his left he could see that it was not his father. It was some kind of huge animal, and the ghostly whiteness of its body as it moved violently and shook the bushes some more had Sean holding his breath.

Cautiously he stretched to see the animal more clearly. *It could be a Badger. Badgers are dangerous.* Now he began to crawl along the top of the ditch with his breath coming in quick silent gasps from fear and excitement and before he knew it, he was sliding back down the ditch. He landed almost beside the creature.

"A deer!" he exclaimed, startling the frightened beast that was trapped by sharp barbed wire wrapped tightly around one of its hind legs. Sean could see that the animal's leg was bleeding, and its large, glistening eyes blinked as it studied him. Suddenly its body heaved as it struggled more fiercely, but this only succeeded in making it bark louder with pain.

Unafraid now, Sean moved right up to the deer. "Easy, boy, easy now," he whispered reaching out his hand to stroke its fearsome antlers. As he did, the deer pulled its head back and butted at Sean's hand, but he was just quick enough to pull it away.

"Whew," he exclaimed. "'I'd better be more careful."

Trying again to rise to its feet the deer struggled, all the time barking with pain, but it could not get free.

"Easy boy!" shouted Sean. "Easy now!"

His shouting startled the deer and it stopped and watched Sean as he slipped around behind to its trapped leg. Suddenly it butted at Sean again, but it was trapped in such a way it could not reach him. Sean could see the barbs of the wire were tearing into its flesh every time the deer moved.

"I'll have tay go home and get me da's wire cutters," he muttered as he stood up, then without a word he was climbing the ditch and racing home. Ten minutes later, he was on his way back with the wire-cutters clutched tightly in his hand.

The deer stared at him as he bent to the barbed wire, but it began to struggle again. "Easy boy," whispered Sean. Immediately the deer stopped struggling and seemed to understand that Sean was trying to help it. Soon Sean's tiny hands had manipulated the wire cutters between the deer's leg and the barbed wire and seconds later the wire was nipped. Sensing its release, the deer struggled to its feet and attempted to run away, but instead it fell back on its injured leg with a painful bark.

"Stop it!" shouted Sean. "Stop it now!"

Startled, the deer froze. Once more Sean bent to examine its leg again. He could see the wound was beginning to bleed and quietly he coaxed the animal to be still. He squinted to try to get a better look at its injury, but all the time he was examining it, he was aware of the deer's large brown eyes studying him.

"Right," he said after a while. "We'll have tay get those cuts washed and see if we can get them to heal."

Taking his handkerchief out of his pocket, Sean then began to search along the narrow path until he found a small mossy puddle and there he soaked his handkerchief in it. Returning to the deer, he squeezed the cold dirty water over its injuries and slowly and gently began to clean away the blood. Sean returned to the puddle several times until he was satisfied that the wounds were clean, and then he bandaged the deepest laceration with his handkerchief. When he was finished he stood up and smiled down at the creature, whispering, "There now, boy. That's okay, isn't it, eh?"

The deer barked as if to say it was, and Sean lay down beside it. The bright moon shone on their innocence; the deer with its legs bent as it lay sideways, with its antlers held erect on its noble head, and the little boy who had somehow managed to fall asleep.

Sean's small head rose and fell as the animal breathed deeply, and it was almost bright morning when Sean woke with a start. He looked around, shivering he stared at the deer. "Jeepers deer, I'd better get home. Me da will be home by now. I'll have to slip in real easy in case I wake him." He looked up the path. "But first I must get ye hidden until yer well again."

Away up near the top of the bordering ditch, Sean knew there was a hollow where the whin bushes overhung to make a shelter. He had often gone there in the summer with his pals, and once it had started to rain and they had been perfectly dry in the overhang. *I'll take it there,* Sean thought, knowing the deer would be warm and safe in the overhang.

He also knew he had to keep the deer's existence a secret. *If Mickey or Jim knew about it, they might harm it.*

He studied the deer, feeling sorry for it, knowing it would be a painful walk to the overhang. "Come on, boy. We have tay get ye on tay yer feet. Come on. We must get up tay the top of the Whinnies." Sean grabbed the deer's antlers and began to pull, but the creature wouldn't move and gave a couple of quick snorts.

Sean tried harder. "Get up," he grunted. Still the deer didn't move. Sean studied it for a few seconds then he moved to the animal's behind and tried to shove it onto its feet. The deer stared at him with unblinking eyes, almost as if to say, "What do you want *me* to do?"

"Oh come on, boy," exclaimed Sean. "Get on yer feet." He was beginning to panic now. The sun had been up for over an hour and he knew he would have to get home before breakfast or his parents would have to know about the deer. *Me da might guess I saw him hide the guns, too.*

His panic gave him strength and with one great heave, he had the deer up on its feet and stepping back, Sean looked up at it. The animal towered above him its wide, pointed antlers looking even more fearsome. It studied Sean and seemed to be wondering what he wanted it to do. It waited. Sean was almost exhausted, but he knew he could not rest. He was afraid the deer would sit down again so he grabbed the thick hair on the deer's chest and tugged hard saying, "Right now, boy. Come on! Come on!"

Barking softly with pain, the limping deer allowed Sean to lead it up the path, and they arrived at the overhang twenty minutes later. There were a few beer cans, some cardboard boxes, paper, a bottle and other rubbish inside so Sean quickly cleared out the back of the overhang then began to pull the deer inside. Making sure there was no glass lying on the dry ground he pulled the deer right to the back. Moaning with pain, it stared at him and then suddenly collapsed onto its side with an exhausted bark and lay there breathing heavily.

Sean examined his makeshift bandage again and made sure it was secure. "Now tay get ye covered in," he muttered. Making sure not to prick himself, he broke off some thin whin branches and built them up in front of the overhang until it was well camouflaged. "There now boy," he said smiling. "Ye'll be safe there until I can get up tay see ye after school. I'll bring ye some food and water." He looked back as he headed down the path checking again that all was well and then he was running for the ditch.

When he came to the back door, Sean checked before going inside. His parents weren't up yet. Quickly he brushed himself down and then quietly slipped upstairs, where he changed into his pajamas and eased into bed. It seemed to the excited boy a long time before his mother was calling him for breakfast.

Mickey was waiting for him at the end of the street and as they walked to school Sean asked, "Did yees go lampin' last night?"

"Naw, sure it looked like it was goin' tay pish earlier on and Jim didn't want to go if it was raining. We might head up the night, though."

Sean stopped. "Are yees goin' up tay the top?"

"Naw, sure ye know the rabbits stay near the big holes at the bottom," said Mickey.

"I forgot," said Sean, breathing a quiet sigh of relief.

After school, they walked home together but Sean was quiet, for he was thinking about the deer. He couldn't wait to get up to see it.

"Sean, are ye goin' down tay the Community Hall the night?" asked Mickey.

"Naw, I think I'll stay in the night," said Sean. "Me da says I have tay do some studyin', ye know?" He felt a twinge of conscience about telling the lie, but he had to think about the deer. He had to get up to it.

Later in the kitchen, he hurried through his homework and waited impatiently for his tea. As they were eating, he asked, "Da, what do deers eat?"

"Deers? I'm not sure, son. I think they eat leaves of trees, probably grass too. Stuff like that. Why? Were ye learnin' about deers at school the day?"

"Naw, I was just wonderin', that's all."

When his parents were in the sitting room watching television later that evening, Sean searched the kitchen for a plastic bag and then filled an empty milk bottle with water. Outside in the lower fields, he began to fill the bag with grass.

It was raining as he hurried up to the Whinnies, and as he approached the overhang, he was dismayed to see that some of the bushes had been pushed away from the entrance. *Oh no, it's gone!* But when he came closer and peered into the overhang, he saw the deer was still there and greeted it with a smile. "Hello, big boy! Hello. Here we are."

As he reached out the plastic bag of grass, he startled the deer and it butted at the bag, knocking it from his hand. "Ah, now don't be silly. There's no need tay be afraid. It's only grass. Here look, and I've brought ye water as well."

Barking softly, the deer watched Sean spread the grass on the ground in front of it. Then holding the bottle, he poured some of the cold water onto the deer's nose. With a surprised snort, it pulled its head away, but soon it was licking greedily at the water, its long, pink tongue flicking in and out of its mouth.

After the deer had eaten some grass and the bottle was almost empty, Sean knelt and undid the handkerchief around its leg to examine the deer's injuries. The lacerations looked clean and any blood that remained had congealed around them. Sean poured some of the remaining water in the bottle onto the handkerchief and washed and cleaned the deer's injuries again. Then he stood up and said, "I'll have tay get a blanket tay cover ye up with. I'll bring it the night. Maybe if ye were warmer ye'd heal quicker." He reached over to stroke the beautiful creature's neck. With its head held back from him, the deer stared into Sean's tiny face and then began licking at his hand. Laughing, Sean pulled away.

"That's tickly. Ha, ha, ha, don't..."

The deer snorted, obviously enjoying the small boy's reaction. After a while, Sean pulled some more bushes around the entrance to the overhang and lay beside the deer, his head resting on its warm body. "Ye know ye'll have tay exercise yer legs soon or they'll stiffen up and ye'll not be able tay walk properly tay get home again. Where did ye come from, I wonder? I suppose yer a bit homesick, eh?" Playfully he grabbed at the deer's antlers.

"Where were ye? Luk at the state of yer clothes! Get up tay the bathroom and get yerself cleaned up. Here. Leave them mucky shoes where they are!" screamed Sean's mother, "Where were ye?"

"I was out with Mickey and Jim, Ma. I'm sorry..."

"Aye, well get up tay the bathroom now. Put on yer pajamas. I'll make yer supper and yer straight fer bed."

The gate slammed at 12:22 when his father went out, and it woke Sean up with a start. Suddenly, he could hear dogs barking in the distance. *Dogs*, he thought sitting up. *What if they have my deer trapped? Oh God they'll kill*

him. Trembling, he quickly pulled on his dressing gown and slippers and two minutes later, he was running up the fields.

When he came to the overhang, he saw everything was all right. There were no dogs about. He listened and far away to his right he could hear the dogs still barking. "I thought the dogs had ye," he said as he pushed into the back. The deer licked Sean's face and he laughed. Sitting down beside it, he talked quietly to the deer, relieved that it was safe. The rain was growing heavier, however, and Sean realized he would have to stay until it was over. He shivered, his light clothing feeling cold against his skinny frame and so he snuggled closer to the deer for heat. "Ye seem tay be always warm, don't ye boy, eh? It's a good job, too. I think me ma would have missed a blanket if I'd taken wan."

The deer looked sideways at him, gave a heavy sigh, and licked its heart shaped lips, easing slightly back as it felt Sean's weight push against its white body. They both lay listening to the heavy rain tear into the whins above them. When Sean eventually got back to his bedroom, he saw that it was 5:31. *Me da must be back by now,* he thought. Hanging his slightly damp dressing gown on the radiator, he went to bed.

6∂9

"O'Hara!"

"Eh?" Sean gave a start at the sound of McLaughlin's voice.

"O'Hara come up here at once!"

"Yes sir."

The teacher glared at him, his ruddy face growing redder with anger. "O'Hara, this is the last straw. I want you to stay after school and I'll speak with you then. Now stand in that corner until dinnertime. I'm fed up with you, boy. I'm fed up with you and your daydreaming in class."

After school, the teacher called Sean to him. "Aren't you getting enough sleep O'Hara? Tell me why are you sleeping in class?"

"I don't know sir, honest. I..."

The teacher sighed. "Look O'Hara, I will be very lenient with you this time, but if I ever have to talk to you about sleeping in class again, then I'm afraid I will have to inform your parents. Now I want you to write out one hundred times, 'I will not sleep in class.' Have you got that?"

"I will not sleep in class. Yes sir. Thank ye, sir," Sean said quietly.

"Very well then, off you go—and O'Hara, heed my warning."

Outside Mickey and Jim were waiting for him.

"What did he say, Sean?" asked Jim.

"Ah nothin'. He gave me a hundred lines tay do. I'll soon scoot through them," said Sean as he walked on. His pals raised their eyebrows to each other then hurried after him.

"Sean," asked Jim. "Are ye goin' down tay the Community Hall the night? There's a man comin' tay show us how tay make knots and stuff."

"Naw. Sure I have me lines tay do."

That evening when Sean reached the overhang, he saw the deer was standing up. While it ate, he examined its leg. *It's healin' fast and it seems much stronger, too.* The deer barked with pleasure as Sean rubbed its neck.

"I'll have tay take ye out of here and exercise ye fer a while. Just fer a wee while ye understand." Sean pulled back the bushes from all around the entrance to give the deer a good clearance to get out. Then he tugged it to force it onto the path. The deer barked loudly once, but limping slightly it allowed Sean to lead it out of the overhang. "That's it, boy, yer doin' well. Good boy. Good boy."

After about a half hour of walking the deer up and down the path, Sean led it back to the overhang. "I'll have tay go now deer, but I'll see ye the morra. Okay?"

That night he dreamt of the deer. It was jumping over high ditches, and he was riding on its back, holding onto its antlers. A loud explosion followed by breaking glass and people shouting woke him. It was 3:10, and his scream brought his mother into the room. Her worried face told him who had caused the explosion. "Go tay sleep, Sean, she whispered. "It's only a bomb away down near the bridge. Go back tay sleep, yer safe here. Go tay sleep. That's a good boy."

That evening he caught a glimpse of the news from the sitting room door. Scenes of the wrecked Spencer Road were shown. Houses and shops were completely wrecked, including Hill's store, which had taken the full blast of the bomb. Nobody had been injured as the I.R.A. had phoned in a warning to the Police Station in Spencer Road. Hundreds of thousands of pounds of damage had been caused, however, and now a reporter was speaking to two old women, sisters whose house in the road had been destroyed.

"Everything's gone," one of the women was saying, her eyes full of tears as she pulled her coat tightly around her. "All our precious photographs and my father's pictures, all gone. And we... we can't even find Darkie..." She turned to her sister and began to cry on her shoulder.

Sean frowned when he heard the other woman say, "Darkie's our cat," her hairy chin quivering as she held back her tears. "He's lived with us fer sixteen years and we can't find him." She looked around and scenes of the devastated building were shown as she added, "Darkie will hardly be alive among all this."

Sean turned away from the television when he heard his father snort, "Christ a cat. Is that all they have to say about the bombin'. They only put... What?" Angry he turned to his wife, irritated by her tugging on his arm. She nodded to Sean.

"Have you nothin' better tay do!" Sean's father shouted. Sean stared at him for a few seconds and then hurried upstairs to his room.

Later that night, he got ready to go out again. He had been thinking about the deer. He didn't want it to go, but he knew it had to. That evening he made up his mind to stay all night with it in case it took off before he could see it go. He carried a light blanket with him, but when he came to the overhang, he saw whin branches strewn all along the path. His deer was gone.

Nearly crying, he went to the back of the overhang and sat down. It was cold and he pulled his blanket around his shoulders. Tears ran down his pale face as he muttered, "It might have waited tay see me one more time before goin'."

He awoke to feel the deer's wet tongue on his face.

"Yer back!" He exclaimed tossing the blanket aside. "Ye've come back and I thought ye'd gone away without sayin' goodbye tay me. I might have known ye wouldn't. Yer better now, aren't ye? Aye, ye are! This will be our last night together, so I'm goin' tay stay all night with ye! That's good, isn't it boy? Eh."

He smiled as he rubbed at the deer's neck. It lay down on the ground and Sean snuggled into it, pulling the blanket around himself and the deer's legs. "Ye'll wait until the morning and then ye can go back tay where ye came from. No one will be about in the mornin'. If people see ye they'll catch ye and put ye in a zoo or somethin'. Ye wouldn't like that, would ye boy, eh?"

Sean thought about his deer in a zoo. *At least then I'd be able tay see it any time.* "Naw, deers like tay be free," he muttered, and gradually, as he began to get warmer, he drifted off. As morning approached, the restless deer woke Sean by licking his face. Shivering, Sean rose, stretched his arms above his head and yawned. "It's time, isn't it boy, eh? Come on then."

Followed by the barking, excited deer, Sean moved out onto the path. "Well, boy yer free tay go now," Sean whispered sadly. "Ye can't stay here any longer. Go quickly before the people see ye. Go on. Go. Go!"

The morning mist still clung to the dewy grass growing along the edge of the path and as the deer pushed past Sean, its nostrils flared. In tears, Sean reached to pat its back whispering hoarsely, "Goodbye…"

The majestic deer stepped away from him, and studying its tiny savior again, its huge bright eyes glistened. Then it gave a long loud bark and began stamping its feet. Suddenly it was running swiftly down the path and with a mighty leap, it rose into the air, clearing the ditch by a good half meter. The morning sun caught the graceful creature in mid-air for a long moment before it vanished. Sean scrambled up the ditch with a cry and was just in time to see the deer bounding across the field. At the far side of the field, it jumped the low hedge and was soon out of sight.

"Goodbye deer!" he cried sadly, then he headed down home.

That day at school, he tried hard to concentrate on his lessons but it was no use. He felt tired and depressed.

"O'Hara!"

"Yes, sir?"

"You haven't left up your homework."

Sean felt the hair crepe along the back of his neck. "Ho… homework?"

"Yes, O'Hara, homework," exclaimed the exasperated teacher. "Are you telling me you haven't done your homework?" With a huge sigh, the teacher rose to his feet and addressed the rest of the boys. "Boys did I, or did I not, set out extra work for you to do on, 'The Battle of the Boyne'?"

"Yes sir," chorused the boys, some of them looking at Sean.

Sweat broke out on Sean's brow and he could feel the stickiness of it on the palms of his clenched hands.

Shaking his head the teacher said, "You haven't done your homework have you, O'Hara?"

"No sir," whispered Sean.

"Pardon, I didn't hear what you said."

"No sir," repeated Sean.

With a sigh the teacher said, "O'Hara, I want you to stay on after class this afternoon. This carry-on has to stop. Now sit there and pay attention to the rest of the lessons."

That afternoon when the rest of the boys had gone home, McLaughlin beckoned Sean to his desk. "You didn't hear me set the extra work did you, O'Hara?"

Sean's face grew red and he lowered his eyes under the teacher's piercing glare. "No sir, I didn't."

"Look boy, I gave you a chance to stop daydreaming in class. You have ignored my warning. Now sit down and write out two hundred times, 'I will be attentive in class,' and O'Hara, I want you to take a note to your father. I will tell him about your behavior. Now get on with your punishment."

Sighing heavily, Sean returned to his desk.

A few seconds later. "Sir."

"Yes?"

"Could ye spell, attentive?"

"Attentive. A-T-T-E-N-T-I-V-E. Have you got that?" the exasperated teacher shouted.

"Yes, sir. Thank ye, sir."

Around forty minutes later, McLaughlin looked at his watch and closed the book he was reading. "That will be all now, O'Hara. You can finish the rest of your lines at home. Be off with you and take this note to your father."

Sean gathered up his books and the pages of lines he had written and hurried over to the desk. "Make sure your father gets this," said the teacher, handing him the note. "I'll expect to hear from him soon."

It was nearly 5:00 before Sean got home.

"What kept ye?" his mother snapped. "Yer father has tay go out early. Now hurry and get yer homework done. I'm makin' the tay now."

After tea when his father had gone, Sean sat in the sitting room with his mother. While he wrote out the rest of his lines, his mother was watching the six o'clock news. The distraction of the news was too much for Sean, and he sat worrying about the teacher's note. He had not given it to his father and he was trying now to summon up the courage to give it to his mother.

Suddenly he sat upright as he stared at the screen for there was his deer. He gaped at the television as he listened to the reporter.

"And the deer—a white deer—was seen grazing with Farmer McCafferty's cows. It is still there. All efforts to catch it have failed. The farmer noticed it this morning when he went to bring in his herd for milking..."

Another scene showed Sean's deer happily grazing with the farmer's cows.

"God," exclaimed Sean's mother. "And just up in the hills above us, too."

Sean stared at the television, anxious for more news about his deer. *It mustn't have found its way home after all.*

"It is hoped," continued the reporter, "that the deer will stay with the farmer's herd until the experts from Belfast Zoo can come and decide what to do with it. It is a mystery to everyone how it came to be in the hills above Derry..."

Sean's mother turned to him. Her face was paler than usual as she said, "That's a warnin'. There's never been a deer up there before and a white one, too. It's very strange. It's a warnin' of no good." She frowned. "I wonder where it came from?"

Sean was overjoyed. He would be able to see his deer again.

"Sean! Sean!" It was Mickey calling at the back door.

"Did ye hear about the deer up at McCafferty's?" exclaimed Mickey when Sean let him in. "Are ye headin' up?"

"But it's nearly dark," said Sean, suddenly annoyed by his friend's excitement.

"I'm goin' up, anyway," said Mickey. "I'm headin' over fer Jim."

Making up his mind Sean said, "Howl on and I'll go with ye. I'll get my coat."

"I'll scoot intay the house and get me flashlight," said Mickey.

On their way over to Jim's house, they met a couple of their classmates.

"Hey, Sean! Did yees hear about the deer?" one of them asked.

"Aye," said Sean. "We're goin' over fer Jim and then we're headin' up tay see if we can see it. Mickey has a flashlight."

"Come on with us, Mickey," said the other boy, thinking about the flashlight.

Impatient to get up to the deer Sean said, "Aye, come on, Mickey. We can see Jim later." Before Mickey could say anything, Sean walked over to the other boys and they began to walk away. Flashing his flashlight on and off, Mickey hurried after them.

It took the boys about twenty minutes to reach McCafferty's big field. When they arrived, Sean saw a number of children were already there. Some had flashlights. The cows had already moved down to the gate where the children were gathered. It was eerily dark and the flashlights pierced the sky in lines of misty light, but the deer was nowhere to be seen. A few minutes later as the clouds parted and the moon lit up the whole field, everyone saw the deer standing silhouetted in the middle of the field.

"There it is!" shouted a boy.

Some of the mooing cows ran back up the field away from the gate, frightened by the yelling children. Sean could see the deer quite clearly now as it raised its head and looked in the direction of the shouting children.

"Deer!" shouted Sean. "Here, boy! Here!" Then he began to climb up onto the shaky gate.

Standing proudly its regal head held high the deer looked towards the gate and when it spotted Sean, it gave an excited bark and then began to race down the field towards him.

"Look out!" screamed one of the younger boys. "It's attackin'!"

Immediately all the children rushed back from the gate but horrified, Mickey saw Sean jump into the field. "Sean, look out!" he yelled.

Now Mickey and the other children watched in awe when Sean ran to greet the deer. When it stopped beside him, Sean whispered, "Hey, boy. Ye stayed, didn't ye, eh? Aye, ye stayed."

He rubbed the deer gently on its neck, and it barked softly and looked past him at the other children.

"Sean!" shouted Mickey. "Get away from it quick. It'll butt ye."

"Naw, it won't. It's alright, Mickey. See? He wouldn't hurt anyone. See? He wouldn't even hurt a fly."

Pulling on the deer's chest, he led it over to the gate. "Come on, Mickey, pet him. He won't hurt ye."

"Ye must be jokin' Sean," exclaimed Mickey. "I'm not goin' near that thing. Them horns it has will poke me eyes out." He stared fearfully up at the deer's huge antlers.

By then some of the other boys who had stones in their hands had returned to the gate. They watched as Sean eventually coaxed Mickey to pet the deer.

"It's okay," said Sean. "He won't hurt yees, any of yees. It's okay."

A few older boys now began to reach through the gate to stroke the deer. One of them exclaimed, "God, look at the size of them horns it has."

Soon all the children were inside the field and gathered around the deer, eager to pet it. Barking and snorting softly, the deer's alert eyes fixed on Sean as the children pushed to pet it. Suddenly it jerked its head up.

"Hey you wains! What's goin' on down there?"

"Jesus, it's McCafferty!" someone shouted, and immediately the children dived for the gate, clambered over it and ran away.

Watching, the deer stamped its feet, then barking loudly it thundered away up the field. But Sean had stayed and now he slipped along the side of the hedge near the gate to hide. He wanted to see his deer again after the farmer had gone.

When they came to the gate Sean heard the man who was with the farmer say, "Ye'll have tay get the baste caught, ye know, or ye'll be tortured with the wains comin' up here at the week-end."

"Ach I'll have tay put up with it I suppose," said McCafferty. "The zoo guys are comin' early on Monday mornin'. They'll sort it all out." He checked the bar on the gate. "No harm's been done, anyway."

Sean listened and waited impatiently for the two men to go, and when eventually they did, he slipped towards the gate to see if he could spot the deer. He waited until he thought the farmer and his companion were well away before calling out to it. He called out a few times more, but there was no sign of it and a few minutes later, he headed home.

Next day, early in the morning, children and some of their parents, newspaper reporters and photographers headed up to Corrody Hill. Notices posted on the gate and along the hedge warned people to stay out of the field. The main crowd soon gathered along the hedge, trying to see through the hawthorn bushes.

Sometimes the deer would wander close to it, enabling the people to get a good look at it. Sean was there too, but he stayed at the back of the crowd near the gate. One time, the deer spotted him but it stayed back too, only going so far then moving away again.

All that day and until Sunday when it began to rain heavily, Waterside and Cityside people trekked up through the fields to see the white deer. It rained so heavy on Sunday that Sean could not get up to see it. It was still raining hard when Mickey called for him. His freckled face was pale and agitated.

"Did ye hear about the deer?" he asked.

"What?"

"Someone shot it. It's dead."

The terrible words numbed Sean. "Dead?" he muttered. "What do ye mean?"

"Someone shot the deer," said Mickey. "It was on the news."

Sean studied his pal's face. Dead. He could see it was true. *Dead.* The word raced through his mind. Was it really true? With a little cry, he pushed past his startled pal and was soon running up the fields as fast as he could. *It couldn't be dead, not my deer. It couldn't be.* By the time he reached the field he was soaking wet.

McCafferty and his nephew were standing looking down at the carcass of the white deer. Its stiff body lay in the back of a long wooden trailer hooked to the farmer's tractor. Dried blood covered a hole about the size of Sean's fist that showed were the creature had been shot. Its beautiful large eyes were now dimmed and unseeing, and it lay at the side of the trailer. Part of its antlers had been broken off.

Sean, with tears running down his face, was suddenly clambering into the trailer before any of the men could stop him. With a cry, he fell on the deer his thin arms trying to hug it. "Why would anyone kill ye? Why would anyone want tay do such a vile thing?" he cried bitterly.

Disturbed by the little boy's grief, McCafferty gently pulled him away from the deer and out of the trailer saying, "Come on now, son. Sure, it's only an animal. It's dead so what's the difference?"

At this, Sean stopped struggling and stared at the farmer. "What's the difference?" he cried. "My lovely deer is dead, just like Darkie. It's gone. I'll never see it again. It's gone. It's dead."

A few minutes later and still crying, he stood beside McCafferty as the trailer was towed up the field to the farmhouse.

"Son," said the farmer studying him. "Ye'd better get away home. Yer soaked through tay the skin. Ye'll get pneumonia."

In a trance, Sean walked slowly down the field and with the rain driving into him drenching him further he arrived home in a distressed state crying and shivering uncontrollably. His mother couldn't understand what had happened but she dried him off and made him some soup, then put him to bed.

During the night, Sean woke screaming from the horrible nightmare of the dead deer's eyes floating all around him.

Next day at school, he sat in class unable to concentrate on anything. The teacher frowned when he noticed this. He said nothing, but made up his mind to call on Sean's parents.

In the playground at dinner-time, Sean was very quiet and withdrawn. He listened, growing angrier as the boys talked about the deer. Then Mickey said, "I wonder who killed Bambi?"

Suddenly rising to his feet Sean shouted, "His name wasn't Bambi! What a stupid name. It's a stupid name fer a deer. Why is everyone callin' him Bambi? His name wasn't Bambi!"

At his outburst, Mickey's face grew suddenly red with anger. "How do ye know what ye called him?" he shouted. "I call him Bambi and if I want tay call him Bambi I will. Right!"

Suddenly with a sigh, Sean relaxed. "I knew him, ye see," he said quietly. "I knew him and I know his name wasn't Bambi," he whispered to no one in particular. "Anyway!" he shouted suddenly glaring at Mickey. "What does it matter what ye call him! He's dead! He's dead!" Abruptly he swung around and walked away. Mickey, Jim, and the other boys stared after him. Mickey scratched his head wondering what was wrong with him.

That evening after he had finished his homework Sean sat in his bedroom. He didn't want to go downstairs in case he would see the news of his deer's death on the television and he still hadn't given his father the teacher's note.

Five minutes later, his mother called up to him. "Sean! Yer tay's ready!"

A minute later, she called again. "Sean, if ye don't come down this instant, ye can stay in yer room all night!"

With a sigh, Sean rolled off his bed and went downstairs to the kitchen. As he sat looking at his plate, unable to eat, he heard his father say, "Christ, there's more talk about that stupid deer than there is about the bomb in Spencer Road."

Sean clenched his fist and for the first time in his life, he wanted to punch his father in the face. *What sort of a man is he?* he wondered. Then, unable to listen anymore to his father going on about the bomb, he rose from the table.

"Sean," said his mother. "Ye've hardly touched yer food. Are ye alright?"

"I... I don't feel too well, Ma."

His mother studied him. "Go up tay the bathroom and take an aspirin. Ye'll soon feel alright. I hope yer not takin' the flu from that drookin' ye got yesterday."

As Sean walked past the sitting room door he could not help overhearing the reporter saying, "And the two old ladies are now living with relatives. I see ye have a lovely cat."

"Yes, but it's not Darkie is it?" said one of the women. "There was only one Darkie."

Sean stuck his head around the door and looked at the television. He was just in time to see the close up of a tiny black kitten sitting in the sad old woman's lap.

"Well," concluded the reporter. "It looks like it's been a bad week for the animal world. Only three days ago we reported that a beautiful white deer had appeared in the hills above Derry and that it was happily grazing with Farmer McCafferty's cows. We are sad to report now that the deer is dead, shot by someone unknown..."

Sean turned to go unable to listen anymore but the reporter's next words held him.

"The sad thing about the death of the deer was that it was found lying in a hollow, a path with whin bushes growing over it in a place known locally as the Whinnies. The farmer had noticed that the deer was missing from his field. Earlier he had heard a shot and when he went to investigate, he saw a trail of blood that he followed. He found the poor creature lying down, dying in the hollow..."

At this Sean gave a cry. "No!" His badly wounded deer had crawled to the overhang to wait for him to come and heal it. *It must have been in terrible pain. It must have suffered and I didn't know. It must have waited fer me fer a long time. Didn't it know I wouldn't come? I didn't know! How was I to know?* Suddenly crying bitterly, he ran upstairs to his room and flung himself onto his bed.

Thirty minutes later, he was slipping out of the back door. As he made his way up to the Whinnies he muttered, "Them that killed my deer deserve tay die too."

6❦9

"Is Kevin in, Kathy? Quick Kevin, Johnny's been lifted."

"What happened?"

"Dunno," said Joe Lynch a thin faced scruffy man. "About two hours ago the Brits surrounded the street. They tuk him away."

"Right, Joe," said Kevin. "I have tay get up tay the Whinnies. I'll have tay shift the cache. Johnny knows where it is. He might talk."

"Do ye want me tay come with ye?"

"Naw, it's better if I go alone. There's no tellin' how long before they make Johnny talk. I'll meet ye at the usual place later."

Seconds later Lynch and Sean's mother watched as Kevin disappeared into the darkness and headed up to the Whinnies.

Breathing heavily, Sean's father reached the hiding place and after checking to make sure there was no one about, he began digging with his bare hands at the clay. Unearthing the cloth, he pulled. He almost fell back as it flapped out easily from the hole.

"What the hell! They're gone. A trap. It's a trap. Johnny must have broken." A scuffling noise to his left had him instantly sweating and he turned slowly in the direction of the sound. In the moonlight, he could make out the tiny figure that had stepped out onto the path.

"The guns aren't there, Da," a familiar voice said. "I have them."

Kevin heaved a sigh of relief when he recognized his son. "Sean. Thank Christ it's you. Ye have the guns, good boy. Where are they? I have tay get them away from here fast."

"Naw, Da," said Sean quietly. "Yer not gettin' them. They'll never harm anyone again. Never."

Angered, Sean's father took a step towards him, but he stopped when he saw his son raise his hand. He gaped in astonishment when he saw what was in it—a revolver—and Sean was pointing it at him.

"Jesus, Sean," he gasped. "Put it down. It's dangerous. It might go off. Put it down." He took a step towards him.

"Stay where ye are, Da!" shouted Sean. "Ye'll never harm anyone again." He began to cry. "Why did ye have tay kill my deer? Why, Da? He wouldn't have harmed ye. Why did ye have tay kill him?"

Kevin studied his son. *What the hell is the matter with him?* "What are ye talkin' about? I didn't kill the deer."

Sean raved on, almost screaming now. "Ye killed Darkie, didn't ye? Aye, ye killed him! But ye shouldn't have killed my deer!"

What the hell is wrong with him? Kevin edged closer.

"Stay where ye are!" shouted Sean. "Just stay where ye are." He took a step back as his father edged even closer.

"Come on, son. Put the gun down. We'll talk about this."

He was just about to spring towards his son when a voice rang out in the clear night air. "We have you surrounded! Drop your weapons or we will open fire!"

Startled, Sean turned in the direction of the voice. As he did, he stepped on the piece of whin bush he had used for digging earlier and lost his balance. As he hit the ground, the gun went off and fired into his stomach. The last thing his father saw before the bullets tore him apart was his son dying in the moonlight, his eyes bright and clear, with a smile on his face.

2

FIRST COMMUNION

Kevin turned on his hard mattress when he heard his young sister, Siobhan, whisper to him from the far side of the bedroom. He could hardly see her in the darkness, but she was sitting up and listening to their parents quarrelling.

"Kevin, me da's drunk again. Kevin."

"Go tay sleep, Siobhan," he hissed. "They'll hear ye." He sighed for he knew it was no use; she wouldn't listen and would stay awake.

It was just after 1:00 in the morning, and he knew his mother had been waiting up for their father.

"Well!" he heard his mother shout. "What's yer excuse this time, eh?"

"Ach, leave us alone, woman. I'm tired."

"Tired! Tired! Hah!" Remembering her children, Kathleen lowered her voice. "Tired," she repeated. "What doin'? Not workin' anyway. Ye've lost all the jobs ye've had through yer drinkin'. God, when I think what ye were like before... before..."

Repeatedly banging his head back against his pillow, Kevin tried to drown out the sound of his mother crying. It always ended like this.

Five minutes later the twanging of the bedsprings told him his father was in bed. They would soon be sleeping. Pulling himself up on his elbows, he tried to see if Siobhan was sleeping, but the sound of her muffled sobbing came to him. Pulling back his patchwork quilt he slipped out of bed and padded softly across the cold oil-cloth covered floor to his sister's bed. Tugging gently on her blanket, he whispered, "Ach, Siobhan don't be cryin'. It's only me da. Sure ye know him. He's always drinkin'. Don't cry. Sure it'll be all right in the mornin'."

Peeping out from under the blanket, Siobhan wiped her nose with the back of her hand and sniffed before saying, "Aye, Kevin it's always all right in the mornin' isn't it?"

The tone of Siobhan's voice disturbed him, but trying to get her mind off their drunken father, he said, "Siobhan, look, why don't ye practice yer prayers, yer Hail Mary especially. Ye know it isn't long till yer First Communion. Ye'll need to know all yer prayers."

His sister stared up at his dark face for a few seconds, and with a heavy sigh, she began. "Hail Mary. Full of Grace. The Lord is with thee..."

Kevin sat a while listening to her rhyme off her Hail Mary's, and he gently eased away, returning to his own bed. Snuggling as deep into it as he could, he was soon feeling sleepy. He could still hear Siobhan praying.

"Holy Mary, Mother of God, pray fer us sinners, now and... Kevin. Why does me da have to drink so much?"

He screamed silently, fully awake again. Hissing as loudly as he could, he said, "I don't know, do I? Siobhan, fer God's sake go to sleep. I'm tired."

"Hail Mary, full of Grace..."

Sighing, Kevin tossed and turned, but it was no use. He could not get back to sleep. He thought now about his sister's question. Why did his father have to drink so much? His thoughts drifted back to happier times not so long ago.

One day when Siobhan was nearing her sixth birthday, she came home from school very excited. She had brought a thick book back from the school library. It was filled with colored drawings of prehistoric animals.

"Creatures that lived on earth millions of years ago," her father read out.

Thumbing through the pages, Siobhan looked at each drawing. "Aren't some of them funny lookin', Da? Aren't they? What do ye call that one? I like it the best of all."

"A Diplodocus," said her father turning to her. He smiled at his daughter's expression. Her green eyes were wide and questioning. "And yer my little Diplodocus," he said suddenly grabbing her and swinging her high in the air. "Yer my little Diplodocus." He winked at Kevin as he swung his squealing daughter around and around. "Ye've got the same long neck as a Diplodocus and yer nearly as beautiful. Ha, ha, ha, ha..."

Later when they all sat down to tea, Kevin's father said, "Kathleen, I have tay play a darts match the night so I'll probably be back late."

"Och, Barney not the night again," said Kevin's mother. "I thought we could go around to yer sister's the night."

"I'm really sorry, luv. They need me the night. I can't let the lads down. We're playin' in the Oval bar down in Duke Street. Och look, luv, I'll make it up to ye."

Kevin's mother said nothing, but it was obvious by her expression she was disappointed. Later, out in the scullery when his mother was washing the dishes, Kevin heard his father say, "Look, Kathleen, we'll go to the Midland on Friday night. *The Long Gray Line* is on. Tyrone Power. Ye like him. It's supposed to be a great film."

Kathleen smiled. "We'd need to pay the insurance man on Friday night or he'll lapse us off."

"Ah sure he can wait, it's time we had a night out together," said Barney.

It was late that same night when Kevin was awakened by loud banging on the front door. Slipping from his bed, he tiptoed to his bedroom door. Easing it open, he crawled out onto the landing and peered down into the dark hall. His heart began to pound when he saw two men supporting his father.

"Jesus, Mary, and Joseph!" exclaimed his mother. "What's happened? Barney yer cut. Yer bleedin'."

"Ach, he'll be okay, missus," said one of the men. "The B. Specials gave him a bit of a goin' over down at the bottom of Fountain Hill. He's just a bit dazed. It'd take more nor that to hurt Barney. He'll be okay. He'll come round in a minute."

With his heart still pounding, Kevin slipped downstairs to listen at the sitting room door. The B. Specials were the auxiliary police for the Protestants—why were they after his da?

"It was lick this, missus," said the man who had spoken earlier. "We whipped a bunch of Orange men at the darts the night, and they couldn't tick their oil. Jesus, but they were really ragin'. Barney here won the game fer us, finishing on the hard double, too. Man, ye shoulda seen them Orange men's faces. Anyway," continued the man, "wan of them effers called Barney a Fenian bastard, and Barney decked him. There was a whole row. It was soon settled though and after a while Barney said he had to go home. Goin' up lower Fountain Hill he was stopped by the B. men. It was wee Danny Simpson who came runnin' in to tell us about the doin' Barney was gettin'. We all piled out of the Oval and down to Fountain Hill. We were just in time, too, though Barney had already got a clout from wan of the B. men's rifle butts. We were all nearly lifted, but because there were too many of us they allowed us to get Barney home."

Just then Kevin heard his father groan. "Ahhh God, me head. It's bustin'."

With a cry, Kevin rushed into the sitting room. "Da! Are ye all right? Da!"

Grabbing him by the arm, his mother pulled him back. "Shhh. Be quiet Kevin. Get back up to bed."

"But Ma..."

"Up!"

Holding his head between his hands, Kevin's father groaned. "Go on up, son. I'm okay. I'll see ye in the mornin'. Go on. That's a good boy."

Since his father wasn't too badly hurt, Kevin gave in to his mother's persistent tugging on the sleeve of his pajamas. "All right, Da," he said. "I'll see ye in the mornin'." That night as he lay trying to sleep, Kevin clenched his fists. He felt angry when he thought about the B. Specials attacking his father.

It was shortly after that his father began to change. He began to drink more frequently and became aggressive and quick tempered. Kevin noticed the change in Siobhan, too. Whenever their father was at home, she would slip up to her room and play by herself. There she would stay until she heard her father go out.

Six weeks before Siobhan's First Communion and two weeks before her seventh birthday, they were out in the hall putting on their coats and getting ready to go to school when Siobhan suddenly blurted out, "Mammy, could I get a watch fer my birthday? Daphne Miller got one fer hers and it only cost two pounds nineteen and eleven pence. Not even three pounds she told me, and it has a blue strap and a funny face and the hands on the funny man's face tell the time and..." Breathing hard from the effort of saying this in one breath, she looked expectantly at her mother. It was obvious to Kevin that she had been rehearsing her request.

Their mother, tightening the scarf around her daughter's throat, said quietly, "Ye'll get yer watch some day, luv, but not this birthday. Don't ferget we're havin' a birthday party fer ye and yer Aunt Joan is comin' over." She studied her daughter's disappointed face. Suddenly she snapped, "Ach sure ye know yer father isn't workin'..." As soon as she said it, she regretted it.

But quick on the uptake, Kevin pushed Siobhan in the back, saying, "Come on silly, or we'll be late fer school."

A shadow at the top of the stairs caught Kevin's eye as they walked to the front door. He knew it was his father. He had been listening to everything they had been talking about. The shadow disappeared, and Kevin heard the click as the bedroom door closed.

Siobhan's seventh birthday arrived. Her Aunt Joan had bought her a pair of Rosary beads made of imitation pearls. She also gave Siobhan a shiny half crown. "To start that lovely purse yer mother bought ye," she said smiling.

Delighted, Siobhan showed her mother and Kevin her presents.

"Och ye shouldn't have, Joan," said Kathleen. "It's far too much."

"Ach, Kathleen," said Joan smiling at her. "Sure it will help her remember her seventh birthday. I wish I could remember mines." She turned to Siobhan. "Well Siobhan, do ye know all yer prayers? Do ye know how to make yer first confession?"

"She certainly does," said Kathleen proudly. "Go on Siobhan. Let Joan hear ye."

"The whole lot?" asked Siobhan, frowning.

"Aye luv. Go on. From the start."

Putting her Rosary beads into the tiny white box with a brass clasp they came in, Siobhan handed it to her mother. Positioning herself in front of her mother and her Aunt, she nervously wiped her lips with the back of her hand and began. "When I'm in the box I say, 'Bless me Father fer I have sinned. This is my first confession.' I tell the priest my sins. The priest gives me abso... abso... lution. That is the cleansing of my soul. Then I say the 'Oh My God'."

"The Act of Contrition," corrected her aunt.

"The Act of Contrition, I mean," said Siobhan. "Then the priest gives me my penance."

"Why, that's really very good Siobhan," said her aunt. "How long is it now to the day?"

"Only thirty one more days, Aunt Joan," squealed Siobhan excitedly. "And we're havin' a big party afterwards up at the boy's school in Chapel Road."

"Ye'll be partied out," said her mother, smiling. "Come on, let's start this party now."

The small table was laid out with sandwiches, a plate of jam tarts, two big bottles of Ross's lemonade, a plateful of custard creams (which were Siobhan's favorite biscuits), and in the middle of all the dishes was a tiny sponge cake with seven candles stuck firmly into the thick pink icing.

Bending over the cake, Joan flicked the wheel on her silver lighter and one by one lit the seven candles. "Now," she said, smiling. "After we sing happy birthday to you, Siobhan, ye must make a wish, and then blow out all the candles with one breath. Are ye ready?"

Joan began and Kevin and his mother sang happy birthday with her as Siobhan looked at the candles, a happy smile on her shining face.

"Happy birthday to you. Happy birthday dear Siobhaaan, Happy..."

Suddenly there was a loud banging at the door, and Kathleen hurried to see who it was. As she opened the door, Barney came staggering in. His suit was covered in stale vomit and he waved his arms about wildly as he made his way to the sitting room.

"Whaaas all thish?" he slurred. Blinking his bloodshot eyes, he looked at the table. Swaying, he squinted down at the seven candles. Already the wax was melting from them onto the icing. "A party, eh? A birthday party?" He looked over at Siobhan who was seated at the far side of the table. Her knees were pulled up tight to her chin, and her eyes were wide. "So it's my little Diplodocus who's havin' a party, is it? Eh?" Pushing roughly past his sister, he had to bend over to get closer to his daughter. As he reached out, he noticed she was cowering away from him. "Ah, Siobhan," he said. "Don't be like that. C'mere. C'mere tay yer da."

Leaning further towards her, he suddenly lost his balance, and his heavy limp body slid past Kevin dragging the contents of the table with him. On his way down one of his flailing hands caught Siobhan a sharp knock on the side of her face, and crying hysterically, she ran to her mother. Everyone except Siobhan—who had her face buried in her mother's apron—stared down at Barney. He was looking up at them, unable to get to his feet. His glazed eyes were partly covered by his long greasy hair. Clumsily, he tried to get to his feet. Kathleen, with tears running down her face, clutched Siobhan tighter. Kevin's father now looked at him and held up his hand. With Joan's help, Kevin managed to get his father to his feet. As the three of them staggered upstairs Siobhan's crying grew louder.

In the bedroom, Kevin managed to get his father undressed and into bed. Later, as he left the room, he heard his father cry out, "Tell her I didn't mean it, Kevin. Tell her I'm sorry. I didn't mean it..."

Three days later he was dead.

All during the wake and even on the day of the funeral, Kevin noticed that Siobhan showed no emotion at her father's death. She seemed happy as she played with the doll Joan had bought her. That night Kevin listened to hear if she was crying, but all he heard was her steady snoring as she slept peacefully.

Four weeks later it was her First Communion Day. Radiant in her white dress, Siobhan came walking jerkily up from the altar. Her face was beaming as she kept the Eucharist firmly against the roof of her mouth.

After a short sermon, the chapel emptied and the parents and relations of the first communicants gathered outside in the yard to wait until the photographers had taken all the photographs. Then it was time for all the boys and girls who had made their first communion to visit their relatives to show off their clothes—and receive money from their relatives in honor of the occasion.

That afternoon, Kevin went to the pictures. When he returned, Siobhan and his mother and Aunt were home. Siobhan showed him how much money she had been given. "Aunt Joan gave me this ten shilling note," she said showing Kevin the red note. "Mrs. Tegan gave me a half crown and Mrs. McKinney gave me two shillings. They were nice, weren't they?"

Kevin smiled as Siobhan spread all her money out on top of the table; sixpences, shillings, five florins, six half crowns and a number of three-penny bits, pennies and half-pennies. She began to count. "Two pounds nineteen and four-pence," she said.

As she counted her money again, Joan gave a sudden start. "Oh God," she exclaimed. "I almost forgot. Before Barney died he asked me to keep this fer ye and give it to ye on yer First Communion Day. It was only now I remembered." Digging deep into her handbag she pulled out a small brown package and handed it to Siobhan.

Siobhan frowned as she looked at it, and then at Aunt Joan and her mother.

"Aren't ye goin' to open it, luv?" asked her mother, wondering what Barney had given her.

Gingerly Siobhan unwrapped the paper, and soon she had uncovered a tiny blue box. Her hands shook as she opened the box. "A watch!" she exclaimed. "It's a watch! Look!" She held it up for everyone to see. "A real watch!" Suddenly, she dropped the box and ran crying to the scullery and out the back door to the steps that led up to the back garden.

Her mother moved to go after her but Joan stopped her, saying, "Leave her fer a wee while, Kathleen."

As his mother and Joan discussed Siobhan's present, Kevin slipped out to Siobhan. She was sitting on the top step crying repeatedly, "Oh Da, Da..."

With tears brimming his eyes, Kevin sat down beside her. Turning to him, Siobhan handed him the watch to look at and suddenly cried into his chest. As he put his arm around her, holding her close, he held the watch up and read the inscription on the back of it through tear filled eyes.

For My Lovely Diplodocus
From Daddy

3

THE MEDAL

M r. Carlin carefully placed his buzzing metal detector on the leafy ground beside him when he heard his son's excited cry.

"Hey daddy look! Look what I found."

"Let me see."

His son handed him the round muddy object that was about the size of a ten pence piece. Spitting on it Mr. Carlin gently rubbed at one of the faces. "It looks like some kind of medal. There's something written on it. A date, looks like 1942. Here Tommy, watch my detector. I'll wash this in the river. It looks like silver."

After slithering down the muddy bank to the river, he carefully dipped the medal into the clear water. Then he rubbed the faces of it. He repeated the operation twice more until he was satisfied that it was clean, then he squinted at the inscription.

MAY BYRNE
CARRICKMACROSS CONVENT
1942

It had been drizzling nearly all afternoon, but now the rain was getting heavier. Scrambling back up to his son, he handed the medal to him saying, "It's a medal, all right. Look, we'd better head for home. We don't want any rain to seep into our detectors. Put the medal in your pocket. We'll get a better look at it when we get home."

As they hurried along the muddy path, Mr. Carlin thought about the medal and the date, 1942. *It had to be been buried there for sixty years. I wonder what May Byrne was like?*

Back home, they quickly changed and in their bare feet they carried their finds out to the kitchen sink to clean them. Mrs. Carlin watched them as they cleaned the mud from a few pre-decimal halfpennies, pennies and one 1935 sixpence. Soon they were all examining the medal.

"Carrickmacross Convent? It doesn't look like a holy medal," said Mrs. Carlin as she turned it over in her hand. "Why has it got flowers on it? Those are definitely roses. I'd love to know the story of how it got there."

That evening at tea, Mrs. Carlin said to her son, "Thomas, why don't you write to the convent and see if they knew who this May Byrne was... or is. You never know—she could still be alive."

Mother Superior folded the letter and smiled. Grunting with the effort, she rose from her well-worn leather chair and shuffled over to the window. Gazing out over the convent's beautiful gardens, she could just about see an old priest and a short, portly nun busy raking fresh manure over the ground. She smiled again. Returning to her desk, she rang a small brass bell and seconds later, a young nun opened the door.

"Would you fetch Sister Breda from the garden?"

Minutes later Sister Breda knocked gently, then came into the office. "You sent for me, Mother Superior?"

"Yes Sister Breda. Would you read this?"

The Mother Superior studied Sister Breda's appearance as she read the letter. She wore a pair of muddy black Wellingtons that peeked from below her muddy habit, and on her hands she wore a pair of fingerless, tattered woolen gloves with hard pieces of mud clinging to them. A pair of clear-framed spectacles was balanced precariously on her stubby nose. The smell that wafted from sister Breda finally reached the Mother Superior, causing her to move back towards her desk and wrinkle her nose with disgust.

Sister Breda's round red face broke into a smile when she had finished reading the letter. "Good heavens," she blurted out. "Imagine that. Was it really that long ago?"

"Will you answer the letter?"

"Oh yes, I think I should," said Sister Breda removing her spectacles and shoving them inside her habit. Folding the letter in two Sister Breda said, "Is that all, Mother Superior? I have to help get the manure dug in to prepare our vegetable garden. I'll answer this now though, just a quick note to tell the boy how I lost it. Is that all?" she repeated.

"Yes, that's all, sister."

With a smile, Sister Breda turned and walked to the door. As she opened it to go she heard Mother Superior call after her, "For heaven's sake, May, get yourself cleaned up."

With a mischievous smile, Sister Breda whispered, "Yes, Joan." She closed the door behind her and hurried to her room. She sat down in the chair in front of her tiny table and whispered to herself, "Sixty-four years ago! My, how time has flown."

She and Joan were teenagers that long, hot summer all those years ago, and they had been sent to Ardmore on a working holiday away from their studies, five months before they were to take their final vows. Ardmore was a small farming village on the outskirts of Derry that lay in a valley through which flowed the trout and salmon rich River Faughan. That first day they had waited in a tiny room just inside the parochial house for Father O'Kane.

As he came in, he smiled. "Hello. And what have we here, eh? What do two pretty girls want with an oul fogy like me, eh?" He had been expecting them, of course, with advice from the Mother Superior to look after them and make sure they had plenty to occupy them and keep them out of mischief. "Well now, girls," the stout, gray haired, red-faced priest boomed. "Let's get ye both settled in, then I'll show ye the gardens."

That afternoon he showed them the beautiful gardens, and in the long back garden that stretched down to the River Faughan, he nodded towards two people at the bottom of it. The old gardener and his son, Peter, had a huge task on their hands to get the garden ready for Bishop Farren's visit at the end of August.

As they walked down the narrow path between the shoulder high bushes and flowers, the girls had to admit that this garden was the loveliest of them all.

"We need to create more space for the vegetables," explained the old priest. "Jim and his son will need help to dig out all the weeds and stuff. Do you two think you could lend them a hand?" He smiled at the girls. "It'll be hard work. Do ye think ye'll be up to it?"

Joan looked at May. They both smiled and nodded.

"Good. C'mon then. I'll introduce ye to Jim and Peter."

With a quick snap, Jim pulled his battered corduroy cap from his bald head and smiling extended his hard-calloused right hand to the girls. Peter brushed his fingers through his long blonde hair that had been hanging over his tanned face before he shook May's hand, and she blushed under his piercing blue eyes as he stared at her. She hoped he didn't hear her heart pounding.

That first afternoon the girls worked in the sun under Peter's directions, tearing up the weeds with their bare hands and using a rickety old wooden wheelbarrow to dump them down along the edge of the river. Occasionally Peter would come over to them, and he would ram his spade into the ground and dig out the more stubborn weeds with a heavy grunt. By 6:00, the girls were sweaty, hungry and tired.

Every day after that, they worked in the garden… and May looked forward to it. Whenever it was Joan's turn to barrow the weeds down to the river, she would stop working to watch Peter. She sighed as she saw the handsome youth carefully examining the pink roses that grew over at the far end of the garden. Once he caught her looking at him, and he winked at her with a smile. This made May blush, and she bent to the ground quickly to tear like a mad thing at the weeds.

Two weeks later and after much hard work, the ground was cleared and ready for spraying. While Peter's father sprayed the ground, May and Joan helped Peter with the roses. May's shyness soon disappeared with the easygoing Peter, and he warmed to the happy, lively girls.

The following evening as all three walked up the garden to the parochial house, Peter said, "Are you going to the annual sports day on Sunday?"

"Sports?" frowned May. "I don't fancy that much. All that running and jumping."

"Oh, but I love athletics," Joan gushed excitedly, clasping her hands together. "I hope I can go."

"It's not all running and jumping," said Peter, looking at May and winding her heart up again. "There's the flower show and horseshoe throwing. It's always a great day. Anyway, Father O'Kane is opening the sports, so I expect you two will be there."

It rained the following four days, turning into one of those hot, clammy periods that seemed to last forever. At least it seemed that way to May, for she longed to be out in the garden with Peter. On the fourth day, the two girls were sitting in a small room at the back of the parochial house that overlooked the back garden, trying to read. With a heavy sigh, May threw her novel on the table and looked at Joan, who was sitting with her bare feet resting on Father O'Kane's leather pouffet, reading a book about the Irish Saints.

"Joan, what do you think of Peter?"

Looking over the top of her book, Joan studied May for a few seconds, and said with a frown, "He's like most boys, I suppose."

"He's not a *boy*," May snapped.

Frowning again, Joan put down her book and sat up. She took another long look at May and whispered. "May, it won't be long now before we take our final vows, so you had better not let Mother Superior hear you talking about boys."

May sighed. "I'm sorry, Joan. I didn't mean to snap at you. It's this rain and the heat. It's getting me down. It's so pleasant out in the garden. Don't you think so? Especially when Peter..."

Joan glared at her. "Is that what's bothering you? Peter? Ach, May, for goodness sake catch yourself on. You're infatuated with someone you don't even know. Don't be so silly."

Blushing, May stammered, "It's... it's not sinful... or wrong... to like someone, is it?"

"No, there's nothing wrong with that. But we are going to take our final vows soon, so you'd better watch out. This temptation is something you will have to overcome."

"Temptation!" shouted May. "What temptation? Oh, for goodness sake, Joan, all I asked was what you think about Peter, and you're talking about temptation? We are allowed to talk to each other, aren't we?"

"Not about boys," Joan snapped, shaking her book up in front of her face.

May glared at her, and with another heavy sigh, she picked up her novel and tried to read.

ᏯᏇᎧ

The rain stopped on Saturday, and by the evening the beautiful pink sky told everyone in Ardmore that Sunday was going to be a perfect sports-day. On Sunday after dinner, Father O'Kane hurried away to get ready. The girls changed into their light, ankle-length summer dresses and at 2:00, the three of them were making their way down the lane to an iron bridge that crossed the river. Turning left without crossing the bridge, they passed the bleach green mill and fifty yards on, they came to a field.

The field was the local cricket pitch during the summer, but now it was lined out as a running track. Several marquees had been erected bordering the track, and hundreds of villagers were already there, with more and more of them coming through the gate.

Father O'Kane turned to the girls and said, "Here girls. Here's six-pence each. Enjoy yourselves. I have to go on up to the top of the field to start the first race. I'll see ye later." With that, he hurried away.

The two girls wandered across the field, to the other side of the running track, where May could see a marquee with the words "FLOWER SHOW" painted on a piece of wood that hung above the entrance. Suddenly the loud-speaker crackled.

"Oh! They're starting the first race!" squealed Joan excitedly. "Come on!"

With that, she hurried up to the top of the field, and May reluctantly followed her. After the first two races May was bored. "Joan," she whispered. "Would you mind very much if I went across to the flower show? I'll be back after a while."

"No, you go ahead. Oh look!" she shouted. "The quarter mile race is about to begin."

As May walked towards the bottom of the field to the flower show marquee, she heard a starting pistol fire and the crowd cheering behind her. A few minutes later, she pushed the canvas flap back, stepped into the marquee and took a look all around.

Then she saw him.

Peter was sitting on a bench seat near the front beside a group of women who were chatting loudly. On the stage above them, an old woman with a shock of white hair and a burly, red-faced man were judging the displays of flowers that lined a long table.

"Hello, Peter," whispered May as she sat down beside him. "What are you doing here?"

Peter blushed, then stammered, "I... I've entered some of my roses."

"You have? Oh, do you think you'll win?"

Peter nodded to a fat, jolly looking woman at the far end of the bench. "Dunno. Mrs. Titser has a great bunch of yellow roses entered. She'll be hard to beat."

"Where are your roses?" May studied the flowers. "The pink ones?"

"Yes."

"Oh but they're lovely, Peter. Ah, you'll win for sure." May smiled at him. Peter smiled back, and they silently watched the judges making notes on each entry.

At 3:15, the judging was over and the noise of the people in the now-packed marquee stopped as the red-faced judge held up his hands.

"As usual this year," he began, "the flower competition has attracted some of the loveliest displays Mrs. Harding and I have ever seen." He turned to smile at the white haired woman. "And we have had quite a task choosing the winner. But we have agreed that first prize should go to Mrs. Emily Titser, who wins the Ardmore cup outright."

"Oh, Peter," whispered May, disappointed for him as the crowd clapped. Peter clapped too, his eyes glistening.

"Second prize, a silver medal, goes to Peter Ward!"

"Second!" squealed May, trembling with excitement. "Peter, your roses have come second!"

With a great sniff Peter controlled himself as Mrs. Harding said, "I must say that it was extremely hard to choose between Peter and Emily's entries, and if there had been a joint prize we would have awarded it. However, congratulations to you both. Now if you could just come up to the stage to receive your prizes."

Later outside, Peter showed May his medal. As she looked at it he said, "May, I'm going for a spot of fishing along the river. Why don't you come with me? I've my rod in the shed at the bottom of the garden."

"Fishing?" exclaimed May, frowning. "Oh, but I..." Then she looked across at the cheering crowd as the puffing athletes raced around the field. "Yes. Why not?" she said, smiling.

"Good. Come on then," said Peter, taking her hand.

Twenty minutes later Peter cast his fly into the easy flowing river. May was lying on the grass above him on the hillside, just beneath a wooden cross that stood in the center of a grove of trees. As he tied on the fly, Peter explained to her that during the time of the Penal Laws, when the English declared it against the law to be Catholic, Mass had been held there in secret.

Birds chirped lazily in the chestnut trees above them, and flies drifted over the water under the overhanging branches. Over a period of ten minutes, May saw several silvery trout rise out of the water and snatch at the hovering flies. Now she gazed at Peter as he cast his line and let the fly drift with the current. She studied his handsome face, sighing contentedly as he concentrated on his fishing.

Suddenly he was into a fish and with a loud "Yahoo!" he struck. May immediately sat up, her eyes wide with excitement. The line was taut and quivered excitedly as Peter played the fish. After a few minutes, May got to her feet and moved closer to the edge of the river.

"Quick!" whispered Peter. "Get the net ready, May."

"Net?" May looked back at Peter's fishing bag, quickly diving up the bank towards it. After much reeling in and slacking off of the line, Peter began to play the exhausted fish closer to the bank.

"The net! Get the net ready! Easy now, easy."

Stretching towards him, May held out the net and as Peter pulled the flopping salmon towards him, she lost her balance and tumbled into the cold water.

Spluttering, she surfaced. Peter dropped his rod and grabbed hold of her, hauling her onto the side of the bank as the salmon, now feeling itself free gave a huge leap and was gone. By then May was lying on the bank.

"Oh, Peter," she gasped, "The fish! It got away. It was my fault."

Peter smiled at her. "There's plenty more in the river. But you need to get back up to the parochial house and get changed. You'll catch your death of cold."

Two minutes later they were hurrying back to the parochial house, but by the time they reached it, May was sneezing.

"Pe... Pe... Peter, I'll be all... all... Atchoo! I'll be all... all... Atchoo! right. You get back to your fishing. I'll change and hurry back to the sports field. I don't want Father O'Kane to find out."

"Are you sure you're all right? You're shivering." said Peter, studying her.

"I'm... I'm... Atchoo! Okay. I'd better get... get... Atchoo! inside and get changed. I'll see you later."

Ten minutes later and still sneezing, May was hurrying down to the sports field.

Father O'Kane sent for the doctor later that evening, who left instructions that May was to stay in bed, keep warm and take plenty of hot drinks.

It was a long and miserable week for May. When Joan and Father O'Kane went into Derry to do some shopping on Saturday, she rose and went down to the reading room. She still felt weak, but she had to see Peter.

As she stood looking out of the window, Peter saw her and hurried up the garden. Opening the window, May smiled at him.

"How are you now, May?" asked Peter, smiling back at her.

"Grand. I think I'm over it now."

"That's great, M... May," he stammered, lowering his head, "I'm really sorry, it was my fault. I shouldn't have taken you fishing. I..."

"Your fault?" exclaimed May. "Oh, of course it wasn't. It was my own fault."

Peter smiled and then reached into his pocket to take out the box containing the medal he had won. "May," he whispered. "I'd like for you to have this."

May's eyes widened when she saw what Peter was giving her. "Your medal!" she exclaimed. "Oh, but Peter—I couldn't..."

"Please, May, Take it. I'd really like you to have it."

May stared at him. "Because of the drooking I got? But Peter, sure it was my own fault. It..."

"No," said Peter, "not because of that. Because... because... Well, just because."

May looked into his sad, blue eyes, and took the box from him with a gentle smile. Then she opened it, and he watched her take the medal out.

"Thanks, Peter. Thanks..." Suddenly she felt the tears welling up in her eyes, and she whispered as she tried to stop herself from crying, "I'd better go now."

"Will I see you later?"

"Yes. Later."

"May?"

"Yes?"

"Are you really going to take your final vows?"

Suddenly, she closed the window and hurried away, crying.

⊙≫☉

The following day, Father O'Kane informed the girls that it was time for them to return to the convent, and all the way back to Carrickmacross, Joan wondered at May's mood. She just stared listlessly out of the carriage window.

The next day, May took the medal to the jewelers and had it inscribed. She also bought a thin gold chain for it.

⊙≫☉

They had been back at the convent two weeks when the Mother Superior sent for Joan. After Joan left, the Mother Superior sent for May.

"I am not the only one who has noticed your behavior; it's the other novices. May, are you sure you are ready to take your final vows? You have to be sure."

"Oh, but Mother Superior, I *will* be sure," cried May, "if only I could see Peter again. Just once. Then I'll know."

The old nun's mouth tightened into a thin line as she studied the crying girl. Then turning her back to May, she walked over to her desk. "Very well, May. Go back to Ardmore. See this... this Peter, and may God help you to make the right decision."

⌒∽⌒

The train journey back to Ardmore seemed to take forever, and May clutched the medal that hung around her neck. When she arrived at Ardmore, Father O'Kane was there to meet her as the Mother Superior had phoned him to explain the situation.

"Peter's father is down in the garden," he said, his old eyes flitting over May's pale face. Hurrying out to the back garden, May shaded the sun from her eyes as she searched for Peter. She could only see his father and she ran to him.

"Hello," said the old gardener, pulling off his cap." Are ye back fer another while?"

"Yes. No. I... I... Where's Peter? Is he about?"

"Peter?" said Mr. Ward, staring at her. "Sure he's away to Belfast. He's won a scholarship to study agriculture at Belfast University. Imagine that, eh?"

May's face fell. "Belfast? When did he leave?"

"He went shortly after you girls had gone back to the convent."

"Oh!" exclaimed May. Suddenly, with a choking cry, she ran past the surprised gardener and on down the path to the river. She didn't stop running until she came to the wooden cross. Crying bitterly, she threw herself down on the grass and lay there, her heart breaking.

Later she sat up, remembering how Peter had tried to hide his disappointment at losing to Mrs. Titser. *What is he doing now in Belfast? Is he thinking about me?* Rubbing her eyes, May gazed at the river and thought about that memorable day with Peter. But it was hot in the grove, and suddenly, she felt very tired. Lying back, she drifted off to sleep. When she awoke, it was late afternoon and sadly, she hurried back to the parochial house.

That evening she took the last train to Carrickmacross, and as she sat staring at her face in the rain-splattered train window, she felt for her medal.

It was gone.

Where is it? In a panic, she searched through her underclothes. *Maybe it has dropped on the floor?* Seconds later, she found the broken chain.

"It's gone. It's gone!" she cried, and as the train thundered along the tracks to take her back to the convent, a new thought came to mind. *Maybe this is God's answer. Maybe he meant for me to lose Peter's medal. Maybe...*

Sister Breda folded her reply to the letter, put it into an envelope, and sealed it. Then pushing her chair away from her tiny table she shook her head with a soft smile. *After all these years,* she thought as she rose from her chair. Quickly she hurried downstairs and dropped the letter in the mailbox. She hurried out to the garden.

From her office the Mother Superior saw Sister Breda lift a rake and go over to the old priest. She couldn't hear the words Sister Breda spoke to him, but in her mind she knew what she would be saying.

"Peter! Remember that medal you gave me years ago?"

4

COUNTY CHAMPION, THREE TIMES

J ason loved his grandfather. He loved the smell of his grandfather—the deep smell of tobacco that wafted from the contented old man as he sat puffing on his pipe in his favorite armchair. Jason loved the look of his grandfather, too, especially during the summer holidays when the old man's hair seemed to get even whiter and his usually pale face turned red and gradually tanned to a leathery brown color. But more than anything else, Jason loved his grandfather's company.

Every day during the summer holidays, they would take Jason's golden Labrador, Lady, out to the park. Lady was older than Jason, and according to his grandfather, she was the same age as he was... in dog years, that is.

"A dog's year is equal to seven human years," he told Jason one day as they watched the old dog chase after some tiny birds that had been searching for worms among the freshly cut dry grass.

As the smells of summer surrounded them, the memory of that year's school sports day came to Jason. He had just been beaten into second place in the one hundred meters sprint, and he was feeling very disappointed and more than a little annoyed with himself, as he had beaten the winner twice before. As he bent over beside the other runners, panting from his efforts, the sound of his grandfather's voice made him raise his head.

"Well done, Jason!" shouted the old man bending under the spectator rope and coming over to him. "Second's not bad. Ye've won a runners up medal, son."

"I should have been first," snapped Jason, then he turned his back on his grandfather, and without another word, he hurried after the other runners to get his photograph taken by one of the local newspaper photographers.

After the photographs were taken and the medals and cups had been presented, the boy who had beaten Jason came over to him. "Hard luck, Jason," he said with a grin as he stuck out his hand for Jason to shake it.

"Hard luck had nothing to do with it, ye won well," Jason replied. "But I'll beat ye next year."

"Aye, ye might," said the taller boy, smiling. Jason smiled back. The boy asked, "Who was yon oul fella, yer Da?"

"My Da? Yon oul cod?" sneered Jason. "Of course not, wise up."

Immediately he felt ashamed, but before he could say anything more, one of their teachers came over to get two more photographs for the school magazine.

Later Jason searched for his grandfather and found him standing with old Father Murray. They were both laughing loudly as Jason walked over to them.

"Here give us a look at yer medal, son," said Jason's grandfather.

"You must have a bit of yer grandfather's legs in ye, boy," said Father Murray as Jason's grandfather examined the medal. "Man, but he was some runner. There wasn't a man in the county could beat him."

Jason looked questioningly at his grandfather, who just smiled and handed the priest Jason's medal to look at. When Father Murray handed it back he said, "Jimmy, ye must have some pile of cups and medals?"

"Ach, they're in a box up in the attic somewhere. I put them there after Mary died."

That evening after his mother and father had gone out, Jason looked at his medal again. His grandfather was smoking his pipe in the armchair, as usual. As Jason replaced the medal on the mantelpiece, his grandfather took the pipe from his mouth and said, "It looks kind of lonely there all by itself. Ye'll have to train and get a lot fitter if ye want to win more." Drawing on his pipe, he looked thoughtful for a moment, then he stood up, walked over to the mantelpiece, and put his pipe beside Jason's medal saying, "Tell ye what, son. C'mon and give me a hand and we'll see if we can get my medals and stuff down from the attic."

Minutes later the rickety steps of the ladder creaked as Jason stepped from the hole in the attic onto them. Moving slightly to one side he called, "Is this the box, Granda?"

"Is Lifebuoy Soap written on the side of it?"

"Aye."

"That's it, then. Now, be careful. It'll be right heavy, so ease it down the steps, one at a time. Easy now, easy."

Step by step, Jason carefully lowered the weighty box to the bottom of the ladder. With his grandfather's help, he carried it into the sitting room and they lifted it onto the table.

"Let's see now," said the old man, pulling back the lids and reaching into the box. One by one, he withdrew cups and medals, handing each one to Jason to look at. "That's real silver there, son—none of yer silver-plated rubbish."

Lastly, he reached to the bottom and gently lifted out a small, brown, varnished box with dull brass hinges. Blowing some dust from the dark wood, he handed it to Jason.

"What do ye think of that?" he said smiling.

Gingerly, Jason snapped up the brass clasp and opened the box. His eyes widened as he stared inside, for lying on a purple velvet cloth was the biggest medal he had ever seen. On it he saw the raised figure of an athlete surrounded by a laurel wreath. When Jason turned the heavy medal over, he saw the engraved words:

THREE TIMES COUNTY CHAMPION
JAMES BRADLEY

He looked at the old man in amazement. "Whew Granda! Did ye really win this?" he gasped, feeling the weight of the shiny medal in his hand. "Ye must have been some runner!"

His grandfather smiled; his secret, wise smile, but he said nothing. Jason examined the medal again, carefully placed it back in the box and handed it to his grandfather.

"Naw son," said the old man. "You keep it. I'd like ye to have it. In fact, I'd like ye to have them all. They're no use to me sittin' up in that dusty oul attic."

Jason gaped at his grandfather. "Yer giving all yer medals to me?" he gasped. Suddenly the words, *was yon oul fella yer Da?* came to him and tears filled his eyes.

His grandfather stared at him. "Well, if I thought ye were goin' to take on so, I would've left them up there."

So Jason told his grandfather what he had said to the boy.

"Ach son, don't worry about anythin' like that. Sure I understand."

Jason searched his grandfather's face for any sign of hurt, and when the old man smiled and reached out to playfully ruffle his hair, he felt better.

"Granda? Ye know I love ye?"

His grandfather coughed a few times, his own blue eyes glistening as he whispered, "Aye, and that's all that matters, isn't it, Jason?"

Jason shivered in the cold graveyard as he held tightly onto his weeping mother's hand. He had been glad when the undertaker had screwed the coffin lid over his grandfather's white, expressionless face earlier that morning because it hadn't been *his* granda. It hadn't been his granda, either, who had cried as the ambulance took him to hospital three weeks before he died. All through that cold winter, it hadn't been his granda who had coughed bloody phlegm into a bucket by the fire, nor was it his granda who had changed into a crabbed old man best left alone.

Back at the house after the funeral, Jason sat on the sofa staring into the fire. He could just hear his mother on the phone out in the hall speaking to his aunt in Canada.

"Ach, it was better for him. Sure what could ye have done? Sure, I know ye couldn't get here in time. Naw, naw I'm fine, really..."

As his mother continued talking, Jason's eyes drifted to the mantelpiece. He stood up and reached for the brass hinged box, carried it to the sofa, and sat down again. Hunched over the box he opened it and stared down at the medal, then gently, with trembling hands he turned it over, and his tears trickled onto the words:

THREE TIMES COUNTY CHAMPION
JAMES BRADLEY

5

BARRIERS

Nineteen year old Joe Doherty sighed heavily, then hunched his back, pushed his hands deeper into the pockets of his blue jeans and quickened his step as he headed towards the Police barrier on Spencer Road. The barrier was there to protect the Police Station from terrorist attacks. A Sangar jutted from the reinforced wall of the station like a monstrous gargoyle and between the two halves of the barrier was a wooden hut. On each side of the road two policemen carrying rifles were on duty.

"Shit," he muttered. "Not that wee bastard again."

As Joe came to the first half of the barrier, the hair on the back of his neck bristled, and he almost tripped over an uneven flagstone as he walked faster.

"Ah sir, excuse me!" a voice called.

Pretending not to hear, Joe walked on.

"I said, excuse me, sir!" the voice repeated, louder this time.

Joe stopped, and turning slowly around he said, "Who, me?"

His heartbeat quickened as the constable came towards him. Holding his rifle against his chest with one forearm, the policeman pulled a small black notebook with a pen attached to it by an elastic loop from his pocket. He leaned his rifle carefully against the low window of the house they were standing outside. As he did, Joe lowered his head and moved back a bit. Out of the corner of his eye, he saw the other policeman across the road watching them.

"Now sir, would you mind telling me your name?" asked the constable. He was at least a foot shorter than Joe, and his piercing, blue eyes flitted over Joe's pale face.

"Doherty. Joe Doherty," said Joe looking away. But when the constable began writing down his name Joe stared at him.

"Address sir?" said the policeman, looking up at him.

"Eh?" said Joe, looking away again.

"Where do you live?"

"Forty, Anderson's Crescent, Gobnascale," said Joe quietly. *Wee bastard,* he thought as the constable wrote his address down.

When the constable put his notebook and pen back in his pocket, Joe got ready to go.

"Have you any identification on you, sir?" asked the constable.

"Naw, but I have me Bru card," answered Joe.

A nerve worked on the side of the constable's face as he snapped, "Well, would you mind showing it to me, sir?"

With a disgusted sigh, Joe patted the breast pocket of his denim jacket. He withdrew a small sports wallet and handed it to the policeman.

"Would you mind opening it yourself, sir?"

Tearing the wallet open along its Velcro closure, Joe showed the policeman what was in the wallet by holding open the compartments.

"Let me have a look, sir," said the constable, taking the wallet from him. Joe grit his teeth as the policeman pulled a sealed condom from one of the compartments. "What's this sir?" he asked, a half smile playing on his face.

"What the hell does it look like?" snapped Joe.

The constable sniffed and replaced the condom. Joe stiffened as he saw him slip a small photograph from another compartment. Holding it between his forefinger and thumb as if it was contaminated, the constable asked, "Who's this?"

"You know who it is," snapped Joe. "Sure ye looked at it yesterday. I told ye then who it was."

The constable's eyes narrowed. "Sir, I asked you who it was," he said coldly.

"It's my brother," muttered Joe looking down the road.

"Pardon, sir?"

"It's a photo of my dead brother, Pius," answered Joe.

"Pius?" said the constable. "That was a Pope's name, wasn't it?"

Joe said nothing, still looking down the road.

"The Pope wouldn't like you using condoms, would he?" said the constable, stepping back as two elderly women carrying shopping bags came walking past.

Suddenly one of the women stopped. "What's the point in all that, eh?" she shouted. "Stoppin' the young fellas? Sure yer only drivin' them intay the Provo's hands, that's what yees are doin'. Recruitin' them fer the IRA!"

The constable ignored her and handed Joe back his wallet.

"Come on, Lilly," whispered the other woman.

"Can't they see what they're doin' is stupid?" Lilly went on. "What's the point in it anyway? Sure, no young fella would be stupid enough tay be carryin' guns or anythin' walkin' past here. They're not stupid, ye know!" she shouted, glaring at the constable.

"Lilly, come on," hissed her companion. "Fer God's sake, come on."

Lilly gave Joe a sympathetic look, and then gave in to her friend's persistent tugging on her coat sleeve.

"Now sir," said the constable as the women walked away, "would you mind turning around and raising your hands? I'm going to body search you."

Blowing out his breath and shaking his head from side to side, Joe raised his arms and turned around until he was facing across the road. As he did, he saw the other policeman approaching them. Joe gave a start as the constable roughly ran his hands under his jacket and across his shoulders. The hands quickly patted his chest and stomach, and he stiffened as he felt the hunkered constable now run his hands up the insides of his legs. Seconds later the search was over.

It was beginning to rain and as Joe put the wallet back in his pocket, he waited to see what the constable wanted next.

"Where are you going, sir?"

"The Bru," snapped Joe glaring at him.

"The Labour Exchange, you mean," corrected the constable smiling at the other policeman.

"Aye," snapped Joe glaring at them. "That's what I mean." *Asshole*, he whispered under his breath.

"Okay, sir you can go."

"Thanks a bunch," snapped Joe. As he turned to walk away, the other policeman spoke.

"Doherty?"

"What?" snapped Joe, swinging around.

"You *know* we'll be watching you, don't you?"

"Big deal, bastard," Joe whispered under his breath and began to walk away. As he did he began a shaky, nonchalant whistle.

The two policemen smiled as they looked after him until a horn sounded behind them. One of them ran to the hut to raise the barrier to allow two army Land Rovers inside.

⟨⟩

"Which of them was it?" asked Johnny Murray as he and Joe walked up Asylum Road to the Labour Exchange. "The wee, fair-haired bastard?"

"Aye," growled Joe. "That's three times he's stopped me this week."

Murray stared at him. "Why don't ye go down Simpson's Brae? Ye don't have to go down Spencer Road past the barrier, ye know."

"Aye, I know," snapped Joe as they walked through the gate. "But I wouldn't give the wee prick the satisfaction."

6

DEPRESSION

Sergeant Bernard Burke stared out of the Sangar window. It was Sunday afternoon and the police barrier was unmanned. Spencer Road was deserted except for two old women who stood gossiping at the corner of Malvern Terrace. The usual Sunday Mass crowd had gone and Burke's thoughts were on the argument he had had with his wife that morning. It was the same argument they had been having ever since his best friend, Constable Jim Thompson, had been blown to pieces near Claudy recently.

"I'm goin' to England and I'm takin' the wains..."

He frowned as he remembered the determined look on his wife's worried face as he looked up from his bowl of porridge at her.

"This is no bloody way to live..."

What could he say? The brick that had been thrown through their sitting room window three weeks ago when he had been on nights had been bad enough. But when Jim was killed shortly after that, it put Daphne over the edge and every day since then she begged him to pack in the Force and go to England.

"You'll get a job there, with better pay, fewer hours and peace of mind! My brother Trevor says there is plenty of work in London, and he could put us up until we get settled."

Burke sighed aloud. *What would I do there?* he thought. All he knew—and all he had ever wanted since he had left school—was to be a policeman. Even now, when it all had changed in 1968, he still wanted to stay in the Force. A car horn sounded suddenly, and he looked towards the barrier, glancing up at one of the screens. He could see his father-in-law get out of the car and look up at the camera.

"Hey, Barney! It's me."

Burke pressed the button to release the catch on the automatic barrier, and a few seconds later the car drove through. Pressing the "close" button, Barney watched with his heart pounding as the car stopped just beneath the Sangar. *What's up now?* he wondered as Daphne's father got out of the car and walked to the steel door by the big, reinforced gate. Pressing another button, Burke released the catch and with a loud click the door opened.

Breathing hard, the old man climbed the steep concrete steps to the Sangar door, and Burke's heartbeat quickened as he opened it to let his father-in-law inside. "Barney," the old man said quietly, the tone of his voice telling Burke that this was not a courtesy visit. "Is it okay to talk in here?" He looked around the cold interior of the Sangar.

Burke studied him for a moment or two. "Aye," he said quickly. "Here, George, sit here. What's up?" He pushed a swivel chair at the old man.

"It's Daphne..." his father-in-law said without sitting. "and the wains. They've gone to London, to Trevor. Barney, I didn't want to do this, but Daphne told me to tell you. I tried to persuade her to wait until you came home, but it was no use. She... she said she couldn't take it anymore. She said it was the only way."

Barney sighed deeply, gripping tightly on the edge of the steel shelf that ran around the wall. "We had a terrible row this morning," he said. "You know the pressure she's been under. It got worse after the brick, and then Jim's death." He stared at the old man. "George, can't she see I can't pack in the Force? It's my whole life. It's all I've ever wanted to do. You know that. So does she," he added bitterly.

"I know, I know, Barney. But Daphne and the wains must come first. You have to realize how desperate she is... to do this... to leave you..."

"She hasn't left me," snapped Burke. "She'll be back. She'll... she'll have to come back."

"Barney," sighed the old man as he took a step towards him. "Daphne's near crackin' up. She's a nervous wreck. She can't go on much longer like this without crackin'." He studied his son-in-law. "You know it's *you* she's worried about."

Burke turned away to look up Spencer Road.

"She says you're not the same," continued his father-in-law. "She says you're always bad-tempered with her and the wains."

Barney sighed heavily. "I've been working long hours, George, you know that. It's not like the old days... before the troubles. I don't get much sleep—especially since Jim got blown to bits."

George stared at Barney's stooped, broad back. "What are you going to do?" he asked.

Barney turned, tears in his dull blue eyes. "I... I don't know," he whispered. "I really don't know, he sniffed. "George, couldn't you speak to her? Tell her I said she can stay with Trevor for awhile. Tell her to take a few days, but then she should come home."

The old man sighed now, half-turning to go. "I'll tell her," he said. "But I think the only thing she'll want to hear is that you've quit. Barney, I'll have to be goin' now. I've to pick up the wife. She's very upset by all of this, too."

"I'm sorry," whispered Barney, unable to stop a tear sliding down his ruddy face.

"Aye, well, I'll be goin' then."

"Aye," sniffed Barney, following him to the door. "I'll see you later, George—and thanks for callin'."

Half a minute later the car was driving back through the barrier, and as the pole sealed it Burke began to cry. Fumbling in his breast pocket, he pulled out a small wallet of photographs. The tears flowed faster as he flicked through them, stopping at one that showed himself and his children smiling up from the back beach at Portrush. It had been a hot day—one of the few last summer. He remembered that his son had kicked sand into his daughter's eyes, and he had lost his temper and hit him. The beach had been crowded, and his loud shouting as he remonstrated with his son had spoiled their day.

"Bad tempered," he choked, the smiling faces on the photograph blurring as his tears ran.

Suddenly a horn sounded, and looking up at the monitor he saw two gray Land Rovers. The patrol was back. Sniffing, he wiped the tears from his face and reached to press the button. As the Land Rovers drove to sanctuary, he slowly pushed the wallet back into his pocket.

7

THE BIRTHDAY SASH

It wasn't that he didn't want them to know he was a Catholic, he did; but not yet; not until they knew him better.

Johnny tossed and turned, but it was no use. He could not get to sleep. Johnny was eleven years old, and he had only been at Templegrove College for ten days. Templegrove was a State School, and the majority of its pupils were Protestants. He could still picture the scene now, remembering the determined look on his mother's face as she broke the news to his grandfather. "It's better if Protestants and Catholics mix."

The old man had bristled, shaking his head wildly, his dull, gray eyes sparking with anger as he gripped the arms of his chair. "He'd be better off goin' tay St. Columb's. Sure he'll learn nothin' at yon place," he exclaimed.

"Wise up, Da. It'll do our Johnny no harm. Sure, we can always send him to St. Columb's if it doesn't work out. Sure it'll be good experience fer him. It's better if they mix. There's too much division nowadays. Schools is the best place to start, and besides, Templegrove is only up the road. St. Columb's is miles away."

Johnny remembered the color of his grandfather's face, and how it grew redder and redder then almost purple beneath his snow white hair until at last he turned on Johnny's father, exasperated. His father had buried himself beneath the newspaper during all the arguing.

"And what have *ye* tay say about it all, eh?" the old man had shouted, as he smacked the paper from his son-in-law's hands.

"Ach, c'mon John," whined Johnny's father, sitting up straight. "Sure, what does it matter? One school's as good as another. Sure, there's too much oul religion these days. Our Johnny'll get on all right no matter what school he goes to. Jesus, it's not as if they'll turn him or anything."

"They'll not learn him properly! Ye'll see. Aye, ye'll see, alright. He'll learn *nothin'*. And he'll be treated differently," persisted the old man, turning to glare at his daughter.

"Look," Johnny's mother had finally shouted before going into the kitchen. "There are other Catholics at Templegrove, and I don't care what ye think. Our Johnny's goin' to there, and that's that! And if he has any problems, I'll sort them out. RIGHT!" And with a final glare at her father, she stamped out of the room.

Any problems! Any problems! Johnny sighed, pushing deeper into his bed as he thought about the present one. How could he solve it?

The next evening after dinner, he waited impatiently until his grandfather had dozed off. His mother was out in the kitchen washing the dishes, and his father was watching television and trying to read the newspaper at the same time.

"Da," whispered Johnny, kneeling down beside him and glancing quickly at his sleeping grandfather. "Da," he repeated louder, tugging at his father's shirtsleeve.

"Eh, what is it son?"

"Da, it'll be my birthday next week, and..."

"Yer birthday? Will it, son?"

"Aye, on Thursday. And..."

"Thursday, eh? Ye'll be a big man, then. Er... what age are ye, son?"

"I'll be twelve, Da, and..."

'Twelve, eh? God, son, ye'll be a full-grown man soon." He smiled. "Yer Mother'll be bakin' ye a cake. We'll have to have a birthday party, eh?"

"Da," Johnny whispered angrily, "'I don't want a birthday party!"

His father stared stupidly at him for a couple of seconds, and then his attention was drawn back to the television.

"Da," Johnny whispered louder. "Are ye listening to me? Da!"

With an annoyed sigh his father turned to him. "What is it, son? What do ye want?"

Johnny looked quickly at the kitchen door, at his grandfather, and then back to his father.

"A sash, Da. That's what I want, a sash fer my birthday." He turned again to look at his grandfather.

His father's eyes widened, and then he began to smile. "Ye know what I thought ye said, son?" he chuckled. "'I thought ye said ye wanted a sash fer your birthday." His eyes twinkled as he laughed, but he stopped suddenly when he saw the look on his son's face. Wide-eyed he sat up. "Yer... yer not serious, son?"

Johnny nodded

"A sash! A friggin' sash!" shouted Johnny's father. They both swung to look at the old man who suddenly snorted. Lowering his voice Johnny's father whispered, "Son, ye can't really be serious. Ye can't want a sash! They are for Protestants—not a Catholic boy such as yourself. Yer grandfather'd have a fit! It'd kill him if he found out. Ye must be mad to even think..." He studied his son's serious face. "What the hell do ye want a sash fer, anyway?"

"They're all gettin' them, Da, all the boys in my class. If I don't get one they'll know I'm a Catholic. I don't want them to know—not yet awhile. Not till they know me better."

His father studied his son's pale face. "But son," he said. "'What do ye want a sash for? I mean, ye can't even wear it! Why, if ye even brought it into the house, yer grandfather'd have fit!"

"I *know* that Da, but if I could get one, then they'd think I was okay fer awhile. Later on, I could tell them that—"

Just then, his grandfather turned in his armchair and snorted loudly a few times. Johnny and his father held their breath, but a few moments later the old man's steady breathing resumed and they relaxed.

With his eyes fixed on the old man, Johnny's father whispered, "Them sashes would be very dear, son—and where would ye buy one?"

"I don't know, Da. I'll try and find out tomorrow." Johnny turned and looked hopefully at his father, whispering, "Ye *will* help me Da, won't ye?"

His father smiled and reached to ruffle his son's hair. "Don't worry, son. Between the two of us, we'll sort it all out." Picking up the paper again, he turned the pages to search for the classifieds, muttering to himself, "I wonder can ye buy them things second-hand?"

6∞9

The next day at his dinner break, Johnny stood with two of his classmates and watched some of the older boys playing cricket. Beside him, Richard Thompson was busy squeezing a pimple from his chin; on Johnny's other side, Phillip Clark stood with his school cap pulled down over his eyes to shade them from the bright sun.

Taking a deep breath Johnny said quickly, "Have ye got yer sash yet, Richard?"

"Naw, not yet," said Richard, wiping his fingers on the right sleeve of his pullover. "Me ma's ordered me one though."

"Ordered ye one?"

"Aye, up at Ballymena. There's a place up there that makes them."

Ballymena. Johnny heaved a sigh of relief. He could get one at Ballymena.

"Ye know, Johnny, you don't know what yer missin'."

"Eh?" Johnny's face fell. "What?"

"The lodge. It's great craic."

"I'm gettin' me oul fella's sash," butted in Phillip, before Johnny could speak. "Aye, you Roman Catholics are missin' out, alright. The Lodge is cracker, especially on the Twelfth."

Johnny's face grew red. His breathing increased rapidly and he felt faint. *They knew,* he almost screamed. They had known all along... and it didn't seem to matter to them that he was a Catholic.

That afternoon, Johnny came dashing into the sitting room. "Da!" he shouted. "Da!"

He startled his father, who looked up from his paper.

"It's okay, Da! I don't have to get a sash after all," exclaimed Johnny.

"A sash?" exclaimed his mother frowning, as she put down her knitting. "What's this about a sash? What would ye want a sash for?"

"A sash!" his grandfather spluttered, struggling to his feet. "I told yees, but yees wouldn't lissen. He's a bloody Orangeman already!"

Johnny gaped at him, looking over at his father, who was giggling hysterically. Johnny began to laugh, too. Stumbling past his mother, he flopped into the armchair on top of his father, and they laughed louder as they listened to the old man shout.

"Yees wouldn't listen. I told yees. But naw, yees wouldn't listen. Now see what's happened. He's a bloody Orangeman!"

8

GOLDEN DAYS

The old man laughed aloud as he thought about the young reporter's last question. *"And how much would you sell your cottage and land for now, Mr. McCool?"* He laughed again as he remembered his own quick reply. *"I'd want no less than a million pounds fer it."*

Gold. Who would have thought his cottage and two fields were sitting on the biggest gold find in Ireland—maybe in the whole world? What would Maggie have said about it all? Would she have wanted to sell?

He turned to look through the half-door at the pink sky and the setting sun. The shadows had almost finished creeping down the wide valley below, and a frosty mist was beginning to grow. He sighed deeply and turned back to the turf fire. *What good would a million pounds be to me now? I'm too old to enjoy it.* Reaching for the poker, he stabbed it at the dying fire. It had been a hard life for him and Maggie. Would the money have made them any happier?

He sighed again. *Aye, it had been a hard life, but we were happy,* he thought. Raising his head, he squinted up at the faded photograph on the mantelpiece. Smiling shyly, Maggie was posing beside one of the three cows they had owned back then. She was wearing her Sunday dress and her black hair was tied up in a bun near the top of the back of her head. Beside her was their only son, Frank, and his thoughts now went to him.

It had been Frank who had showed him how to take the photograph; the camera had been his fourteenth birthday present. What would Frank have to say about the farm? "Ach!" he muttered as he reached for his matches. "Sell. That's what he would say."

With a grunt, he rose from the stool, went over to the table and slowly began to pump life into the oil lamp. Moments later as its cozy glow filled the room, he went to the door and stared out. Without taking his eyes from the night, he felt for his pipe and filled it, fingering the tobacco tight into the bowl. His eyes fell to the flame as he lit the pipe and took a long drag. Waving out the match, he turned and threw it in the direction of the fire, as he sucked hard on his pipe he reached to bolt out the darkness.

Returning to the fire, he sat down. His thoughts once more drifted to his son. How long ago had it been since he had last seen Frank and his wife? He shook his head trying to remember. Time seemed to pass more slowly these days, yet the rest of his life—the happy times—seemed to have gone by in a flash. He wished he had given more time to his son, built up more memories. He had very few he could reminisce about except the day he had taken Frank fishing.

"Da! Da! The sun's up! Wake up! We're goin' fishin', remember? Da!"

"Eh?" He woke, staring for a few moments at his excited, curly-haired son. He felt for Maggie, but she was already up. The morning smells drifted to him.

"Aw aye, the fishin'. Right son, give me a coupla minutes and then we'll get diggin' fer some bait."

Five minutes later, he was splashing cold water onto his ruddy face. With a loud, "Ahhh," he stepped away from the basin and reached blindly for the towel. As he dried his face, he was aware of Frank watching him. With a smile, he reached out and ruffled the grinning boy's brown hair. "Right son, let's get some food intay us."

At the table as she filled their mugs with tea, Maggie remarked, "Ye'd need tay wear yer oilskins the day. There'll be rain fer sure."

Turning, he looked through the open half-door at the black clouds hanging over the valley. "Aye, yer right there, Maggie." Turning to his son he smiled. "All the better fer catchin' trout, eh, Frank?"

"Aye, Da," said his son almost choking as he sipped at the remains of his tea. He rose to stand by the table and waited impatiently for his father to finish.

"Have ye checked that ye have everythin'? Have ye plenty of hooks and weights and things?"

"Aye, Da I have. All we need are the black heads."

"There'll be plenty of them down in the lower fields. Have ye got a jar?"

"Jar?"

"Aye, a jar. How did ye think ye were goin' to carry the worms, in yer pockets? Ha, ha, ha..."

Maggie smiled and said, "Ye'll find an empty jar in the cupboard, Frank, the bottom shelf."

They both smiled as they watched their tiny son stand on tiptoes as he stretched to reach for the crockery jar.

And so, with a spade resting on his shoulder and his son shouting, "Hurry, Da!" they headed down the path to the lower fields.

Minutes later a light breeze whipped at his long hair as he drove his sharp spade into the turfy ground. As his son gathered up the worms, he leaned on his spade and looked up at the cottage. Maggie was standing at the door watching them. With one hand on the spade, he waved. She waved back and then went inside. As he gazed up at the cottage, a single ray of sunshine hit it for a few seconds, moving away as the sun hid behind more black clouds. He smiled, contented.

"Do ye think we have enough, Da?"

He turned to stare at the overflowing jar of angry worms. The shiny mucilage of the black heads sparkled in another brief blink of sunlight. "Aye son, that'll be enough. Come on let's get down tay the river."

He rammed his spade into the ground then hurried after his son down along the trees and across two more fields to the river.

Minutes later and with a gentle "plop," the first wriggling black head was cast into the calm water. As he eased back onto the grass that sloped down to the water, he watched the changing lines of concentration on his son's face as he followed the drifting float.

He sighed. It had been a perfect day; a day he would always remember. He sniffed as he felt the tears running down his face as he now remembered the day Frank told them he wanted to emigrate. Maggie had been heartbroken, but he had kept his feelings to himself.

"Ah, Maggie," he croaked aloud, his thoughts going back to her funeral.

A few distant neighbors had turned up for Maggie's wake, and he had sat by the fire watching his son and his wife greeting them and making them welcome. He had been unable to cope with it all. Apart from Maggie's death, he had not been able to get over the change in his son. He had been shocked by how old his son had looked, and as for Frank's thin wife, he wondered how anyone could love such a dour looking woman. *Why, Maggie looked younger than she did,* he had thought at the time.

What age was his son—over forty? Yes, his son was over forty...

After the funeral and an awkward parting, his son's last words had been, "Ye'll have tay come and visit us Da, one of these days."

As he watched the car drive them away, he remembered thinking that he didn't even know where Frank lived. Maggie had the address somewhere, he was sure. But, at the time he felt glad that his son was gone; glad everyone was gone. Now he could mourn by himself.

A night creature howled, its echoing cry reverberating down the valley. He shivered and reluctantly rose to go to bed. Tapping his pipe against the fireplace wall, he stared into the glowing turf ashes for a few moments, and turned and walked to the door to check the bolt. As he reached for the bolt, he paused and eased it open. A cold wind whistled into the cottage as he gazed up at the frosty, star-filled sky. The night creature cried again. *It seems closer this time,* he thought. *Maybe it's askin' me not tay sell.*

He felt a strange allegiance with it now, and he thought about the many creatures that would have to leave their homes when the machines came... *if* they came, *if* he let them. Could he stop them?

Where would he live if he left here? In Canada, with Frank and his wife? He couldn't imagine living with Frank's wife... nor with Frank, to tell the truth. He'd changed. *She'd* changed him. Maggie had been right about her...

No, he could never leave the oul sod.

But, where would he live? Would he live in the town? He could be rich and living in the town... but what was rich, anyway? Was it money, possessions? Or was it waking up on a beautiful day with all the sounds of summer and Maggie at his side?

As the night creature cried again, he bolted the door and turned to go to bed. As he walked past the fireplace, he glanced up at the mantelpiece and Maggie's photograph. He stopped and reached out, lifting it off the mantle, and with tears streaming down his face he tried to see her face.

Then, shaking with sadness and still holding the photograph, he stumbled to the bedroom door.

9

THE FISHERMAN

H e rowed out into the lough away from the waving woman—and he rowed badly, too. He was unused to the heavy oars and the long, clinker-built boat, and he splashed water up around his legs several times when he missed his stroke. On one occasion, he even fell into the back of the boat when he failed to dip his oars deep enough.

He had spotted the sign on the second day of his holiday as he drove through the village:

FISHING BOAT FOR HIRE
BAIT PROVIDED

After parking his car and walking down a dusty lane, he had come to a whitewashed cottage by a tiny lough.

There had been only one boat tied to the pier; he had hired it for the next day and paid in advance for it and a jar of worms that the woman had told him was the only bait the fish in her lough would take.

"The middle's the best, sir," said the stout woman who had leased the boat to him as she had pushed him away from the shaky wooden pier.

As he rowed, he glanced at the big jar of slimy, black-headed worms and his fishing rod that lay beside his tackle bag. Inside the bag, along with his fishing tackle, was a flask of strong coffee and some cheese sandwiches provided by the hotel where he was staying.

Estimating that he was as near the middle of the lough as he could get, he stopped rowing, shipped his oars, and a few minutes later he was ready. With the reel whining its objections, he swung the squirming worm over the side of the boat. The lead sinker carried the doomed worm to the bottom; when it had settled he set the tension on his reel then laid the rod alongside the oars. Pushing his narrow shoulders into as comfortable a position as he could get he lay back.

Although the sky was a clear blue and the sun burned down on the green fields all around the lough the breeze blowing across the water made him shiver. Pulling his cap over his eyes, he tried to contain his thoughts, but it was no use. He sighed deeply. He missed her. *What would she be doing now? Who would she be with?*

Separate holidays had been her idea; he had been angry at first, but what could he do? He didn't own her. He only loved her.

It was during that long winter in the city that their relationship had deteriorated. Just when he felt they should be getting engaged, he found out that she had been seeing someone else. He remembered his angry outburst. *"But why? Why?"* He also remembered her tearful reply. *"I don't know why. I can't explain it."*

She had promised him never again... and he had forgiven her, though his trust in her was gone. Yet somehow, the row had made him love her all the more.

He sighed again, his eyes snapping open as a screaming bird glided past and brought him from his thoughts. Pushing his cap back on his head, he sat up and reached for the rod. Tightening the spindle on the reel, he slowly wound in the line. As the dark hook and the remains of the worm surfaced, he caught it and laid down his rod again. Examining the piece of worm, he could see that something had been nibbling at it, so he removed the rest of it and tossed it over the side. Reaching for the jar, he took out another wriggling, angry worm and slowly worked its glistening body around the hook so that its black head moved enticingly on the end of it. When he was satisfied the hook was properly baited, he swung it over the side.

It quickly sank with a soft plop. The water sparkled from the spinning reel, and when the line stopped running, he again set the tension. Making sure the line was running over one of the rowlocks, he laid the rod down again. Now shading his eyes, he looked towards the hills, noting the black clouds drifting across them. The lough had been silver calm when the woman had pushed the boat away from the pier; now it was becoming quite choppy.

His eyes dropped to his tackle bag, and he grabbed at it. Taking out the flask, he unscrewed the white plastic cup, placed it between his feet on the bottom of the boat, and carefully poured some hot coffee into it. He pulled out a cheese sandwich, and after tearing at the cellophane paper, he took a bite from it.

He glanced at the hills again. Great dark shadows were now creeping down the valley below them and slowly extending towards the far side of the lough.

As he ate, his thoughts went back to his blonde-haired Carol. He could understand other men wanting her. He could understand his own jealousy. He could not understand why she wanted him... if she did anymore. He remembered a day similar to this, when he had taken her fishing for the first time. His enthusiasm for the sport had made her want to join him, but she had been bored by it.

He had not taken her fishing again. In fact, *he* had not been fishing since then. He thought about their relationship. They both liked different things, it seemed. He liked peace, quietness, and being alone with her. She liked going out to noisy, crowded nightclubs.

Screech!

With his mouth full of bread, he froze and looked at the reel.

Screech!

The spool was revolving slowly. Quickly he put down the cup and gently lifted his rod, tensioning the spindle with his other hand. Feeling another tug, he pulled hard, hoping the hook would bite deep enough into whatever was on the end of the line. Almost immediately, the line went taut as the fish took off.

The boat now rocked wildly as he eased off then reeled in, eased off, and reeled in, playing the fish out. His rod was almost bent in half with the line running under the boat.

"Come on!" he shouted, exhilarated. "Come on, ye boy ye!" His voice echoed across the lough, causing some bobbing ducks to quack their angry reply and rise gracelessly from the water.

For a full twenty minutes, he played the fish until gradually its efforts to escape grew weaker. With a few more vigorous spurts, it exhausted itself and was quickly reeled in.

Reaching down, he slipped his fingers into the helpless fish's heaving gills and hauled it up into the boat. "It must be a good seven pounds," he muttered as he searched in his tackle bag for the bishop. He raised it and was just about to give the trout a sharp knock on its pointed head when he paused. He stared down at the helpless creature. Its large eyes were wet and fearful, and its brown, scaly body heaved as it slowly suffocated.

His hand fell slowly. The sun had gone now and it was beginning to rain. The brown back and speckled underbelly of the fish heaved faster as he raised the bishop again. Suddenly with a curse, he flung it on top of his bag then bending, he examined the fish. He could see the hook was well embedded in its opaque upper lip. Quickly he pulled out his knife and began to carefully cut the gut near the eye of the hook. He forced the hook through the fish's lip and gently placed it back on the bottom of the boat. Still suffocating it flopped about banging its head against the wood.

Making up his mind, he slid his hands under the fish, gently lifted it to the edge of the boat and lowered it into the water. He watched as it turned and twisted on the surface of the water, and with a few flicks of its tail, it disappeared below. By then the water was slapping hard on the sides of the boat, and he hurried to put away his gear. With rain spitting into his face, he rowed back to the pier.

The woman was waiting for him with a plastic coat draped over her head, and as he handed her the mooring rope she said, "Any luck, sir?"

"Aye. I caught a real beauty. It must have been over seven pounds."

Glancing at his tackle bag and into the boat, the woman frowned. "The rain fairly got up; spoiled yer day?" she said quickly.

"No, I really enjoyed myself."

She smiled. "Ye'll be back the morra then, sir?"

"No," he said smiling back at her. "I don't think so. I'm through with fishing."

Still holding the mooring rope, the woman stared after him as he walked past her cottage and up the lane to his car.

Twenty minutes later he was pushing open the door of the hotel. Just as he was about to step inside he stopped and moved quickly aside, holding the door open to allow two girls through. As they passed, one of the girls smiled at him.

Still holding the door open, he watched them skip lightly down the wet steps and walk briskly into the drizzle. The girl who had smiled glanced back and smiled again. He waved at her and she waved back; he turned and went inside with a smile.

As he passed the hotel notice board, he stopped. A poster of the night's entertainment caught his eye:

HOLIDAY DANCE TONIGHT
EVERYONE WELCOME

He read it twice, his lips pursing into a silent whistle. Then smiling, he strode towards the lift.

Aye, he thought. *I'm glad I let her go.*

10

ASYLUM

Roy Rogers was lying beside Trigger when Jack stopped near a small garden on Clooney Terrace. The big palomino was dying, its heaving, pain-wracked body covered in bullet holes. Roy was already dead; the golden cowboy lay with one pearl-handled Colt 45 clutched in his right hand, and his white hat was still on his head.

Jack stared at it. He had often wondered what the cowboy film-star looked like without it. He was about to reach over the wall and pull the hat from Roy's head when the cowboy began to disappear. Frowning, Jack turned and looked for Trigger, but the horse had disappeared, too.

Jack shook his head as he stared at two beer cans and a plastic bag of rubbish that littered the garden. A few seconds later and he was on his way. The biting wind tore at his unshaven, haggard face and he shivered. He still had a bit to go yet.

"Here's lookin' at you, kid."

"Eh? Oh, hi, Bogie." Jack stopped to smile at Humphrey Bogart, dressed in a raincoat with his hat pulled down over his swarthy face; his upper lip was curled.

"Don't call me that," snarled Bogie, his upper lip working overtime. "I hate people calling me that."

"What?" asked Jack, puzzled.

"Bogie. I *hate* being called Bogie."

"But everyone calls ye Bogie!" exclaimed Jack.

"Yeah, well I don't like it, see?" snapped Bogie. "Do you know what a bogie is? Yeah, well don't call me it again. Okay?"

As Bogart prodded him in the chest, a woman passerby slowed down to stare at Jack as he stood talking to a lamppost.

"Sorry, Bog... I mean, sorry. By the way, how's Louis?"

"Who?"

"Louis. Ye know; the chief of the French police, the Gendarmes?"

"Eh?" Bogie stared at him with a look that said "this guy is nuts."

"In *Casablanca*. Oh come on, Bog... er Humphrey. Ye remember, in the film, *Casablanca*, at the end of it, as you and Louis walked through the mist at the airport and you said, 'Ya know, Louis, this could be the start of a beautiful friendship.'"

Bogart stared at Jack, his lip tightening over his protruding teeth. Then muttering, "Of all the bars and gin joints in the world, I have to walk into him," he walked away.

Jack stared after him as Bogie slowly disappeared. Shrugging his shoulders, he began to walk on.

By the time he reached the bus stop outside Bradley's sweet shop, he saw a large crowd spilling out onto the road. They were looking up at a window on the top floor. Looking to his left, Jack saw several policemen lined along the footpath. Suddenly he saw the police chief push through the crowd to the edge of the footpath and holding a megaphone in front of his mouth he shouted, "Give yourself up, Rico! You haven't got a hope in hell of getting away!"

Looking up, Jack saw Edward G. Robinson stick his head out of the window and yell, "You'll never take Rico alive, see!" as he began shooting down at the crowd.

Jack smiled as he saw the police chief fall to the ground, blood pouring through his fingers as he clutched at his chest. Two policemen immediately began to pull him to safety, and as they did Jack shouted, "Don't let them take ye alive, Eddie! Give it to them! Ha. hey. Give it to them, Eddie!"

Suddenly the shooting stopped, and Jack looked up at the window again. It was shut. As he looked back at the seven people standing in the bus queue, he saw a young girl giggle and nod at him. He glared at her. "Bitch," he snapped, and began to walk away. *Aye, You showed them, Eddie.*

It was beginning to rain when he stopped at the traffic light at Dale's Corner. A line of traffic tailed right back up Dungiven Road.

"Hi, Jack!"

He looked up at the rugged cowboy sitting on a horse in front of him. The cowboy wore a button-down blue shirt, leather chaps and a battered hat. It was John Wayne.

"Hi, Duke," called Jack. "Where are ye off to?"

"Gotta find, Scar, Jack."

"Scar?" Jack searched his memory for the name. "Oh aye, Scar. Now I remember. He was the Indian who kidnapped Natalie Wood in the film, *The Searchers*. Well, good luck, Duke and keep takin' the tablets."

"Yo!" shouted Wayne as he pointed down the road towards the roundabout just before he disappeared.

The green blinking of the light drew Jack's attention. When the traffic stopped, he began to hurry across the road, but he stopped halfway across when he saw *them*. Was it really them? A driver hooted his horn for him to get out of the way as the traffic moved off again. He glared at the driver and turned back to look for them; he smiled when he realized that they were still there. He hurried towards them, unaware of the hooting cars as they drove past.

"Yes, ma," he said smiling. "Da," he muttered, staring at the stony faced, burly man.

"Hello, son," said his mother. "Are ye on yer way out there?"

"Aye. Are yees comin' with me?"

"If ye like," his father said gruffly.

Jack frowned and cowered back as his father suddenly smacked his fist into the palm of his other hand. He looked at his mother. She looked so sad. He shivered and pulled his coat up around his neck. His headache was back again.

"How are ye keepin', Jack?" his mother asked as they began to walk along Limavady Road. "I haven't seen ye since the funeral."

"Ach, I'm okay Ma," he replied, his voice sounding like Jimmy Cagney. "Top of the world, in fact... except fer the headaches."

"Are they lookin' after ye well?" his mother asked.

"Okay, I suppose. Sometimes they stick needles in me. I don't like that."

At this his father stopped. With his eyes sparkling he smiled as he asked, "Does it hurt?"

"Aye," Jack said quickly. "It does."

His father's smile widened as they walked on. They were near St. Columb's Park now, and the rain was pelting down. Water dripped from Jack's nose and greasy hair. He noticed that his parents were not wet at all.

Suddenly his mother pointed to a man who came walking out through the park gates. "Oh, oh look! Isn't that Tyrone Power?"

They waved, and Tyrone Power smiled and waved back at them. He was dressed in a matador's outfit, and he slowly disappeared.

"I always liked him," said Jack's mother. "*The Long Gray Line.* That was my favorite film. It was on TV the night I died..."

"Nooooo!" screamed Jack. But it was too late. His mother had disappeared, and his father was disappearing too.

"Were ye a good boy, Jack?" his father whispered smashing his fist into the palm of his hand just before he disappeared.

"Aye Da, I was," Jack cried looking all around. "I was. Ye didn't have to hit me. I was always a good boy." He keened as he reached up to hold his head with both hands. The pounding grew worse. Sniffing as tears ran down his face he hurried on, walking just on the edge of the footpath towards the top of Caw Brae.

When he reached Nelson Drive, four teenagers came walking out of the housing estate to head down Limavady Road.

"How's the Bowery boys?" Jack asked with a smile as he stopped in front of a big nosed teenager who had his baseball cap on the wrong way round. "What about ye, Satch?"

"Hey Jack, whatta ya say?" exclaimed Satch, smiling.

Suddenly a smaller, pug-nosed teenager took off his cap and began to hit Satch with it, shouting in a high-pitched voice, "Never mind whatta ya say, dope. We gotta go. See ya, Jack."

"Aye, see ye, mugs," said Jack as he turned to watch the Bowery boys walk away.

"What did ye say?" asked Satch, turning. He had suddenly become the shaven-headed leader of the teenagers. He narrowed his eyes as he glared at Jack.

"Nothin'. Nothin'," muttered Jack, hurrying away.

"Headcase!" sneered one of the teenagers as they all laughed.

Afraid they would come after him, Jack walked faster. *Not far to go now,* he thought, looking down the brae. *Not far to sanctuary.* Suddenly, bending, and dangling his arms down at his sides he began to shout, "Sanctuary! Sanctuary!"

A man jogging on the other side of the street stared at him as he passed.

"She gave me water!" shouted Jack. With his back still bent and his arms dangling at his sides he ambled on down the brae.

By now he was soaked through, but he didn't care. He was nearly there. He smiled as a wagon train led by Davy Crocket rumbled past. He waved to a cowboy sitting in the back of the last wagon, and the cowboy waved his rifle at him.

Just then, the wagons became army Land Rovers and the soldier in the last one waved to him. Jack walked through the gates and onto the hospital grounds to his sanctuary.

11

Letting Go

The old farmhouse groaned with the noise of the young people; friends of his daughter and her fiancée. He felt out of sorts amongst them as he watched it all from his hiding place by the side of the fire.

She seems nervous, he thought. *Aye, nervous, but happy.*

He tried not to stare at her; instead, he tried to look happy for her, but his head buzzed with the clamor and the drink, and now a girl began her well-rehearsed party piece, the accompanying melodeon trying hard to match her sweet voice.

He clapped vigorously; too long, and then abruptly stopped. Embarrassed, he turned quickly to look down at the fire. As he bent to pick up two lengths of dusty turf, he smiled at a young couple who sat near the black hearth. Placing the turf carefully on top of the burning pieces, he pressed hard and watched the sparks fly up the chimney. Almost immediately, sweat erupted from above the line on his pale brow.

"Here's to Mary and Tom!" a bleary-eyed young man suddenly yelled, holding his drink aloft.

The words, "TO MARY AND TOM," rang around the farmhouse, followed by loud cheers of "Congratulations and best wishes for your future!" as the men and women gathered around Mary and her fiancée, some patting their backs, others shaking their hands. He could just see Mary now, her face red and flushed as she smiled into her Tom's dark eyes.

For a moment he was jealous, but quickly conquered the feeling and reached for his lukewarm, almost empty glass of whiskey. *If only Kathleen were here.* As he drained the glass, his eyes flitted around the room. He needed her now. He was never any good with people, especially the young. Kathleen would have known what to do.

Suddenly he could stand being inside no longer and edged towards the door. Easing open the bottom half, he grabbed for his cap and slipped outside.

"How about a song, Mary? C'mon. Ah, c'mon."

He turned and looked into the room and was surprised to hear Mary start to sing. Her eyes were shining as she sang an old "Come all ye" he had heard years ago when the three of them lived in Creeslough. *She's so like her mother,* he thought as he watched Mary sway in Tom's arms. She sang easily—not embarrassed or shy. *There's strength there; aye, she has her mother's spirit about her.*

Sighing, he turned away from the scene and walked a few steps into the darkness by the side of the doorway. He looked up at the starry blackness and took his pipe from his pocket. Gazing away down the valley to the twinkling lights of the town, he filled his pipe, pressing the tobacco tight into the bowl. A minute later, when the pipe was lit, he drew sharply and leaned back against the newly whitewashed wall, one leg bent, the heel of his new brown brogues scraping black lines down the whiteness.

The clear night seemed to depress him even further, for it was on nights like this that he would have walked with Kathleen down along the river. Every summer's night, hand in hand they would walk down the fields to the river and wander for miles along the fishermen's path drinking in all the river sounds. Occasionally they would stop when they saw a trout leap or a river hen run in a mad frenzy over the water. Later when it was almost dark, they would head home listening to the sound of the night creatures in the fields beside them.

Back then he thought nothing would change, but the night Kathleen told him she was pregnant, he took the news with mixed feelings. Somehow, he knew nothing would ever be the same again. Then Mary was born, and the walks by the river were gone. Drawing deeply on his pipe, he remembered the night Kathleen passed away. Mary was nearly seven, and he could still remember trying to tell his intelligent little girl that her mother had gone. He could still picture the look on her face as she tried to take it in.

The months after Kathleen's death were lost months. The farm suffered, for the heart had gone out of him. Then the Priest came to tell him it was time Mary went to school, so he sold the farm and they moved to Falcarragh.

He bought a smaller farm near the village where Mary could attend school. As she grew older, he came to depend on her for news about the villagers. He kept mainly to himself, preferring his three small fields and his farm animals for company. One day Mary brought Tom to see him and with his heart breaking, he listened to the likable young man telling him how much he loved his daughter. Now they were to be married on Saturday.

Drawing easily on his pipe, he pushed himself away from the wall and walked slowly down the stony path to the gate. He gazed again down the valley. *Kathleen would have liked it here*, he thought, raising his eyes to the star-filled sky. It had been a lovely summer... his last, maybe.

"Are ye not comin' in, Da?"

Startled, he turned and stared at his beautiful daughter. For a second or two, she was Kathleen. Reaching for his pipe, he stammered, "Aye... aye. I'll be in now, Mary. I just came out fer a bit o' pipe. I'll be in now. Go ye on in and enjoy yersel. Yer young man'll be missin' ye."

Mary frowned as she searched his shadowed face. "Da," she whispered tearfully. "Are ye all right? Are ye... are ye happy fer me?"

"Happy for ye? Of course I am," he said brightly. "Why wouldn't I be? Tom's a fine man. He'll look after ye."

Mary smiled and reached to take one of his hard hands in hers. Her mouth quivered, and she was on the verge of tears.

Suddenly a shout of, "Where's Mary? Where's the bride-to-be?" came from the farmhouse, and letting go of her father's hand she half turned.

"I'd better go in, Da," she whispered.

"Aye," he said quietly. "Go on in and enjoy the craic. Sure it's yer night."

His eyes glistened as he watched her walk to the door. *She has to go, I suppose,* he thought with a heavy sigh. Turning away from the farmhouse, he took another look down the valley. Tapping the bowl of his pipe gently against the gatepost, he watched the burning pieces of tobacco stream to the path like a row of falling stars.

He stood for a few more moments watching the tobacco die, and pushed the pipe into his breast pocket and followed Mary into the craic.

12

LAST MILE TO BELFAST

The agitated orderly burst loudly into Doctor Dawson's office. "Doctor! Doctor! She's escaped!"

Startled, Doctor Dawson gaped at the excited man before him. "Who, man? Who's escaped?"

"Mary Duggan, Doctor! She stabbed Nurse McGinley with a pair of scissors!"

Dawson's eyes widened with horror. "Not Duggan!" he said as he grabbed for the phone at the same time he shouted at the orderly. "Sound the alarm! Get everybody out to search for her. She may still be on the grounds." As he dialed 999, he knew it was too late. Mary Duggan was too clever to be caught now, too insanely clever.

❦

The nun staggered along Derry's railway platform to the hissing, impatient Belfast train. The heavy suitcase she carried in one hand made her walk like a penguin. She was gasping and wheezing when she stopped at the first open door; she took a deep breath and lifted the suitcase onto the train.

A minute later her thick soled boots clumped along the busy corridor as she searched for a seat. The train was unusually busy, but eventually she stopped at a compartment with an empty seat and left down her suitcase at the door. A young, fair-haired man wearing a tweed coat jumped to his feet with a smile and easily lifted the suitcase into a rack above his head.

An older man with a neatly trimmed moustache beside him moved sideways to allow the nun to sit down. Opposite them sat three girls; the one sitting opposite the nun sat hunched over her knitting, her needles clicking rapidly as they fed on the thick balls of wool bulging from her plastic bag.

A few minutes later, three sharp blasts on a whistle signaled to the driver. With a few head-wobbling jerks, the train shunted from the station, spewing steam. Soon it had picked up speed, and the station disappeared from view.

❦

"I hear some nutter has escaped from Gransha Asylum. Seems she's a pretty bad lot," said the elderly man as he looked around the compartment at the other five, waiting for some of them to take up his remark.

"It seems that when she is angered, she has the strength of ten men," he said, looking at the thin faced girl opposite him. She gave him a disdainful look and fumbled in her bag for a packet of cigarettes.

The man glanced at the *No Smoking* sign above her head. "Ah, excuse me, young lady. This is a no smoking compartment." He nodded to the sign. The girl turned and glared at him, and then she shoved the cigarettes back into her bag and swung to stare out of the window. Her fingers drummed agitatedly on her leather bag.

Annoyed by the girl's attitude, the elderly man turned to the young man beside him. "That nutter could be on this train," he said. "Even in this very compartment, eh?" He nudged the man in the ribs, but the fair-haired man ignored him and concentrated on the buxom, blonde-haired girl opposite him.

He smiled at her.

She returned his smile.

"I really don't want to meet her, anyway," the girl who was knitting said, her broad Scottish accent ringing around the compartment.

"Don't you worry, love. You're safe here with us men, eh, eh?" the older man cracked. Again he nudged the other man.

The nun was reading a thick prayer book, but she looked up at the girl with a sympathetic smile. The train thundered on, and between its rhythmic "pitter patter, pitter, patter" and the heat in the compartment, she was lulled into a drowsy sleep. Over an hour later, she woke with a start by the noise of the conductor sliding open the door to the compartment.

"Tickets!" he bellowed.

After carefully checking the six passengers tickets, the conductor said as he was leaving, "Folks, there will be a short delay at Belfast station. The police will be checking every passenger who is on the train."

"Are they looking for the nutter who's escaped from Gransha?" asked the elderly man.

"Yes, sir. Apparently she stabbed a nurse at the Asylum, who died from the attack."

When the conductor left, the elderly man looked around at the others and said excitedly, "I told you, didn't I? She really could be in here with us." He looked around the compartment. *Well*, he thought mischievously, *I may as well enjoy the rest of this boring journey.* He looked at the surly girl opposite him. She scowled at him, turning to look out the window.

"One thing's for sure," said the elderly man as he turned to the young man. "It's neither of us two." He looked at the girl opposite. "So how about the rest of you identifying yourselves? Come on, then. Let's start with your names."

The young man stared at him.

"Look, what harm can it do? Let me introduce myself. My name is Tom Painter—Colonel Tom Painter, army, retired."

"Yeah, well yer not in the army now, Colonel Tom Painter, retired," the girl opposite him snapped.

The young man smiled and the girl opposite him smiled back.

The Colonel's face blazed with anger and his short moustache bristled. Just before he was about to repeat his question, the girl opposite the fair-haired man stretched out her hand towards him and said, "Hi. My name's Angela Poole. I live in Belfast."

The young man's face broke into a broad grin. Taking her hand, he said, "Joe Wilkinson, and I'm very pleased to meet you, Angela." He held onto Angela's hand as he gazed into her blue eyes.

"Right then," said the Colonel, staring at the girl opposite him, "That's you two. Now what about you? What's your name?"

"My name! I don't have to tell you my name. You're not the police," snapped the girl.

The colonel smiled, enjoying the girl's discomfort. Turning abruptly away from her he looked at the girl who was knitting. Looking up from her knitting, the girl said, "Oh dear, Morag. Morag McIntosh. I live in Dublin. I have to change trains in Belfast. I'm heading for Dublin tomorrow."

The colonel studied her for a few moments and he swung to the girl opposite him again. With his upper lip curling he snarled, "Now you. What's your name? Come on," he said raising his voice. "Everyone else has given their names. What's yours?"

"Ach, look. Leave her alone. Forget it," said the young man turning to him suddenly. "If she doesn't want to tell you her name she doesn't have to."

The Colonel gaped at him. "I was only asking her name," he said, somewhat subdued.

"The nun didn't tell you her name, did she, you stupid old fool?" snapped the girl opposite him.

The Colonel looked at the nun. "She doesn't have to!"

"Sister Teresa. Navan Convent. I'm staying overnight at a boarding house in Belfast before moving onto Navan in the morning." said the nun, smiling.

"Oh Sister, maybe you could see if there's room for me?" Morag piped up. "I'd sleep anywhere." She smiled at the nun.

"Of course, Morag, I'm sure you could stay in my room for the night. There must be a sofa or something." She smiled back at Morag.

"Thank you, Sister. I didn't like the idea of looking for somewhere to stay so late."

Colonel Painter looked across at Morag again and at Angela, who was still smiling at Joe. He glared at the surly girl. "All I want to know is your name—"

"Look!" the girl screamed suddenly—so suddenly that everyone gaped at her. "Would you leave me alone, you old fool? I won't tell you or anyone here my name! I don't have to, so just let me be. Okay?" She glared at Colonel Painter.

The compartment rocked gently as the train steamed quickly along the tracks. The Colonel sat for awhile with a sneer on his ruddy face, and he spoke again. "What have you to hide, eh? Why won't you tell us your name? Eh?"

The whites of the girl's knuckles showed as she gripped the edge of her seat, but just as she was about to explode the train whistle sounded, signaling it was the last mile to Belfast. As the train drew into Belfast station, the passengers could see many policemen—some with Alsatian dogs—standing along the platform.

Soon it was time for the passengers to disembark and as they did, the Colonel kept his eyes on the girl opposite him. He watched her rise and then dive from the compartment, hurrying along the corridor. Quickly he followed her, and his eyes widened when he saw her open a door and jump down onto the tracks on the other side of the train.

"I knew it!" he shouted. "Stop her! There she goes! Stop her!"

He watched with satisfaction as the screaming girl was soon overpowered by six policemen and dragged off to a waiting police car. Joe and Angela were among the crowd who had watched the drama, and as the police car drove away, Colonel Painter came running up to them.

"I told you," he said triumphantly. "I was right, wasn't I? I was right!"

"Yeah, Colonel you were right," said Joe quietly. Turning, he put his arm around Angela's shoulder and without another word to the Colonel they walked out of the station.

The Colonel followed them, mumbling to himself, "I was right. I told them. I was right..."

"It seems as if they caught the unfortunate girl after all, Morag," said Sister Teresa as the police car disappeared.

Morag shuddered. "Who would have thought it! And she was in our own compartment, too! And I was sitting beside her." She shuddered again.

As the police car sped through Belfast, the handcuffed girl who was flanked by two stout policewomen, sobbed "I'm sorry! It was such a temptation, you see. The safe key was always there and I needed the money. I really needed the money..."

The policewomen stared at each other as it quickly dawned on them. This girl was *not* Mary Duggan.

Sister Teresa opened the door of the room and put down her suitcase. "Whew," she gasped. "I'm glad we're here at last! I didn't think I was going to make it." She looked at the small sofa by the far wall. "Do you think you will be comfortable sleeping on that?"

"I'm sure I will," said Morag, smiling. "Do you think I could use the bathroom first, Sister?"

Morag locked the bathroom door behind her and began washing her hands and face. She felt a lot better now. *They almost had me,* she thought as she dug into her bag and withdrew a shiny pair of scissors. Looking in the mirror, she smiled as she ran her forefinger along the sharp edge of the scissors. *I wonder how I'll look in a nun's habit?*

13

GINGER BAP

The red haired boy stood his ground, glaring fiercely and bunching his hands at the group of boys who were taunting him.

"Ginger bap! Ginger bap! Na,na,na,na,na..."

Just when he was about to launch himself at the nearest boy, he felt a persistent tug on the sleeve of his school blazer. "Ach Tommy, don't mind themmuns. Sure they're only jealous because you're top of the class. C'mon... c'mon," he coughed nervously.

Still angry, Tommy turned to stare at his best friend, Paul Moran. Mary, Paul's sister, stood behind him. She had a worried look on her dark face.

"C'mon, Tommy." Paul started coughing again. "Let's go."

Tommy relaxed a little, but turned back to give his tormentors a defiant glare before walking away. As they walked home Paul's continuous coughing disturbed Tommy.

"Are you still not better, Paul?" he asked.

"Naw. Me ma's takin' me to the doctor's tomorrow. I was up all night sick."

Tommy studied his best friend. His usually chubby cheeks were very pale and slack.

"A neighbor said it might be his lungs, or somethin' like that," Mary whispered.

When they reached the corner of the street where Tommy lived, Paul said, "I'll not be at school tomorrow, Tommy. Me ma's keepin' me off."

"Yer a lucky duck, Paul," said Tommy. "I wish I could stay off. I'll see ye later on anyway. See ye Mary."

"See ye," chorused Paul and Mary.

As Tommy headed down the street, he was unaware that Mary's wide, innocent eyes were gazing adoringly after him. When he turned the corner out of sight, she sighed and swung around to race after her brother.

That evening, Tommy stood in front of his bathroom mirror. He glared at his reflection. His red hair, thick and curly, shone back at him like a fiery beacon. With a sigh he reached for his toothbrush and began to clean his teeth. When he had finished, he bent to the water-tap and with water in his mouth he gargled loudly as he looked into the mirror again. Turning he spat venomously into the sink. "Ahhh," he groaned aloud. "Why me? Why did I have to have red hair?"

"Thomas!" His mother called from downstairs. "Thomas!"

Breathing heavily he gulped, "Yes, Ma?"

"Have you cleaned your teeth yet?"

"Aye, Ma."

"Well hurry up and get to bed. It's almost 11:00."

"Aye, Ma."

With a final grimace at his reflection, he hurried into his bedroom. After kicking his slippers off, he bounced onto his bed. Reaching out for his pile of Marvel comics, he thumbed through them. He tried hard to concentrate on the *X Men* comic he chose, but it was no use. With a grunt, he threw the comic onto his bedside table with the others and lay back staring at the ceiling. *Ginger bap*, he thought. *What a nickname!* He hated it. He hated his hair. Throwing his head back hard against his pillow, he tried to block out the thoughts from his tortured mind, but it was no use. *If only I could wake up in the morning and my hair would be black, or gray, any color but red.*

He growled as he stared at his poster of Elvis. The King's hair was a glistening black, combed to perfection. *I would even swap my hair for a big nose like Dympna Simpsons,* he thought, *or a turn in my eye like Joe McCourt's. Anything would be better than having red hair.* Reaching up, he ran his fingers through his thick red locks. *Maybe when I'm older me ma will let me dye it...*

Next morning, Paul was marked absent and Mary sat beside Tommy in the classroom. It was a hot, end-of-spring day and the portly teacher, Mr. Morgan, sweated profusely, his thick, bulging neck straining at his tight restricting shirt collar and tie.

The morning passed slowly, the heat increasing in the poorly ventilated classroom. At 11:20, unable to bear it any longer and with his handkerchief soggy with sweat, the teacher said, "Class, take out your history books and turn to the Siege of Derry. Read over it. I will return in a few minutes so I don't want to hear any disturbance. Right!" Giving his pupils one of his well-rehearsed glowers, he walked to the door. At the door, just before opening it, he said, "Behave yourselves, I'll be back shortly." He hurried away to the staff-room for a cold drink of water and a fresh handkerchief.

The rustling of pages and the low whispering of the boys and girls filled the classroom. A minute passed and suddenly, there was a loud *thwack* as an ink-soaked piece of blotting paper hit Tommy on the back of his head. Tommy could feel the blue ink trickle down his neck as he reached behind. He stared at the blue ink on his hand. Swinging around, his face white with anger he shouted, "Who did that? Who was it?"

A smirk on Buster Mellon's fat face answered his question.

"Who did what, Ginger bap?" he sneered rising to his feet. "Did someone dye yer ginger bap for ye? Did they, eh, eh?" Suddenly he began to bang on the lid of his desk shouting, "Ginger bap! Ginger bap! Na,na,na,na,na..."

Encouraged by this, some of his cronies joined in and soon the classroom resounded to the thudding noise as more pupils began to jeer Tommy. The noise grew louder until it was almost deafening.

"STOP IT! STOP IT!"

The sharp squeal penetrated the din and startled most of the pupils stopped. Everyone stared at Mary, for it was Mary who had screamed and she was now standing on top of her seat, her eyes filled with tears.

Just then the door opened and Mr. Morgan entered. His greasy hair was combed into place. The smell of perfumed talcum wafted around the room.

"What's all this, Mary? Sit down." He glared at her. "Now," he said as Mary, very embarrassed, sat quickly down. "Let us continue with your history lesson."

After school, Tommy and Mary walked home together.

"I hope Paul's alright, Mary. Tell him I'll be over tonight."

"Sure, Tommy," said Mary with a shy smile.

As they passed the long red-bricked wall that ran along the edge of the school Gaelic pitch, they spotted Buster Mellon and three other boys.

"Look!" yelled Mellon. "There's Ginger bap. Hello, Ginger bap. How's it goin', eh?"

The four boys gathered around Tommy. One of them pushed Mary out of the way. She watched, afraid, as Mellon prodded Tommy in the chest and began to taunt him.

Suddenly, with a snarl that took the bigger boy by surprise, Tommy swung his fist and hit Buster high on his left cheek.

Later, Tommy sat in the kitchen as his mother gently dabbed at his swollen eye and cut lip with an antiseptic-soaked piece of tissue.

"It's not worth fightin' about, Thomas," she scolded. "Sure everybody has a nickname. They used to call me *skinny lizzy from the boneyard*. God, I was so thin in them days," she laughed, feeling her fat-layered midriff. "Ach, sure ye'll soon get used to it. Nicknames don't mean anything. If ye ignore them, those boys will soon leave ye alone. They'll soon get fed up and stop, you'll see."

"Ach Ma," moaned Tommy. "I get browned off with it all. It's my hair. I hate it. I hate the color of it. Is there nothin' you can do about it?"

His mother frowned, trying to understand her son's torment. His hair was very red... but then, plenty of people had red hair. "Plenty of people have red hair, Thomas—aye, and famous people too. They never let it bother them. Besides, I think it's a lovely color. Yer grandfather had lovely red hair..."

"But Ma," began Tommy. "Ah, what's the use talkin' to you," he snapped. "You just don't understand." Pushing his chair back he rose and stalked to the kitchen door shouting, "I hate my hair! Don't ye understand! I hate my hair!"

That evening he called to see Paul. Paul's mother, with her eyes puffy and red, came to the door. Mary stood behind her.

"Is Paul in, Mrs. Moran?" Tommy asked glancing at Mary.

Mary's mother stared stupidly at him.

"Tommy," said Mary pushing past her mother. "Come on in. Paul's away up to the hospital in Belfast fer a checkup. He'll be there a month, fer tests."

"A month? Is... is he alright?" asked Tommy as he passed Mrs. Moran and came into the hall.

"Come on up to his room," whispered Mary, glancing at her mother who was closing the front door. Tommy followed Mary up the stairs and into Paul's bedroom. He sat beside her on the edge of Paul's bed.

"Me ma's very upset," said Mary quietly staring at the floor. "The doctor says Paul will have to get chemo treatment."

"What's that?"

"I don't know, but I hope it stops Paul bein' sick."

"I hope so, too," said Tommy looking at Mary.

"I miss him," she whispered, her eyes glistening.

Tommy reached out to take her hand but stopped. Embarrassed, he said quickly, "Ach, sure it'll only be for a month. Mickey Johnson was in hospital for a whole year and he was okay. Anyway, I wish I could get a week or two off school. Buster and his lot are really gettin' on my goat."

"Tommy, you shouldn't worry about them callin' ye names. Besides, I like the color of your hair, and ye have lovely eyes, too..."

Tommy stared at Mary. Her face grew redder, and she heaved a silent, relieved sigh as her mother came into the room carrying a tray.

"I thought yees would like some biscuits and milk," she said, leaving the tray on top of Paul's bedside chair. She gave Tommy a smile and left the room.

⑤✐⑤

The following weeks dragged slowly by. Tommy tried to ignore Mellon's taunts, but it was no use. He did, however, manage to stop getting into any more fights.

⑤✐⑤

"Tommy, Paul's comin' home today." Mary's excited face beamed at him on the following Monday.

"That's great, Mary. I'll call over and see him this evenin'."

Mary was sitting on the edge of Paul's bed when Tommy was shown into the room. She watched as Tommy's eyes widened with horror when he saw Paul. His friend was propped up on his bed. There were two dark rings around his sunken eyes. His cheekbones pushed sharply on his pale face. On his head he wore his school cap. The sound of his quick breathing filled the room.

"Yes, Paul," gulped Tommy. "How are you?"

"Not too bad," Paul croaked hoarsely. "I have to get injections. That's the sorest part of it."

Tommy noticed that Paul was clutching tightly onto his blanket, the strain of talking obviously painful for him.

"What's with the cap?" asked Tommy at once regretting asking the question.

"Ah it's only the chemo treatment," said Paul. "It's made me loose some of my hair. Do ye want to see?" Tommy nodded. Paul's breathing quickened as he reached up and pulled the cap from his head. His dark eyes studied Tommy's reaction. Tommy gasped. Only small clumps of hair remained on Paul's head and the pale skin that was exposed bubbled with sweat. "Wile lookin' isn't it, Tommy?" said Paul, attempting a smile.

"Naw, naw, sure you're sick," Tommy whispered, annoyed at his own inadequacy.

Mary quickly reached for Paul's cap and put it back on his head. Her brother gave her a grateful smile.

Fifteen minutes later, Mrs. Moran came into the room. "I think Paul needs to get some rest now, Tommy," she said.

Later as Tommy and Mary stood at her front door, Mary suddenly began to cry. "I don't think Paul's goin' to get better..."

"Ach, don't worry, Mary," said Tommy gulping, tears finding their way into his eyes. "He doesn't look too bad," he lied. "He'll soon be up and about. Besides, the summer holidays will be starting soon. He'll be better then." He reached out as Mary's tears trickled down her sad face. "Don't cry, Mary. Don't cry," he whispered softly and put his arm around her shoulder.

This seemed to make Mary worse and she began to cry all the more. "Tommy, do you know what Paul said to me when he came home?" she sniffed, her shoulders heaving as she cried. The summer breeze blew lightly up the dusty street and death walked into the house behind them. "Ma had to get his cap to cover his head..."

A week later he found Mary crying near the school toilets.

"Mary... what's wrong?"

"The chemo, Tommy... it's... it's not working. It won't take the cancer away... It won't take it away."

The word buzzed through Tommy's head as he held the crying girl. *Cancer.* He hadn't realized.

Ten days later, Tommy stood with the rest of the class in the cemetery at Paul's graveside. He blinked through his tears at Mary, who was standing with her distraught parents. As the grave-diggers lowered the tiny, varnished coffin into the ground, Tommy cried harder as he thought about what Mary had said to him at her front door ten days ago. She told him that Paul said he didn't know why Tommy was complaining about having red hair. Paul had said he wished he had red hair. The tears ran down Tommy's freckled cheeks, and he raised his head again to look at Mary crying loudly as she clung to her mother. He remembered her words, too: *"Tommy, you shouldn't worry about them callin' you names. I like the color of your hair, and you have lovely eyes, too..."*

14

THE LADY AND THE TRAMPS

As the Bedford lorry rattled to a stop at the crossroads to turn left for Derry, two tramps jumped from the back of it onto the middle of the road. Breathing hard they watched as the lorry drove away. When it was out of sight they went over to the low ditch and sat down on the grass. The tallest tramp scratched his chest with his dirty fingers and looked around. He had a few days growth on his pale haggard face and his black hair was long and greasy. He wore a heavy gray overcoat, a red scarf wound around his neck, and a pair of scuffed black boots. "The police will never find us way up here," he said hoarsely.

His companion, a ferret-faced small man with greasy, fair hair nodded silently. He was wearing a dirty, brown corduroy suit and light jogging shoes. He groaned now as his stomach rumbled. "Dickie, I'm hungry. When we robbed that oul biddy we should have stopped for something to eat."

"Aye," snarled Dickie kicking out at him. "And then we would have been caught. Use your loaf, Davy. Come on. Let's get a move on." He rose to his feet. "It'll soon be dark. Maybe we can bed down at yon place?" He pointed away to the low hills. On the lea of the nearest hill they could see a solitary white-washed cottage pushing a thin line of smoke into the darkening sky.

Davy stared at the small building and suddenly the hair creped along the back of his neck. He turned. "Dickie…"

"Come on," said Dickie, impatiently marching on up the road.

As he followed Dickie, Davy couldn't shake the feeling of foreboding.

They reached the quaint cottage twenty minutes later and at the gate they looked around. At the back of the cottage they could see a small barn with a rusting corrugated roof.

"Go on, Davy," whispered Dickie when they reached the door. "Give it a knock."

Davy looked at him and knocked loudly on the top half-door. They waited for several seconds, but there was no answer.

"Knock again," whispered Dickie.

Davy knocked two more times, and a few seconds after the second knock, the top half of the door creaked open to reveal a tiny, plump, gray-haired old woman with her hair tied up in a bun at the back of her head. She wore a long flowered apron over her thin gingham green dress that was buttoned to her neck. Her wrinkled face broke into a pleasant smile as Dickie introduced himself.

"Good evening missus, my name is Richard Benjamin McClusky, and my honorable friend here is David Cole. We are very sorry to disturb you, but we just happened to be passing and wondered if by any chance there were any jobs that you needed doing, in return for a bite to eat, of course. You see missus," he continued with his well rehearsed speech, "we have been on the road all day, and I'm afraid we are feeling rather tired and hungry. Do you think you could possibly see your way to assist us?"

The old woman studied the two men for a few seconds, and smiling she unlocked the door and stepped back saying in a quiet voice, "Come right in and sit by the fire. You must be feeling the cold. I have the kettle already boiling, and you can have a piece of my freshly baked pie. I hope you like rhubarb?"

With a wide yellow-toothed grin at Davy, McClusky rubbed his hands leading the way into the cottage. Shortly they were seated at the blazing turf fire drinking hot mugs of tea and eating rhubarb pie. The pleasant smell of burning peat surrounded the tramps as they ate, and as they did the old woman introduced herself. "My name is Kathleen Conaghan. I don't get many visitors up here. In fact, I've not had any company since I buried my husband Patrick three years ago."

"You mean you live here all alone?" asked McClusky nudging Cole.

"Oh yes. All by myself," the old woman said smiling though for a second or two McClusky thought he saw her eyes darken slightly.

By now it was dark outside, and after pouring the tramps two more mugs of strong tea, Kathleen went over to a dark dresser and took out an old red glassed oil lamp. After pumping it, she lit the wick and almost immediately the interior of the room was bathed in a warm, pink glow.

Nudging Cole again, McClusky stood up. "Ahem. Excuse me, missus."

"Yes?" said Kathleen as she placed the oil lamp on the table by the window.

"Would it be asking too much of your generous hospitality to let my friend Davy and me bed down for the night in your barn?"

"My barn?" exclaimed the old woman. "Goodness, I wouldn't want you sleeping in that draughty old place."

McClusky looked abashed. But Kathleen's next words had him smiling. "Why not use the bedroom? There's a big double bed in there, and it hasn't been slept in these past three years. It won't take me a minute to get some clean blankets from the cupboard."

McClusky winked happily at Cole. "That's most generous of you, missus. It will be nice to sleep in a proper bed again. And I do feel tired."

McClusky did feel tired and looking at Davy he could see he was tired, too. The old woman smiled. "I'll get the blankets out now then." Carrying the lamp with her, she went out to the kitchen.

"Davy," McClusky whispered prodding him. He could see that Davy was nearly asleep. "This is great. I wonder if the oul hen will part with some money if we asked her nicely. Get my drift?"

Cole stared sleepily at him. "She doesn't look as if she has very much," he grumbled.

"Shhh, here she comes."

As they followed the old woman out through the kitchen the lamplight cast eerie shadows on the rough walls, and seconds later she was showing the tramps into a bedroom. Dropping the blankets on top of a double brass bed, she said, "Oh, before I go there's one thing I must ask of you."

"What is that, missus?" McClusky asked frowning.

"Do you see that door?" Raising the oil lamp Kathleen showed both tramps a door at the far end of the room.

"Yes," said the tramps together.

"Well, could I ask you not to go into that room?"

"But why missus?" asked McClusky glancing quickly at Cole.

"Just promise me you won't open that door," said the old woman her eyes flitting across both tramp's faces.

"But...?" Cole was about to question the old woman when he felt McClusky's sharp nudge in his ribs.

"Yes. Yes of course, missus. We promise. You have the word of Richard Benjamin McClusky on that missus. Nothing on earth would make us go into that room. We will respect your privacy. Won't we, Davy?"

"Yes... yes, you're right," spluttered Cole. "You can trust us, missus."

With a smile Kathleen said, "Well then gentlemen, good night. Have a peaceful sleep."

"Good night, missus, and thank you again," said McClusky with a wide smile.

When the door closed behind the old woman Cole hissed angrily. "What the heck are you playing at, Dickie? Don't open that door. Are you out of your skull? That's where it is, her money..."

"Shhh," whispered McClusky holding up his hand to silence Davy. Silently he slipped to the door and putting his head against it, he listened. He could hear a scraping noise coming from the kitchen. He could also hear the old woman humming.

"Dickie, are you listening to me?" whispered Davy. "I said that's where her money is... in that there room."

"For God's sake, don't you think I know that? Look, we'll wait until the oul hen goes to bed, and then we'll see what's in there. Okay?"

Davy stifled a yawn as he stared sleepily at the bed, and as he reached to pull the blankets into place he said, "All right, we'll wait. But Dickie..."

"What?"

"I feel very tired."

McClusky sighed heavily, "Well go and lie down and kip for a while. I'll waken you when she goes to bed." He widened his eyes. He too, was beginning to feel tired.

Thirty minutes later and trying very hard to stay awake, Dickie went to the door again. He listened. The old woman was still up. He could still hear her humming and the scraping noise seemed nearer. He stepped back from the door and suddenly swaying unsteadily he almost fell. His stomach heaved as he stared at his sleeping friend. Bending he shook him. He shook him again. But after a few more hard shakes, he realized he could not wake him. The scraping noise was louder now and seemed to be closer. Cursing his nausea, McClusky stumbled across the room to the forbidden door. "I'll see what's in that damned room now," he whispered angrily. Feeling for the handle of the door he tried it. It turned easily and he pulled. His head spun as he stared at... bricks, rows of red bricks had been solidly built into the door opening. He fell, dragging himself along the floor to the bed, his head spinning and lay beside Cole. Later, just before he passed out, he became aware the scraping sound had stopped.

Outside the bedroom the old woman stepped down from a chair and put a rusting trowel beside a small pile of mortar. She had just finished. Raising her lamp she examined her handiwork. Neat rows of red brick now blocked the doorway into the bedroom. "I must get all this mess cleaned up," she said to herself as she carried the lamp and trowel back to the kitchen. As she filled a bucket of clean water she thought about the decomposing body of the tramp in the other room. *It's time I buried him.*

Later, as she sat by the fire, she thought back to the day her husband had invited a tramp in for something to eat. He had been invited to stay the night, too and had seemed very friendly. But in the morning he was gone, and with him their life's savings. A month later her heartbroken husband had died. There had been a few visitors since then. Some of them were buried in the barn. She smiled and the light from the fire shone in her mad eyes as she made a mental note to buy some more poison and cement.

A soft wind soughed outside and the cottage was at peace again.

15

HIS NAME WAS JOSEPH

He had been walking in the heavy rain for over two hours before stopping in the middle of the new Foyle Bridge. He had climbed over the railings and he stood now right on the edge staring at the swirling muddy water forty-meters below. He hoped the fall would kill him. He hoped it wouldn't be too painful.

The wind blowing up the river chilled him, and he shivered. Yet he felt strangely comfortable. He looked towards the glittering lights of Derry. To the right lay the dark shadows of the East bank where he lived. He wouldn't be back. The dread that was his constant companion would end soon. His uncle wouldn't be able to touch him. His uncle... "No!" he screamed suddenly, trying to blank out the memories of his uncle's torture, and it had been torture. He hadn't been able to sleep. He hadn't been able to tell anyone. How could he have told his mother about the things his uncle made him do? She would never have believed him. Not Jim, her brother, not Uncle Jim. If only Daddy had been alive.

A sea gull screamed as it flew past, and he turned to watch it disappear into the darkness under the bridge. It was only then he became aware of the tears streaming down his face. He sniffed hard and stared down at the river again. It would soon be over.

Suddenly he stiffened. He could hear soft-lulling music. It seemed to be coming from below.

"Don't worry. There's someone here to help you." The Samaritan's concerned voice came to him now.

He had eventually phoned a month ago when his uncle's abuses had grown more violent, but he couldn't bring himself to tell Angela-the angel Samaritan. How could he tell her? He couldn't tell anyone. He couldn't tell his school friends, friends; he had none now. He sighed. Better get it over with. He wondered what his mother would think. His letter would explain. Would she believe it? His daddy would have. Why couldn't he have died of cancer like his daddy? He remembered his visits to the hospice and his mother crying all the time. He remembered how annoyed his daddy had been with her. He hadn't cried. Would his mother cry for him? He didn't want her to. He remembered with a sudden shudder his daddy's funeral, and how he had cried then. His uncle had held him close, so close, too close. He had been nine years old.

The music distracted him. He looked at the water again and imagined he saw a face, his father's, beckoning him. "Jump." The music grew louder still and suddenly softer when he let go of the railing with one hand. A gust of wind blasted rain into his face blinding him, and he swayed for a few seconds before grabbing the railing again.

The whiteness of his Nikes, a birthday present from his mother drew his attention. When they found him, would she be able to take them back to the shop? Explain he didn't need them anymore? Maybe he should take them off. But he felt so tired, so very tired.

"Come on!"

Startled, he turned at the sound of running feet, and suddenly he saw two people appear out of the light mist. They wore yellow gore-tex raincoats with the words, 'Foyle, Search and Rescue' written on them in bright, red letters.

The man and young woman stopped about three meters from where he stood. Panting hard, the man gasped. "Don't do it, son." He took a step towards Joseph.

"No! Stay back!"

The man froze and turned slowly to his companion. They frowned at each other. Now the young woman moved to stand beside him. She had dark, oval eyes.

"Nothing can be that bad," she said quietly. "Come on with us. We'll get it all sorted out."

Sorted out, hah. Joseph stared at her pale, smiling face. *What would she know?* "Stay away!" he screamed. "Don't come any closer!"

"Talk to us then," said the woman. She smiled again. "What's your name?"

Joseph shook his head. He didn't want this. He wanted to be left alone. "Go away! Just go away and leave me alone!"

"We will," said the woman. She smiled again. "What's your name?"

Joseph studied her companion. He was smiling too. His uncle had smiled a lot, especially before...

Suddenly the crackling of a hand held radio broke the silence and the man swung around, pulled it from underneath his coat and muttered something into it. Joseph heard the words, *"incident here."* He glanced down at the river again. He would have to jump before more people came.

"Please talk to us," pleaded the woman, taking a step towards him.

"No! You can't help me. No one can. Leave me alone!" Suddenly he frowned. The music had grown louder. He could hardly hear what the woman was saying. Looking down he was surprised to see colors, magic colors swirling on top of the water. He would be safe down there. His uncle wouldn't be able to reach him, to touch him, to... "Joseph. My name is, Joseph." He turned to the woman. She looked relieved and smiled.

"That's what my boyfriend is called," she said. "I'm Justine." Her smile disappeared. "Joseph can you tell me what's bothering you. Maybe I can help."

Joseph glanced at her companion.

"Paddy," whispered Justine nodding for the man to move back. He smiled at Joseph, stepped back a few paces, turned and bending slightly began to speak into his radio. As he did, Joseph stared at the back of his raincoat. Justine was saying something to him, but he didn't hear her. He was remembering his uncle's raincoat-the sweaty smell it had. He was remembering how his uncle had forced him to go for a run in his car. His uncle had bought him an ice cream. He had hardly eaten any and after, he had been sick. The ice cream had stained the raincoat while it rained outside—where he wanted to be.

"Joseph." The woman had moved closer. "You're cold."

"Cold? No." And he wasn't. He was shivering, but he didn't feel cold. He looked down at the colors again as the music distracted him. The colors seemed brighter and kept changing as the magic caught them, throwing reds and blues into tiny fluffy clouds that began to float up to him. In the clouds Joseph could see smiling faces. He wanted to be inside one of the clouds. He wanted to be down there, where his daddy was. He let go of the railing with his left hand.

"Joseph." Justine's raised voice startled him, and he turned to her. As he did, the music grew louder, pulling at him.

Justine had removed her coat. "You must be cold. Put this around your shoulders."

He shook his head. "I'm not cold." Still holding on with one hand he looked down. The magic colors floated higher. He could not see the water now. He turned to Justine again, suddenly stiffened when he saw Paddy turn and it wasn't Paddy anymore. It was his uncle. He could see his hooded eyes, the same cold eyes when he touched him. "Nooooooo!"

By the time Paddy reached the railing Joseph was halfway to the water. The pain as his back broke was momentary, and he disappeared into the colors.

Seconds later the rescue boat arrived.

They found him ten minutes later. His limp, broken body unnerved one of the youngest of the crew as they dragged it from the water, and almost choking, he vomited over the side of the boat.

When they were carrying Joseph to the waiting ambulance, Justine stared at the crooked smile on his pale face, and she wondered what had been so terrible to make him take his life. Tears ran down her face as Paddy put a comforting arm around her shoulders and said, "Come on, Justine. There's nothing we can do for him."

As they were moving away one of the ambulance drivers came over. "Did you get his name?"

"His name," whispered Justine. "Aye. His name was Joseph."

16

HOME FOR AWHILE

The Long Tower chapel bell pealed its welcome loud and clear on that frosty morning as he rounded the corner from Bishop Street. He gazed at the remembered scene before him and his heart leapt, but almost as quickly he felt depressed. Sighing he thought, *Twenty years; twenty wasted years.* The squat, green gas tanks still grew out of the gas yard and a thin line of white smoke fizzled from a pipe somewhere between them. He looked to his left, and somehow the dotted whites of the graveyard seemed comforting. He noted that the graveyard was bigger than he remembered. Two women passed him, and he began to walk down the street joining other people as they made their way to ten o'clock Mass. *Home can wait for another hour,* he thought as he headed into chapel. *Sure after all it's been twenty years.*

He felt nervous as he slid into a seat near the side door and knelt down. He mumbled a short prayer and sat up on the hard seat. Sitting, watching other people coming into the chapel, his thoughts tormented him. When was the last time he had been at Mass? Somehow in America, Mass didn't seem all that important. When was the last time? Now he remembered. It was his son's christening. *What age would he be now? Eighteen? Eighteen,* he thought sadly. He sighed. *What age would she be?* Closing his eyes he tried to remember what his Italian-American wife, Maria, looked like. *I wonder where they are?* He had been married two years before he realized that his marriage had been a mistake. He had fallen in love with the country and the American way of life. He had fallen for Maria—or so he thought. His hair had been black as coal then, just like hers. Now it was gray, and he was dying.

As the congregation stood up, he opened his eyes. The priest began Mass and he knelt. With his head bowed, he stared at his thin, joined hands. *He had been strong then, too.* Strong and a hard worker, America had so much to offer him. Suddenly his face creased with sadness as he remembered the night he left Maria and his son, Angelo. He had drifted from town to town and then got a job working on the American Central Railroad. He had known many women and spent a fortune on drink.

There were times when he thought about his home in Derry. He had written a few times, and once he had received word telling him his father had died.

All he had felt when he received the letter was the dull ache that had always been there. He had never written home again. But now he was back and the familiar smells and sounds surrounded him, the hollow coughing, a baby crying, the murmured praying and the priest's droning voice. He looked around. He recognized no one. If he had stayed, he felt he would have known them all.

Later as some of the people slid from their seats to go to the altar for Holy Communion, a great desire to receive it as well made him say an Act of Contrition. He tried to recall all his sins. There were so many. Almost in tears, he rose shakily to his feet, his hands joined and his head bowed, and shuffled to the altar. Soon it was his turn; "Body of Christ," he said, and then he was heading back to his seat, his step a little lighter.

He stayed kneeling after Mass was over, waiting until most of the people had gone. Rising, he slid past an old couple who were praying loudly, their rasping, whistling prayers echoing through the chapel. As he turned to go, he saw a young girl lighting a candle. Feeling in his pocket for change, he made his way towards the flickering array of lighted candles. The girl blessed herself and moved away.

Dropping his coins into the slot, he picked up a tiny candle. Lighting it from another candle, he stuck it firmly into a three-pronged holder. As he stared at the flame, he suddenly realized he was crying. Tears ran down his pale, gaunt face and dripped onto the brass candle stand. Minutes later he left the chapel. Outside the sun managed to squeeze a gap in the gray misty sky and turning left, he walked down the steps to Lecky Road. Near the bottom was a poster:

CIVIL RIGHTS MARCH
30 January 1972

He looked at the date. *That's today.* As he hurried along past the high gas yard wall he smiled. *Only another bit to go.* Turning the handle on the inside door he took a deep breath and pushed it open. Quietly he went on into the hall and knocked before opening the sitting room door. And there she was, sitting by the fire, her gray hair tied up in a bun behind her head. She was watching television. Startled, she turned, her eyes brimming over immediately as she saw him. She tried to rise to her feet, but he went quickly to her, tears in his eyes.

"Hi, Ma," he whispered brightly. "I'm home for awhile."

17

THE ATHEIST

The doctor patted the woman's arm gently. "I'm really very sorry, Mrs. McGartan. Your husband has just passed way..."

Paul McGartan gaped at the scene below. He could see himself lying in the hospital bed, the doctor telling his wife that he was dead. His mind reeled as he tried to establish where he was. He seemed to be somewhere in the corner of the room, somewhere on the ceiling.

"What do ye mean, I've just passed away?" he yelled. "I'm here, up here! Can't ye see me?" He struggled to try and get closer to his wife and the doctor, but they were beginning to fade away, and all of a sudden, he was being whisked along a dark tunnel. Away ahead he could see a glowing dot growing larger as he drew nearer, and before he realized it, he was passing through a bright shimmering light. As he passed through it, he was filled with a warm peaceful glow, and before he had time to think on this he stopped. Now he found himself standing in a bright narrow room that seemed to have misty walls.

"Would you please join the queue, sir?"

"Eh?"

Paul gaped at the golden haired being that had shoulder-to-heel white wings and long, white, silky hair.

"Would you please join the queue for judgment, sir," said the winged being pointing behind Paul, "It won't take long."

Turning Paul saw the queue of people. He swung back to ask why they were queuing and what he was doing there when he saw the angel fly away. He stared after it until it disappeared, and in a daze, he stumbled to the back of the queue. Still dazed, he tapped the left shoulder of the man in front of him and asked, "Where are ye from hi?"

With a frown, the man turned and said, "Belfast. You?"

"Derry. Tell us, mucker, what happened to ye? How did ye snuff it?"

"Snuff it?" said the man, frowning.

"Aye, snuff it. Ye are dead, aren't ye? We both are, aren't we?"

"Oh aye we're dead, alright," said the man, smiling. "Me, I was shat."

"Shat? What's that?"

The man stared at him for a second or two and said, "Shat... with a bullet. I was shat."

"Aw, ye were shot. Why didn't ye say so? What happened?"

"I was comin' out of church today, and they shat me."

"Church?" exclaimed Paul with a half sneer. "Ye believe in God, then, do ye?"

"Aye, of course I do." The man frowned. "Don't you?"

"Naw I don't," snapped Paul. What am I doing here anyway?

"Well you'd better start believin' in him right and quick. You're about to be judged, you know." Turning, the Belfast man nodded to the head of the queue, and it was then Paul saw them.

An old man, a very old man, with a wrinkled, pink face and a long, wispy, white beard that seemed to melt into his fleecy, white robe stood holding a thick, golden book. Beside him was a beautiful, golden haired woman. Her hair fell to her slim waist. She wore a blue garment that stretched to the top of her porcelain like feet, and on each foot, between her big toe and long toe, was a perfect red rose. Around her waist hung a gold linked belt with a tiny cross-shaped gold buckle. She was the most beautiful creature Paul had ever seen.

A few minutes later, Paul and the man in front of him where at the head of the queue. He watched as the old man closed the book with a loud snap and the Belfast man was led away crying. He looked back at Paul for a moment as an angel tugged at the Belfast man's arm. They disappeared into the clouds.

Now the old man addressed Paul. "Welcome, friend Paul. My name is Peter. You are very welcome here. You are about to enter Heaven."

Paul gulped as he studied Peter. He had the golden book open, and a feathered quill suddenly appeared in his hand. With a quick stroke of the pen he snapped the book shut, and smiling, he addressed Paul again. "A few tiny errors on the way, but you made it. Welcome again to Heaven, friend Paul."

At last Paul found he could speak. "Heaven!" he gasped. "But how can I be in Heaven? I'm an atheist. Isn't that fact in your book? A friggin' atheist. I don't believe in Heaven, or God fer that matter. So what's all this about, mucker?"

Peter smiled at his companion and she smiled back. "Oh we know you didn't believe. That is why you are here. You see, you couldn't commit any sins against God because you didn't believe."

Behind Peter and his beautiful companion, Paul could see angels playing harps and flying in and out of the fluffy clouds, and through a gap in the clouds, he could see a shimmering path that wound away down to a lovely valley of quilted greens and silver rivers. "Is... is that Heaven down there?" he stammered.

"Yes," said Peter. "Come, let us take you there." Reaching out he took Paul's arm. But with an angry grunt, Paul pulled away from him.

"Wait! Wait just a friggin' minute, mucker. I told ye I don't believe in Heaven. I don't want to go down there. Look, there has to be a mistake. Are ye sure ye have the right person? I mean I'm an atheist. A friggin' atheist fer God's sake."

Turning to the woman Peter smiled, and turning back to Paul, he said, "There was only one atheist called Paul McGartan living in Derry. You are he. There is no mistake. Come. You belong in Heaven."

But Paul grew angrier. "I do, do I? Well what about that poor sod from Belfast? What about him, eh? He belongs in Heaven. He was shot ye know. What about him, eh?"

Peter's old eyes grew sad as he whispered, "He will be welcome in Heaven after a time, but he has to be cleansed of some errors. But you, friend Paul McGartan, you can go straight on in."

"Naw. Naw," said Paul growing angrier. "I don't want to."

Frowning, Peter turned again to his companion who smiled but said nothing. Her blue eyes flitted over Paul's angry face. Looking at Paul again, Peter said, "You have to come into Heaven. You can't want to go to that other place? Not with him? Surely? Not with Lucifer? You have to come into Heaven. You belong there."

Paul glared defiantly at old Peter. It was then that the golden haired woman reached out and took his hand. The warmth and gentleness of her touch surged through him, and he immediately felt at ease. Looking into his eyes she spoke, her voice singing and soft. "Come with me, Paul. I will take you down to the golden gates. Come."

Paul hesitated.

"Come," the woman repeated and before he knew it, Paul allowed her to lead him through the clouds past hordes of singing angels and onto the shimmering path that led to the beautiful valley. "You will like it there, Paul. You will be able to have anything you desire."

"Anything I desire?" whispered Paul staring in awe at the scenes all around him.

"Yes," said the golden haired woman smiling.

Soon they came to the golden gates. From beyond them in the light mist, Paul could hear the loveliest singing, but suddenly he panicked, and with a great effort, he pulled his hand from hers. The woman smiled at him. "Don't be afraid, Paul. You have nothing to be afraid of."

"Ach I'm not afraid," said Paul quietly. "It's just... It's just... well... Look I find it all hard to believe. I mean, I've been an atheist all my life. I've never believed in anything. I've never harmed anyone right enough, and I don't think I've committed any big sins, but still I find it all hard to believe that I'm about to go through the gates of Heaven."

"Yes, you are."

Paul studied her for a few seconds and asked, "Look, tell me. When I'm in there, will I be able tay see him?"

"Him?"

"Aye him. God. Will I be able to see God?"

"Of course," said the woman smiling.

"Well tell me then. What does he look like?"

Reaching, the woman took his hand again and as she led him through the golden gates she whispered, "I am God."

And the heavenly singing surrounded him as he passed into eternity.

18

THE VILLAGE OF CHILDREN

He was definitely lost. Driving slowly through the thick Irish fog, his eyes strained for a sign of something recognizable. He was tired, and somehow he had driven off the main road and didn't know where he was. He squinted at the digital clock on the dashboard; it was 8:53 p.m. *I can't carry on in this,* he thought gloomily. *I'll have to pull in somewhere and try and get shelter for the night.*

Twelve minutes later a village loomed out of the fog, and Paul heaved a sigh of relief. A small figure was leading a horse and cart up the street and Paul pulled to a stop and waited until the figure—a boy—drew near. He rolled down his window and called, "Hello. Sorry to bother you, but could you tell me where I am?"

The boy stopped and scratched his head before saying, "Clontallaght, sir. You're in Clontallaght."

"Clontallaght? Is that near the main road?"

"The main road? Ah no, sir. Sure yer miles away from there."

Paul pondered on this. It would be useless to try and get to the main road now. "Could you tell me is there a comfortable inn in the village? Somewhere I could stay the night?"

"The night, sir?" The boy's freckled face twisted into a smile. "Ah, then you'll be wantin' Herrity's Pub, sir." He turned and pointed down the village street. "Aye, there's usually a spare room at Herrity's."

Paul smiled at the boy. "Thanks." Winding up the window, he switched on the engine and drove down the street. *Strange,* he thought looking around. There appeared to be no fog in the village. It was then he saw the sign, HERRITY'S, painted in bright red above narrow double doors. As he pulled on the handbrake and stepped out of the car, he was unaware of the many eyes that peered at him through the tiny windows of the pub. The eyes vanished as he pushed easily on one of the doors, and a bell tinkled above his head as he stepped through the door.

Inside he saw that the pub was packed with children. Frowning and wondering, he stumbled to the bar counter. "Excuse me," he said to the boy behind the bar who was cleaning glasses. "Is your father in?"

"My father, sir? No, sir. May I help you?"

Without answering him, Paul turned and stared around the room at the children. Most of them were drinking. Some sat at tables, others were standing by the counter drinking stout.

"May I help you, sir?" repeated the boy.

"Eh?" Paul turned back to him. "Yes... yes," he stammered. "I'm looking for a room for the night. I was told you might have one."

"A room? Are you sure, sir?" said the boy, leaving down the glass he was cleaning. He had dull red hair, bright green eyes, and wore a white apron that was two sizes too big for him. Under his apron he wore a collarless striped shirt.

"Yes. I would like a room for the night and maybe a little supper, if it's not too much trouble. I'm quite tired and apparently the main road is a fair bit away. I'll never find it in this fog." He gulped as he looked side-ways along the counter and saw a boy quickly throw back a glass of whiskey, smack his lips and shout for another.

"A minute, Paddy!" the bar-boy shouted back, turned to a door behind him, and yelled, "Mary!"

A dark haired girl, with large, brown eyes came out through the door. Her eyes flitted over Paul as she dusted flour from her loose green dress.

"Gentleman would like a room for the night," said the bar-boy.

Mary's large eyes widened even further as she studied Paul for a few moments. She looked at the bar-boy, and he nodded.

"Follow me, sir," said Mary. The bar-boy raised the counter lid to allow Paul through, and with a last look around the room, Paul squeezed through and followed Mary out to a narrow hall, up a narrow staircase where he was shown into a tiny bedroom. The only window in the room overlooked the village street.

"Would ye like me to bring ye up somethin', sir, tay and some scones? I'm after bakin' some."

"Scones? Yes, Mary, that would be lovely. Thank you."

Giving Paul another strange look, Mary left the room.

Removing his jacket, Paul hung it over a chair at the side of his bed, went to the window, and pulled back the curtains. Down in the street he could see two boys, on Daisy-bell bicycles, ringing their bells and whistling loudly at a young girl who was pushing a pram across the street. Another boy, smoking a pipe, drove past on a horse and cart, his whip flicking at the frisky black and white horse. Looking directly below, Paul saw more boys and girls coming down the street and going into the pub. He stood for a few minutes watching and swung away, muttering, "Where the hell are the people, the adults?" These questions and others ate at him as he sat down on the edge of the bed. He yawned as he looked at the soft pillow. *A good night's sleep will help.*

A minute later there was a knock at the door and Mary entered carrying a tray with a mug of tea, some steaming scones and a dish of butter. "Here we are, sir." She beamed, placing the tray on the chair.

"Thanks Mary." As Mary turned to go, Paul asked, "Where are the adults? Are they away? Do they know about the children downstairs, drinking?"

Mary stared at him her brown eyes twinkling mischievously. "Drinkin', sir?" she said.

"Yes, Mary, drinking... drinking," Paul repeated angrily. "Alcohol. It is alcohol they're drinking? They're all far too young. Why some of them are younger than you." He studied her. "Ahm, what age are you?"

With a smile Mary blushed, and whispered, "One hundred and thirteen, sir."

"Eh?" Paul's mouth fell open as he watched Mary turn and leave the room. He stared at the closed door for several seconds and shook his head. No, it must have been thirteen she said. Yes, it must have been thirteen.

Half an hour later Mary returned.

"Is the bar still open, Mary?"

"It is, sir."

"Good. I think I'll go down for a drink later on." He was curious about the children now and knew he wouldn't get to sleep until he found out why the children were in the bar and why they were allowed to drink.

Mary smiled as she bent to pick up the tray. "Of course, sir," she whispered, almost to herself.

Ten minutes later, Paul came through the door to the bar. Smiling, the bar-boy lifted the counter lid, and Paul squeezed through. He looked around the room. He could see it was even more crowded, and he was the only adult there. Frowning, he saw that some of the children appeared drunk, and to his left he gaped at a young girl who had her arms around a boy with dimples. She was lilting a song in Gaelic in a slurred voice into his face. Occasionally one or two of the children would look over at him and whisper to each other. Dazed, Paul turned back to the bar and motioned to Mary, who was cleaning glasses, to come over to him. "Mary," he whispered, "Do you think I could have a whiskey and a stout please?"

As Mary poured the drinks, he turned again to look at the children. *What the hell is going on?*

"Your drink, sir."

Turning, Paul grabbed at the glass of whiskey and in one gulp downed it, almost choking, as the fiery liquid hit the back of his throat. Grabbing his glass of stout he took a long drink of the cold liquid.

As he drank, Mary watched him.

"Mary," gasped Paul when he had recovered. "All these children, their parents?"

Mary frowned her question at him. "Sir?"

"The adults," Paul snapped. "Where are they, the children's parents?"

"Parents, sir?"

"Yes Mary, their parents, their mothers and fathers, where are they?"

"Oh, them," said Mary smiling. "They're all gone, sir."

"Gone?" Paul frowned.

"Dead, sir, many years ago."

Paul gaped at her.

"Same again, sir?"

Dazed, he nodded, and as Mary poured him another drink, he turned back to look around the room. *No parents.* He studied the children for a few seconds, turned back to the bar, and took a good drink from his glass of whiskey. This time the drink slipped easily down filling him with a warm glow.

"Ye'll have one on the house, sir," the bar-boy said coming along the counter towards him. Before he could answer the boy lifted his glass and filled it almost to the brim with whiskey.

"Here, easy on, son," Paul smiled. "That's strong stuff." He looked at Mary as she topped up his glass of stout. The bar-boy stood beside Mary, watching Paul as he took another drink of whiskey.

"Tell me," Paul asked when he lowered his glass. "How long have you worked here?"

"Worked here, sir?" the boy said, smiling at Mary. "I own this pub."

"You own it," croaked Paul reaching for his glass. His hand trembled as he took a gulp of the whiskey. Glaring straight into the boy's green eyes, he snapped, "You're a bit young to be owning a pub, aren't you?"

"No, sir. My wife, Mary," the boy nodded to Mary, "and I have owned this pub nigh on eighty years."

"Eighty ye... Wife?" Paul's hand shook as he took another quick mouthful of whiskey. His eyes watered as he gasped. "Did you say eighty years?"

"Yes, sir. Mary's father owned the pub. I married her."

Paul stared at Mary who smiled shyly at the bar-boy.

"It's a joke. Yes, that's it." Paul smiled. "A mad, crazy joke." His head was beginning to spin and with two more gulps he finished off his whiskey and turned to the crowded bar. "It's a joke!" he shouted. "A mad joke!" The children all stared at him and some of them began to laugh. Swinging around to the smiling bar-boy, Paul waved his hand behind him to indicate the children and snapped, "Tell me, what is the average age of the children in this pub?"

The bar-boy looked around the room and said, "I would say about a hundred years, sir."

"A hun... ye... a hundred... but... but where are the adults, older people like me? Where are they?"

"Like you?" The bar-boy frowned and then smiled. "Oh, I see what ye mean now, sir, like you." Suddenly a shout from a bigger boy at one of the tables drew his attention and leaving down his drying cloth, he said, "Excuse me, sir." Paul watched as the bar-boy ducked under the lid went to the table and began to gather up the empty glasses. As he did he shouted, "Four more pints and three halves, Mary!"

By now Paul's head was spinning so much that he was beginning to feel sick. A heavy tiredness had come over him. Turning to Mary, he whispered hoarsely, "I think I'll go on up..."

"Yes, sir," said Mary smiling as she lifted the counter lid.

Squeezing through, Paul stumbled to the bottom of the stairs, and with his head spinning even more he staggered up to his room.

Next morning a knock on the bedroom door woke him, and with a groan he sat up. His head was pounding like a Lam-Beg drum when Mary entered. She smiled at him. "Yer breakfast, sir."

Placing the tray containing a plate of crisp bacon, two eggs, three scones and a small pewter pot of tea, milk and sugar on the chair, she went to the door. Studying Paul for a couple of seconds, she smiled and left the room.

Groaning, Paul crawled to the edge of the bed and squinted at his breakfast. His stomach heaved, and groaning louder, he pulled himself back to the middle of the bed and huddled under the sheets.

Two hours later he came downstairs. The bar-boy smiled at him.

"Last night..." Paul began.

"Ye had a wee bit too much, sir. Ye drank it too quick."

"Yes, yes. Well, thank you for your hospitality. How much do I owe you?" He gave Mary a forced smile as she came out of the kitchen. Mary smiled back. After settling his bill and groaning as his stomach heaved again, he walked out into the sunny village street.

As he drove out of the village in the direction the bar-boy told him would lead to the main road, Paul tried to reason with himself about the previous night. Five minutes later his mind was still on the children as he drove through a valley. The glare from the early morning sun had become brighter and reaching inside the glove compartment he searched for his sunglasses. As he took his eyes off the road, the car slipped into a pothole and he lost control. The car skidded into a shallow ditch. After trying for a few minutes to drive out of the muddy ditch, he gave up and got out of the car. Looking up and down the road he could see no one about, so after a while he set off in the direction he had come from.

Twenty minutes later he heard the sound of a tractor coming behind him, and a few minutes later he was back at his car. The driver of the tractor was a tall, thin, pleasant man wearing a pair of dirty dungarees and muddy Wellington boots. After pulling a thick rope from the back of the tractor, he tied it to the front axle of Paul's car.

"Get in, sir. I'll tow ye out. You'll have to steer."

Two minutes later the car was out of the ditch, and Paul gratefully thanked the man, explaining how he had landed in the ditch in the first place, and where he had stayed the night before. When he was finished the man scratched his head. "You say you stopped in a pub called, what?"

"Herrity's. Herrity's Pub. It's in the middle of the main street."

The man stared at him. "Sir, I've lived here for fifty years and I can tell you the nearest pub is thirty miles away, Dungloe. In that direction."

Paul gaped at him. "But I tell you, I stayed in Herrity's last night, in the village of Clontallaght. My God man, you should have seen the children. They were all drinking. All of them."

Rolling up the rope the tractor driver asked, "Was everyone in the village children? Were there no older people?"

"No. At least I never saw any. A girl there said all the adults were dead."

The man gasped. Paul studied him and asked, "Do you know the village, then?"

Saying nothing, the man climbed into the tractor.

"Wait," said Paul. "I must pay you."

Turning to him the man said, "No, sir. I don't want anything. It wouldn't be right."

"Eh?"

"Sir."

"Yes?"

"My father used to tell me about the village of Clontallaght."

"Yes?"

"Well, many years ago the villagers there were supposed to have trapped a Leprechaun. During his capture he was fatally injured, and as he lay dying, he cursed the village and all in it, telling them that not one adult in Clontallaght would live to see old age."

Paul stared up at the man. Just before starting up his tractor the man said, "It's just a tale, sir." Without another word he drove off.

A minute later the tractor driver turned and sighed as he watched the car speeding away. He frowned now as he remembered another part of his father's tale—the part about the Leprechaun's curse including anyone who stayed overnight in the village.

Years later, a teenager and a middle-aged woman drove slowly through the valley.

"We must be near the place now, Catherine. Maybe we'll be lucky this time. I think it was near here where I got stuck in the ditch."

"Are you sure, Paul?"

"Yes. Yes, I think so."

Sighing heavily, his wife changed down a gear as she followed his directions. She hoped they would find Clontallaght this year.

19

Pebbles On The Beach

Seven-year-old Danny looked up at his grandfather's pale face. The old man was standing with one hand shading his gray ringed eyes as he searched the stone covered beach. "There are only a few people in the world who know how to recognize a lucky stone and I'm one of them. Did you know that, son?"

It was a dull summer's day and the first day of their holiday. Danny's parents had rented a cottage near the beach in Magheroarty, County Donegal. As Danny was an only child they had brought a playmate along for him. They had brought Danny's grandfather.

"Do you think there are any lucky stones on this beach, Granda?" asked Danny looking along the broad beach at the lawn of many different colored stones.

"There are," said his grandfather, narrowing his eyes as he looked down along the water's edge.

The sea lapped gently onto the stony beach, the incoming tide wetting the stones making their smooth colors glisten like fruit on a dewy morning.

"But a lucky stone has to be wet before I can recognize it," said Danny's grandfather stepping carefully with his size eleven bunioned white feet over the stones and down to the water's edge. Danny followed him.

Suddenly Danny spotted a shiny white stone and quickly picked it up. As he handed it to his grandfather, he asked, "Is this one, Granda?"

The old man examined the stone, occasionally glancing at Danny's flushed excited face. Danny held his breath.

"Aye," said Danny's grandfather looking at the stone again. "It could be. It could be." He glanced at Danny again. The boy's big blue eyes were wide with excitement. "But I don't think so," he said handing the stone back. Danny's face fell, and the stone slipped from his fingers and fell with a sharp click at his feet.

"It looked like one all right," the old man said quickly. "But I knew it wasn't."

Danny looked down at the stone and then at his grandfather. "What does a lucky stone look like, Granda?" he asked.

"Ach sure you can't just tell by looking at one. A lucky stone has to feel right." Bending closer to Danny, he whispered, "You have to be able to feel the magic."

"The what?" exclaimed Danny loudly. "Did you say the magic?"

His grandfather looked all around and held a forefinger to his lips, silently telling Danny to speak quietly.

"Are lucky stones magic?" whispered Danny looking around too.

"Of course they are," answered his grandfather. "I thought you would have at least known that."

"No, I didn't," said Danny quietly, thinking, *magic*. He stared along the orchard of stones, looked up at his grandfather again, and asked, "Can you really tell which is a lucky stone?"

"Of course I can. Sure, haven't I the gift?"

"The gift? What's that?"

His grandfather bent towards him again and whispered, "A gift is something few people have. People who can feel the magic." He sniffed. "I have it."

"You have?" Danny whispered as his grandfather bent to the stones.

"Oh aye, I have the gift all right," he said, picking up a dimpled red stone and examining it.

Danny stretched to look. "Is... is that one?" he whispered excitedly.

His grandfather screwed up his craggy face as he studied the stone. Then he threw it from him. "Nope," he said quickly.

"Do you think we'll find one, Granda?" asked Danny.

The old man looked thoughtful as he scanned the water's edge. "We might," he said. Turning to look down at his grandson, he added, "We might find more than one."

More than one, thought Danny as his grandfather took a few steps forward. Danny followed him.

Away out to sea, gulls screeched as they plummeted to the blue-green water. A haze was forming on the horizon, and the light breeze that had earlier kept the searchers cool had changed direction. Some black clouds were drifting over the sand hills towards the sea.

A few minutes later, Danny and his grandfather where almost halfway across the beach. The sound of the ocean was lost to them as they searched. Suddenly, "Aha!"

Danny hurried forward as his grandfather picked up a flat stone. He could see that several white lines ran through the shiny blackness of it. His grandfather turned it over. The stone had a dimple like an empty eye socket on one side.

"Is... it one?" gasped Danny. "Is it, Granda?" He held his breath as he studied the strange looking stone. When he looked up at his grandfather again he saw that he had his eyes closed. Holding the stone on the palm of his right hand with his thumb resting on the dimple, he raised and lowered the stone several times as if testing its weight.

"Yes," the old man whispered, opening one eye and looking at Danny. "Yes. I can feel it. I can feel the magic. Yes. There's no doubt about it. This is definitely a lucky stone."

Danny released his breath. He stared at the stone. "Can... can I hold it, Granda?" he asked.

"Of course you may son. Here."

Reaching with both hands Danny gently took the stone from him. "Is it really a lucky stone, Granda?" he asked, studying it.

"Of course it is." Danny's grandfather frowned. "Wait a minute. Can you not feel the magic of it? You might have the gift, too."

"Me? No... I..."

"You might have. You're my grandson after all. The gift is supposed to run in the family, you know."

"Is it?"

"Aye."

Danny frowned as he studied the stone again. "But I can't feel anything, Granda. I can't feel the magic." A tear pushed to the corner of one eye.

"Maybe that's because you're not doing it properly. You have to close your eyes and hold the lucky stone in your right hand. You saw what I did, didn't you?"

"Yes."

"Well, why don't you do the same? Go on try it. Hold the stone in your right hand. Yes, that's it. Now close your eyes tightly, tightly now."

Danny did as he was told.

"That's it," he heard his grandfather whisper. "Now feel the stone. Feel the magic. Raise and lower it. Easy... easy now. That's it, son. Feel the magic. Aye, that's it."

As Danny raised and lowered the stone his right hand began to tingle. A strange feeling seemed to surge through him. *It's the magic I can feel it.*

"Can you feel the magic now?" he heard his grandfather whisper.

"Yes," gasped Danny opening his eyes. "I can!" he shouted. "I really can!"

"I knew it. I knew you had the gift," said his grandfather smiling as Danny stared with wonder at the lucky stone. "Well, now you've got the magic, you'll know how to find other lucky stones. Come on, let's look for more."

An hour later, just as the first drops of rain spat onto the beach, Danny and his grandfather returned to the cottage.

As Danny excitedly showed his mother the five lucky stones he had found, his father, who had been reading the newspaper, glanced over at the old man who was standing by the fireplace filling his pipe, watching. Danny's father smiled and shook his head at the old man. Danny's grandfather ignored him and turned to the mantelpiece for his matches.

"Go on out to the kitchen and wash your hands, Danny," said his mother. "Tea will be ready soon."

When Danny was out in the kitchen, his mother glared good-humoredly at her father. "You and your lucky stones," she said, shaking her head.

That night as the rain battered against the cottage Danny lay awake staring at the five stones on his small bedside table. He smiled. The tingling of magic from the stones seemed to fill the room. *I'll search for more tomorrow.*

20

BEWARE THE AGAPANTHUS

Even after all these years, I can still remember the fear I felt as I read that warning on the dried out, worm-riddled, wooden sign that tilted at an impossible angle blocking our path. It was a warm, sunny day when we walked about two miles across the coarse sand to the mysterious island. We, being myself, I was in my early twenties then, and my wife's three young brothers. Paul, the youngest, was a quiet, plump boy aged five, and I was carrying him on my shoulders. We were all in our bathing pants.

In that part of Donegal, called the Ardlands, where we were holidaying near Burtonport, west of Cruit Island, the land was very flat, and when the tide went out it left long stretches of glistening sand. This sand, with its pools of lukewarm water, was our playground that summer, and on that particular day, when the tide was at its lowest, we had decided to go out to the island and explore it.

At the start of our two-week holiday we had spotted the island. In the middle of it, at the highest point, was a solitary derelict house. It seemed to us a strange place for a house, for even though the tide went out a good distance the only way the island could be reached was by boat, except for that day when the tide was so far out we thought we could wade over to it.

I was as excited as my young brothers-in-law as we approached the shallow water that still surrounded the island. With a word to Paul to hold steady, I waded into the warm water feeling unknown water creatures wriggling under my feet and darting for safety. Swaying unsteadily, I shouted back to Martin and Francis, Paul's brothers, to be careful as the water was almost up to my waist. As I waded on, the water got shallower, and breathing heavily, I lowered Paul down onto the hot sand at the bottom of a long sandy path that wound its way up to the house.

Raising my hand to shade my eyes, I studied the path. It was dotted with black and white pebbles and low fuchsia bushes bordered both sides of it. A few bees hummed around the fuchsia searching for nectar. Paul and I turned to watch Martin, a lean, freckle-faced twelve-years-old who wore glasses, and Francis a small, pale-faced ten-years old struggling through the water that was almost up to their necks. Shivering, they reached us, and as they shook the water from their goose-pimple covered bodies, I said, "C'mon." Taking Paul by the hand, I led the way up the path.

As we drew near the house, I could see the patchwork of red bricks that showed through the pebble-dashed, cracked gable. I also noted pieces of brown, brittle leaves protruding from out of the top of the three tall, yellow chimney-pots. I remembered thinking that it must have been quite a while since the house had been occupied. Encouraged by this assumption, I led the boys on.

As we came to the top of the path, beyond which I could see a tiny garden, I stopped and looked around to make sure no one was about. After all, we were trespassing... and it was then I saw it. The sign read:

BEWARE THE AGAPANTHUS

And suddenly my heart began to pound like a drum against my ribs. It was then that Martin saw the sign.

"What's an Aga... Agapanthus? Ahhhh!"

I turned to see him racing back down the path towards the water. By now my heart was really pounding, for Martin's reaction to the sign had panicked me.

"Quick!" I shouted, gripping Paul's hand tighter. "Run! Francis! Run. Run..."

Francis stared at me as I swung Paul up into my arms. Then with a quick double take he looked down the path after his fleeing brother and back at me. With a stifled cry he was away. Carrying Paul, I raced after him. As I did, I could feel the hairs creeping along the back of my neck, and as I flew down the path unaware of Paul's weight, I imagined all types of fierce beasts tearing from the thick bushes at my bare legs. Seconds later I slithered to a stop at the bottom of the path, turned quickly to see if I was being followed, and it was then I swear I heard a low growl. With a terrified leap, I plunged into the water passing Francis and Martin mid-way between the island and the sanctuary of the sand on the far side. When I reached sanctuary, spluttering and out of breath, I lowered Paul gently onto the sand and flopped down to watch his brothers wade towards us. I ventured a look towards the island again and shuddered. As I did, little Paul, with his chubby face wrinkled with puzzlement at our actions, stared at his brothers as they threw themselves down onto the sand beside us.

"Wha... what's up?" he stuttered.

Ignoring him, I scrambled to my feet and a few seconds later we were heading back along the beach. As we walked, we discussed the warning sign and took an occasional fearful look back at the island vowing silently never to return.

"But what the heck kind of creature is an Agapanthus or whatever it is?" Martin questioned.

Behind us the black clouds drifted ominously over the island.

That evening as the rain tore at our little rented cottage, and the wind shrieked like a banshee through the cracks in the doorjamb, I took a long look through the window at the island. The tide was fully in now, and I thought I saw two bright lights bobbing about like the eyes of some strange night creature.

It was quite some time later before we found out that an Agapanthus was a type of flower.

21

THE FAIRY

Mary sighed as she studied Paddy's stubborn face. They sat together on their rickety old summer-seat that was half hidden amongst the rhododendron bushes at the back of the garden. Their cottage was the only building on the narrow road that ran adjacent to the river.

"I couldn't live without you... and I won't."

"You're only being silly, Paddy."

"No," he snapped, turning away.

Mary sighed again, as her hand strayed to gently touch the swelling cancer on her left side.

"Paddy," she said quietly, reaching to take his hand and lovingly caressing the familiar calluses on his. "It would be wrong."

Paddy's face tightened and his gray ringed eyes glistened as he croaked, "It's wrong what's happening to you."

The evening that Mary had told him what the doctor had diagnosed, Paddy had gone out to the big field and had roared and cursed his anger at the moon, the stars, and God. Crying, he had slumped to the ground. He had lain there for over an hour before Mary came for him, and like hundreds of nights before, they had walked down to the river, only that night was different. Paddy, with his arm gently wrapped around her slender waist, was afraid to let her go. Once they had stopped, and with tears running down his face, he had kissed her softly. She had given him a half smile, each knowing she was being brave, and each knowing she was terrified.

"Please, Paddy. Promise me you won't."

"No. I..." He studied her pale face. "But... what am I going to do?"

"Go on," she whispered. "Live your life until it's your time. Don't go before then. Paddy, promise me you'll go on."

"Promise," he muttered. There had been no promises between them. No need, until now. "What's my life going to be like without you? I'd rather be dead." He turned away when he saw the dreaded grimace as her pain began.

He couldn't bear to look at the growth anymore. With a grunt Mary rose. "I... I have... to go in." He rose to go with her, but she pushed him back with unusual strength, and groaning, stumbled up the garden path to the cottage and disappeared inside.

Paddy stared at the back door, then raised his eyes to the barge-board and the flaking paint. He had intended to paint the cottage before Mary took bad. He tried to remember the last time he had painted it. He couldn't, yet he could remember the first time, all those years ago. They had been married only six months. That was the year they saw the Fairy down along the river.

It was one of those late summer evenings, one of the special times that invaded all your senses and stayed with you forever. The fields sang with a cacophony of sound, the sky was slowly turning a magical pink, and the river meandered like a long drop of dripping golden syrup to the carry to tumble white over the moss-covered green rocks to the lower water.

It was on the way back they saw it—at least, Mary did. They had been kissing near some bushes that grew on the edge of one of the many fields. Mary had seen it watching them and with a cry had suddenly pulled away from him and pointed. For a few seconds she couldn't speak as Paddy stared in the direction she had indicated. The rustling of the bushes told him someone or something had been there, but he could see no one. Afterwards, Mary quickly told him what she had seen.

That evening as they lay in bed talking about the Fairy, Paddy wondered what Mary had really seen. He didn't believe in fairies, or any of the silly stories he had heard when he had been growing up. Still, he thought, as he drifted off, Mary had seen something.

A month later, when they were on their way back along the river just as the sun was setting, they were startled by a shrill scream coming from a low hawthorn hedge. At first Paddy had thought it was a badger, because on earlier walks they had seen badgers, and a couple of mink in the long fields. But as they approached the hedge it began to shake violently. Telling Mary to stay where she was and careful not to prick himself, he eased back a section of the hedge and peered into the semi-darkness. What he saw shocked him so much he staggered back into Mary, almost knocking her over. But seconds later they were both staring at the fairy.

It was repulsive, yet the feeling quickly vanished when they saw it was in pain. The tiny, man-shaped creature wore clothes that appeared to be made of leaves and grass. Its eyes were piercing, yet seemed dark with wisdom. Thick hair grew on the parts of its exposed body, and its dirty face was deeply etched with wrinkles. It was bare-footed, and they saw that one of its feet was caught on an old rusting steel trap that must have been set years ago. Though it was quickly growing dark, Paddy could see the creature's ankle was badly torn. Blood was pumping from one of the big veins on its tiny leg.

Wary, Paddy and the creature studied each other, until Paddy said, "You're badly caught. I'll have to go up to the cottage for a crow-bar and some tools to free you."

The creature hissed sharply though it seemed to understand.

"Mary," he whispered. "I don't want to leave it alone. Will you be all right? I won't be long."

Mary's eyes widened with fear.

"I won't be long," he repeated and gently pulled her out onto the path. "Mary." She seemed to be in a trance and was trembling. He shook her.

Mary stared at him. "Wha... what is it, that... that thing?" she asked.

Paddy shook his head. He couldn't say "fairy;" in fact, he didn't *want* to say it. "I don't know. But it needs our help. Look I have to go up to the cottage for tools. I'll only be five minutes. Will you be alright?"

Mary shook her head. "Paddy, I..."

"Mary, it would be better if you stay with it. The thing's leg's badly mangled and it's frightened."

Mary looked at the hedge, and whispered, "Hurry back."

In a moment he was away. Once he had glanced back and in the dying light he saw Mary pushing into the hedge. He returned to find her pale and trembling holding the fairy's hand. He shuddered now as he remembered how it had been a long time before he could hold that hand.

It took him three minutes to spring the trap open without causing the fairy too much pain. With a cry that sent the hair creeping along the back of Paddy's neck, it stood up. It glared at them, with what seemed to Paddy to be undisclosed hatred. It was as if it hated to have been freed by *them,* the humans. Suddenly with another cry it leapt backwards through the hedge and was gone.

Later they talked long into the night about the fairy, each coming to their own conclusion that it must have been a real one. But during the following mild winter, they saw it again.

They had been at a farewell party for neighbors of theirs who lived three miles away and who were immigrating to Australia. As it was a beautiful moonlit night, they decided to go down to the river. They had only walked about four hundred yards when Mary stopped and pointed. Thirty yards in front of them, the fairy had stepped out onto the path. It was studying them and by the look on its face it seemed to have an awareness of something they couldn't see—a presence of some kind. Suddenly it pulled a small bag from its belt and bent to place it on the middle of the path. In the time it took Paddy and Mary to look at the bag, the fairy had disappeared back into the bushes.

When they reached the bag they saw it was made of leather. Inside were five gold sovereigns: a present.

"Paddy," Mary whispered looking all around. "We can't accept it."

"What! Why not?" He was already planning to spend the money on seed and a new scythe. "The fairy gave it to us. You saw. There was no mistake. It gave it to us freely."

"Yes, but we can't take it," said Mary. "Paddy, please leave it here. Please."

At first he had been angry with Mary, but he realized she was right. They couldn't accept the fairy's gift. They had helped it, freed it, but they had done so willingly.

Early that morning Paddy thought about the bag of sovereigns lying on the path. Someone else might come along and find it. They had been foolish. When he had hurried to the place, the bag was gone.

Over the years they saw the fairy often. It stayed well away from them and never offered anything again.

Mary's crying brought him out of his thoughts, and he clenched his fists. God, he thought, will her pain never end? He couldn't bear to hear her in so much agony. But what could he do? Sighing he hurried into the cottage.

Over the next seven days Mary grew worse, and on one of the bad nights Paddy went down to the river. He stood staring at the carry as the water gently tumbled away just like his Mary's life. *It would be a good place to end it.* He stood there for over an hour, thinking back on their life together. It had gone so fast. Mary couldn't have children, and they had never regretted it. All they needed was each other. She had been the best... was the best.

As he turned to go, a movement along the bank caught his eye. It was the fairy, and beside it stood a tall, stick-thin thing. It was green in color and had bright piercing eyes. Paddy couldn't quite see its face, but there seemed to be something familiar about it. The fairy pointed to the thing and then at Paddy. The fairy did this three times, before Paddy realized it was offering its strange companion to him. Horrified, he backed away, and turning, stumbled along the path to the cottage. He lay awake all night thinking about it.

Three days later the doctor ordered Mary to the hospital.

Five days later before going to visit Mary, Paddy went down to the river again. He didn't know why he went now. It would never be the same without Mary. The river had lost all its magic. Nothing would ever be the same without her. He stood, tears streaming down his face, as he remembered the good times, the special times when they didn't want the day to end. Suddenly a noise made him turn. It was the fairy. Horrified he backed away as the fairy offered its companion to him again. The thing had changed, no longer thin, it had filled out. Its hair the color Mary's used to be. Its eyes sad and beautiful like hers. The Fairy moaned and pointed at it, offering it to Paddy who suddenly screamed with fear and ran for the cottage.

That night Mary died and later Paddy cried himself to sleep vowing that in the morning he would take his life.

When he woke, the sun was shining through the bedroom window. *It's time,* he thought. Slowly he rose and walked to the window and looked out. Beyond the garden he could see the river. But just as he was about to turn away, a movement near the summer-seat caught his eye and he saw her.

Quickly he dressed and hurried out to the garden. As he ran down the path to the summer-seat. he was unaware of the fairy pushing into the rhododendron bushes out of sight. He stopped now when the thing that resembled Mary said, "What kept you, Paddy? I've been up for ages."

22

HOME FOR CHRISTMAS

Clare stared stupidly at the ticket the boatman had handed her:

TICKET TO TORY—ONE WAY

One way, she thought. *Aye. I'll hardly be returning.*

As the boat putt-putted into the narrow inlet that led to the pier, Clare's heart gave a little flutter as she watched the young boatman edge along the rim of the narrow craft and get ready to leap. Quickly cutting the engine, the Captain swung hard on the steering wheel, and the boat bobbed gently to a halt against the pier. At the same time the boatman sprang to the pier and bending quickly, looped the mooring rope around a rusting bollard, and then turned to the boat and waited.

As Clare made to disembark, he gallantly held out a tanned, freckled hand to help her, at the same time blushing when she thanked him. Gently he helped her onto the wet pier, and there Clare waited beside the bollard until the boatman climbed on board again and returned with her small suitcase.

She could feel the two boatmen staring after her as she walked slowly up the slippery green steps past the fishermen's hut, and onto the grassy path above. A few seconds later, breathing heavily, she stopped to catch her breath and lowered her suitcase to the ground. Small beads of sweat glistened on her pale brow in the hot summer sun, and a warm breeze whipped at her long black hair. She opened her light raincoat and, removing it, she draped it over her suitcase and set off again.

Ten minutes later and gasping for breath, she reached the top of the winding path. Leaving down her suitcase again, she sat on a flat, lichen covered rock. From there she had a good view of the little harbor. Looking down she saw that the boat she had arrived in was already on its way back to the mainland. She sighed heavily, her tiredness making her lower her head, and her eyes fell on her thin hands.

Paul had always admired her hands. Not now. She stared at them, bony and veined, ugly things. Her shiny wedding ring looked out of place on her hand and, twisting it nervously, she gazed again after the boat. On further out to sea she could see the screaming gulls gliding gracefully catching the wind and then plummeting to the green blue swell of the ocean. As she watched the gulls, their piercing, haunting cries took her back. It had been over five years since she had last sat here and over six years since her mother had died.

She had been twenty when her mother had suddenly passed away. Her mother's death had so affected her father that he changed from the cheerful, loving man Clare had always known into a crabbed old man who rarely left the fireside. All day long he would sit staring wistfully into the fire. There was always a fire in the cottage. Even during that following hot summer, she never failed to awaken to the sound of her father raking and poking at the turf ashes. Soon she began to grow discontented with her lonely life on the island and on the day of her twenty-first birthday, she told her father she was leaving to find work on the mainland. At first he had objected, but he soon realized that she had made up her mind.

Sighing as the memories came to her, Clare reached down and pulled at the dry lichen on the rock between her legs, thinking about the day she had left Tory. She remembered the tiny figure of her father standing on the cliffs looking down as the boat carried her away. She had so wanted him to wave, but he had remained motionless. When the boat had rounded the headland she had lost sight of him.

She sighed again. Grunting with the effort, she rose slowly and headed on up. The familiar smells hit her as she walked slowly up the fuchsia bordered path to the cottage. White smoke curled into the blue sky from the cracked chimney, and as she drew nearer the familiar smell of turf made her feel even more melancholy. Changing her suitcase over onto her other hand, she automatically hooked her thumb over her wedding ring to keep it from sliding from her finger and this action immediately brought her thoughts back to Paul again. They had been married for four happy years. Those years would have been complete had they had the baby they both longed for.

But after a second internal examination, her happiness was shattered when the doctor told her she could never have children. In fact, he told her she had very little time left. She made the doctor swear not to tell Paul. A month later, after more tests and another conclusive diagnosis, she decided to leave Paul. The letter she wrote telling him to find someone else, someone who could give him children, had drained her.

She loved him. Oh, how she loved him, but she had to leave him. She couldn't bear to see his disappointment. She knew how much he wanted children. He would be happier with someone who could give him a family... and she was dying anyway. It was better this way. She waited two months before returning to the island.

A cow mooed loudly as it stared at her over the low hedge bringing her quickly out of her reverie. A few moments later she was smiling sadly at the rusting, three-legged pots on each side of the cottage door. White carnations, her mother's favorite flowers, grew in profusion out of them. Quietly she put down her suitcase and reaching over the lower half-door, she eased back the bolt. As she pushed the creaking door open and stepped inside, an excited bee buzzed inside the cottage with her.

Her father was sitting by the fire, his greasy cap pulled tight over his long white hair. Startled, he turned towards the door, his pipe quivered in his mouth, and immediately his eyes brimmed over when he saw her. He tried to rise from the chair, but in an instant she had reached him. Falling to her knees, her thin arms surrounded him and with tears in her eyes she whispered, "I've come home for a while, Da—until Christmas."

The wild winter waves crashed upon the bleak inlet, scattering white spittle onto the gray rocks on each side of it. Clare huddled in her favorite place, staring out at the misty horizon. She had come here often these past months, as often as her strength would let her. She didn't know why she came, except that somehow she was comforted by the untamable sea as it thundered against Tory.

This evening—Christmas Eve—she felt stronger, and she had stumbled from the cottage and down to the rocks. She shivered now, pulling her heavy coat around her thin shoulders. She could hardly breathe, and all of a sudden her head felt so heavy. She could hardly hold it up. The wind howled like a banshee shrieking louder than the crashing waves. Then suddenly, above the sound of the wind, she heard a voice calling to her.

"Clare!"

Standing up, she saw him now, away out. His face was tanned and his dark hair was blowing across his handsome face. He was smiling as the boat sailed towards her.

"Paul!" she gasped, stumbling from her shelter and blindly making her way over the wet rocks to the water's edge. Her heart was pounding and with a smile, she moved into the water. The waves tugged and pulled at her and she fell. She struggled to rise and looking out over the waves, she saw him again, and her heart swelled to almost bursting with love for him. His arms were reaching out to her, and he called her name again.

"Clare!"

And the creeping tide reached out and carried her away.

23

THE PORPOISE

From early morning they had been walking along the railway line that ran from Derry to Belfast. This part of the line they were on skirted the east bank of the River Foyle. It was a cold misty morning and their breaths smoked steadily from their numbed, somber faces as their tired eyes searched the black mud that would soon be covered by the incoming tide. On out from the line, a clinging, ghostly mist capped the river, and a half mile away the top of the 40 meters high New Foyle Bridge was just visible.

He'd been a good boy, thought May as she stumbled after her husband over the rough stones that lay at a slant and under the knotted sleepers on each side of the line. *Danny had been a good boy, but a bit wild.*

The policemen had called in the early hours of the morning, and she would never forget it. Standing between two policemen was Sheila, her son's girlfriend. May's heart had pounded so hard that she thought it would burst as she listened to Sheila's tearful explanation of what had happened to Danny. They had been drinking at the Strand bar and due to over indulgence of a mixture of vodka and coke, they had quarreled on their way home across Craigavon bridge.

Sheila told Danny they were finished. Danny roared at her that without Sheila he didn't want to live and before she could stop him, he climbed the steel railing that bordered the bridge and leapt into the cold, heartless river. Sheila begged May's forgiveness; but what was there to forgive? It wasn't her fault. It wasn't even the alcohol.

All that day May stood on the lower deck of Craigavon Bridge watching the police divers search the river. Her husband was too distraught to go with her, but next day he did go, when the two Derry Sub-Aqua Clubs and the Strabane Sub-Aqua club volunteered to help in the search. Two days later the search was called off and a policeman called to tell them that Danny's body would probably surface on the next high tide. But three days later the high tide did not bring Danny's body to the surface, and they began the search along both sides of the wide river. Their friends, neighbors and people they didn't even know searched with them, spending long hours walking along the riverbank. But eventually they realized it was futile and now only May and her husband walked the familiar riverside every day.

At 11:45 the tide was full in and the mist had lifted. As they headed onto the wide arc that would take them around Rosses Bay to the New Foyle Bridge they saw Joe Houston, the railway man, coming towards them. His head was bowed as he inspected the line. When he saw them he greeted them with a pleasant smile addressing May first.

"Mornin' Mrs. Carlin. Mornin', John."

"Mornin' Joe," they said together.

"Cowl wan," said Joe still walking.

"Aye," said John. May nodded and looked along the line. She wanted to get on.

Joe walked for about ten meters and suddenly stopped. "John!" he called. "The twelve o'clock will be along shortly so watch out fer the drag!"

Half turning John waved a reply.

Joe stood for a few seconds watching Danny's parents as they stumbled along the line, and with a deep sigh and shaking his head from side to side, he turned and continued on.

At five to twelve the sun was breaking through. By then they had reached the middle of the curve of the bay. In the reed-thick lake five meters from the side of the line a Cygnet on the far bank flapped its wings and hissed loudly attracting their attention. Still walking, John and May watched the beautiful creature. Now they saw a Pen and its beautiful mate swim from the reeds bordering the lake and head towards the Cygnet. But as they did the young swan began to swim on out to the middle of the lake. Two minutes later John and May saw the three swans swimming together towards the hide in the reeds.

Suddenly a movement in the water to May's left caught her eye and she stopped. "Look! There!" she cried.

They both stared out into the bay watching the ever-increasing ripples tumble towards the bank.

"What was it, May?" asked John turning to her. "What did ye see? Was it Danny?"

May shook her head. "I don't know what it was, a creature," May whispered. "There was something in the water... There!" She pointed again and her husband, bending closer, followed the line of her arm. They stood motionless, unaware that behind them the swans had come out of the reeds and were swimming towards the middle of the calm lake.

"There!" exclaimed May, and hardly daring to breathe, they both watched the *creature*.

Water glistened in the sunlight on the graceful porpoise's sleek body as it broke the surface, and in bounding arcs the creature—poetry in motion— knifed through the muddy water until suddenly, with a higher dive, it disappeared below again. May and Joe watched it, their troubles forgotten, as the porpoise appeared again racing up and down the bay near the edge where they stood, entrancing them with its seemingly boundless energy.

Suddenly a loud horn sounded and turning, John gasped, grabbed May's arm and gently helped her down to the low wall that bordered the left side of the line. Again the sound of the horn echoed across the river as the train rattled under the bridge and around the corner. Hugging the wall, John and May froze as the train thundered towards them. Clinging tighter to each other they felt the drag of each carriage pull at them, threatening to suck them under the wheels, but a few seconds later the train was past.

May and John looked after it, only relaxing when it disappeared around the corner, and remembering their purpose, they began to head on around the bay. Once or twice May looked for the porpoise, but she never saw it again.

24

The "R" Months

The water slapped gently on the side of the boat as he heaved the lobster pot onto the edge of it. Making sure the attached line wasn't snagged, he pushed the pot towards the water, and with a splash, it quickly disappeared below. As it did, the memory of the first day he had gone lobster fishing with his father suddenly came to him.

There were plenty of the big blue shellfish back then, and he could still hear his father's hearty laugh as he pulled two lobsters from one pot. He remembered his fear of the fierce looking creature as his father held one out to him, its fan-like tail jack-knifing rapidly as it tried in vain to tear away from the five-fingered vice that held it captive.

He sighed as he baited another pot with the head of a dead pollack, remembering the happy days of his youth. Was that why he had returned? To try and recapture that happiness? Why had he come back to his island home? Why had he left the comfort of his successful solicitors practice in Galway for the inconvenience of living on this remote island?

A seagull shrieked excitedly before plummeting to the calm water, and shading his eyes, he looked towards the craggy rocks that outlined the cloud-crowded sky. With a grunt, he lifted the baited pot to the edge and pushed it over the side. Why did he welcome the loneliness of the coming hard winter, he thought dejectedly, why had it all gone wrong? What killed his ambition? Had he any to begin with?

Checking the bobbing marker buoys attached to each line one more time, he began to row towards the pier. A few minutes later, he was slipping into the small harbor, and with a final pull, he quickly shipped the oars and his boat bounced gently as it hit the pier wall. After securing the boat, he walked past the slipway and on up the narrow lane to his cottage.

He had been back three weeks, but her face still haunted him. Even now as he breathlessly climbed the steep path, she seemed to be everywhere. He wondered why he had never brought her here. Would she have liked his island home? What did it matter now? It was all over.

Stopping at the door of his cottage, he turned and gazed away to the mainland. In the distance, he could make out a few, ruck-sacked holidaymakers standing on Magheroarty pier getting ready to board the boat that would take them to Tory.

Looking to his left he could see the neat, whitewashed cottages and bungalows of Falcarragh, and further to his left the horned rocks of the headland jutted menacingly towards the islands. Looking up now, he searched the sky. The coming rain would maybe spoil the visitors' trip, he thought as he went inside.

He brewed himself a mug of strong tea. Tea had never tasted like this on the mainland. Later, taking a bite from one of the addictive scones he bought daily from the only shop on the island, he smiled. Already the island was beginning to weave its enchanting, delightful spell as it tried to capture him forever.

The beautiful sunsets that usually fired the summer sky did not come that night, and for the first time since his return he felt uneasy. Later that evening as the rain tore at the cottage, a thousand strange sounds surrounded him. He tried to read. He had brought two boxes of books with him, books he had always meant to read, but never seemed to have the time. He could not concentrate on the books now, and his thoughts drifted to his past years. When had it all begun?

He remembered the night the teacher came to the cottage. He could still hear his words. "It's a waste for the boy to stay here, John. He's got a sharp mind. He would get better schooling on the mainland. I can only do so much."

He remembered his father's face and his words as the light from the oil lamp eerily lit it up when he turned from the turf fire. "But I'll need him. He's strong enough now to help me with the lobsters, and there are the mussels too..."

"Ach, John, can't you see there's a world out there? I've taught here for twelve years and your son is the brightest pupil I've ever had. It would be a waste to hold him back. Look, I'll recommend him. He'll pass his college examination. I'll help him."

That was how it began. He didn't want to leave the island, and for days afterward he hated his teacher. That spring, he went to stay with an old aunt in Letterkenny where he attended college. Each summer he returned to the island and helped his father fish for lobsters and mussels. The years at college passed slowly, and he easily gained the qualifications he needed for Galway University.

It was during his final year there he received word his father had drowned. "Carried to the bottom by one of his pots, the line snagged his leg. A tragic accident," the priest told him when he went back home for his father's funeral. After his father had been buried, he had all the lobster pots brought to the cottage and put into a hut at the back of it. He also had his father's boat pulled up the slipway and stored near the pier. Then locking up the cottage, he returned to Galway.

It was that year—that Christmas—that he met Grainne. He had been persuaded to go to a Christmas party by one of the lecturers at the university. Grainne had been the center of attraction at the party, eulogizing and arguing the rights of Catholics and Sinn Fein in the North. Her zest for life had fired him, and that night he wondered if any of the others had fallen in love with her. Nine months later, after his graduation, they were married and two months after that he opened his solicitor's office in Galway. He employed a secretary and an assistant, and his business quickly prospered. The amount of legal work increased to such an extent that he took on a partner. Even then he had to work most evenings until late.

Grainne, too, was busy. She worked as a councilor in a home for battered wives. When she had applied for the position, they had had their first argument, but secretly he was glad she had got the job for she had become restless, complaining how life bored her. She worked every evening, too, and they saw very little of each other except at weekends. He began to dread their weekends together for they argued constantly. He wanted to start a family. She didn't.

Then everything changed.

Early that summer, he was surprised one evening to find Grainne waiting for him. He had had a particularly bad day with a client, and he was feeling irritable and tired. As he came into the hall, he saw her suitcase. The bombshell hit him when she told him she was leaving. She had fallen in love with one of the women at the home. At first he was stunned, then suddenly his anger exploded, and he hit her, knocking her hard against the sitting room wall. As she scrambled to her feet, he would always remember her face as she screamed defiantly, daring him to hit her again. Immediately ashamed of his violence, but still angry, he stalked from the house and spent a sleepless night at the nearest hotel.

When he returned home, she was gone.

A week later, as he sat staring out of the open window of his office, unable to concentrate on the pile of work on his desk, his secretary brought in the mail. Among the letters was one from Donegal. An islander had written to ask him if he would be willing to sell him his father's cottage and boat. He read the letter three times, his heart beating faster each time. Putting it down, he turned to stare out of the window again. Smells of the island seemed to drift into the room, and before lunchtime he had made up his mind to return home.

When he had been on the island a week, he wrote to his partner telling him what had happened. He also told him that he didn't know when he would be returning to Galway. He finished the letter with the words, "I need to be alone for a while."

Summer passed, and that autumn he began making plans for the winter. He had enough turf sent to outlast even the longest winters. He also ordered more books and magazines. The island's shop was always well stocked with food, and he felt confident he would have everything he needed.

His days on the island didn't vary much. Depending on the weather, first thing every morning he would check and bait his lobster pots. He would spend the rest of the day raking in mussels. Mussel gathering months were from September to April, the months with an R in them, and most of the islanders worked at bringing in the small shellfish. In the evening the bags of mussels would be weighed and washed ready for sending to the mainland the following morning. When the weather was bad, he repaired his pots and read.

Winter came early, with fierce storms cutting off the island for weeks, and on Christmas Day he went with the rest of the islanders to the church hall for the Christmas Ceildh. Two well-inebriated accordion players and a teenage fiddler belted out sometimes recognizable tunes to the eager dancers.

Early on Boxing Day, he staggered home with the wind tearing at him. The following days he rarely ventured from the cottage, as the winds grew stronger. On New Year's Day, he woke to a calm cold start to the year and with the dawning of the day came the realization that he could not quite remember what Grainne looked like.

Towards the end of January, he had a visit from his partner and eagerly he agreed to sell him his half of the practice. He left it up to his partner to finalize the legalities.

Spring came with the bright fuchsias bursting from every hedge, and the sun grew kinder with each day.

One morning towards the end of May, he rowed slowly around to his patch of the island to empty and bait his pots. It was a particularly warm day, and the water was a strawberry calm in the early morning sun. When he had checked and baited the pots near the shore, he moved out to his furthest buoys and began to haul one of the pots aboard. Inside their caged prison, two blue lobsters waited, bravely snapping as he expertly pulled one out and put it into a box at the back of the boat. As he pulled out the other lobster, he held it up and laughed as it rapidly jack-knifed its shiny body, trying to get away from him.

The sound of his laughter echoing across the water startled him, and for a moment he was back with his father. As tears ran down his tanned face, he looked towards the mainland. The dotted whites of the dwellings sparkled in the warm sun, and he shivered as he thought about the long winter to come.

25

THE STRANGER

As Father Doherty shuffled from the confession box, the rattle of Rosary beads brushing against the door alerted the man who knelt in the shadows to the left of the candlelit Grotto and he gave a soft cough.

"Who's there? Are ye for Confession?"

No answer. The old Priest peered closer, and gave a start.

"Who's there?" he repeated almost in a whisper, knowing even as he asked the question, who it was. *So he's returned,* he thought. He suddenly found his mouth was dry. "I'll be goin' over to the parochial house. We can talk there." Then digging his hands deep into his long black coat, he stumbled down the aisle past St. Anthony's statue towards the sacristy.

As he did, the man stood up and then slid sideways out of the long seat. He hesitated for a few seconds, then followed the priest.

In the sacristy he watched as the priest struggled to unbutton his coat. Neither of them spoke. Their eyes met. The man was the first to turn away.

A sharp wind tore at them as they made their way across the open tarmac chapel yard to the parochial house. As they climbed the steps and came into the hall, Mrs. Fahy, the housekeeper, came out from the kitchen.

"Mary, would ye be kind enough to bring us some tay? We'll be in the study," said Father Doherty.

Mrs. Fahy studied the stranger, then said, "I'm just after takin' some scones from the oven, Father. I'll bring some with the tay."

"Thanks, Mary. This way," he said to the man, opening the door of the study. He stood back and ushered him inside. Pointing to a leather armchair, he said, "Sit down. Take your coat off."

As the man removed his coat, Father Doherty walked to the far end of the room, pulled the curtains together, and then turned. "How are ye? How long have ye been back?" He forced a smile to hide his tumult. *Why has he come back? Why now?*

"How's my Ma?" the man asked looking steadily up at the Priest.

"Yer Mother," Father Doherty whispered, turning away from him. *So that's it,* he thought. Reaching for the packet of Senior Service cigarettes that lay on the table, he shook one out. "She... she passed away, a month ago."

A long sigh hissed from the man, and he bent to hold his head in his hands. "So I'm too late after all. I've come too late."

"She had a peaceful death, Michael. She didn't suffer." The old Priest stared down at him. "She missed ye, Michael. Ye could've come home... why didn't ye at least write? A letter would have—"

With tears in his eyes Michael suddenly shouted, "You know why! How the hell could I have stayed here after I found out?"

"Aye. I... I..."

Just then, Mrs. Fahy knocked and entered, carrying a tray. Butter was already melting onto the plate from the steaming scones.

"They're a bit hot, mind," she warned, going to the table.

"Lovely, Mary. Thanks."

Mary studied the stranger again, and placing the tray on the table, she took another long look at him before closing the door after her.

"Sugar?" asked Father Doherty, holding out the bowl and spoon.

"No. What was my Ma's last years like, Father? Was she happy? Did you see her much?"

Holding out the plate of scones to him, Father Doherty replied, "She was happy, Michael. She would have been happier to know ye were all right. Where did ye go? What has *yer* life been like?"

"My life?" Michael sighed heavily. "My life... remember how angry I was when I found out? About a month after, I joined the Army in Liverpool. I spent six months training and then I was posted to Germany. I was there nearly two years and I was just coming to terms with everything when I heard my unit was being sent back to Northern Ireland, so I left."

"Left? Ye mean ye deserted?"

"Aye."

"Then what?"

Looking down at his cup, Michael continued softly. "I spent the next couple of years bumming around Europe. Then I met Monique, in France. I'm married Father, with three kids. We live in Marseilles."

"Three wains. Have ye brought them with ye?"

"No."

"Does Monique know about... ?"

"Aye. I told her everything."

"What did she say?"

"That it didn't matter."

"She's right. It doesn't."

"Is she right? You know she's not."

Sighing, the Priest reached and put his cup on the tray. "I don't seem to know very much these days," he said. "This mess, the Troubles here, I just can't come to terms with some of the things that are goin' on."

"But you came to terms with my Ma."

"Aye. It wasn't easy. But Aye."

Michael looked up. He studied the old Priest. He had aged. "Are you keeping well, Father?"

Father Doherty smiled, his smile failing to hide his troubled eyes. "As well as can be expected," he said quietly. "Fer a man my age..." He stopped. "Yerself? What about yerself?"

Michael looked down at his cup again. He seemed to be caught unaware by the simple question. His reply was barely audible. "I'm dyin'."

"Dyin'?" The priest's hands suddenly clenched as if to erase the word. "How long? I mean, how do ye know?"

"I've about six months, if I'm lucky."

"Six months. Then that's why ye came back."

"I came back to ask my Ma to look after Monique and the kids, see that they're all right. I came back to be buried here." Tears suddenly streamed down his face. "I'd like to be buried with my Ma."

"With your Mother?"

"Aye. Father, would... would *you* look after my family?"

"I'll do whatever I can, Michael."

"Thanks." He looked down at the floor. "Father, I... I'm afraid."

Father Doherty's eyes glistened as he said, "Would ye like me to hear yer confession?"

"It's been so long. Aye. Aye, I'd like that."

A few minutes later, Mrs. Fahy knocked gently on the door and opened it. She paused when she saw that the stranger was on his knees in front of Father Doherty then quietly she stepped back and closed the door. As she hurried back to the kitchen she realised now what had been familiar about the stranger. He looked a lot like Father Doherty when he had first come to live in the parochial house all those years ago.

26

MAEVE

On a cold February day, old Johnny Collins hurried from chapel. At the top of the street he stopped to catch his breath, lungs aching from the smoke he had inhaled when the young arsonists had tried to burn him out. The wind threatened to topple him off his spindly legs, but taking a deep breath and with one of his bandaged hands clutching his Sunday cap, he struggled against the elements.

Two minutes later, he reached his house. He took a deep breath and coughed several times to try to clear his lungs while he fumbled inside his greasy waistcoat pocket with the hand that had been less severely burned for the door key. As he pushed open his new front door and stepped into the hall, the lingering smell of smoke hit him. Still there in the recently decorated hall, was the sickening odor. As he locked his front door he called. "I'm back, Maeve!." Seconds later he was opening the sitting room door. "I'll stick on a pot of tay, and I'll get the fire goin'. I'll not be long."

Out in the scullery, he half filled his kettle blackened from use and placed it on the gas ring, wincing as his shirtsleeve rubbed against the forearm burns. As the blue tongues licked at the drops of water dripping from the kettle, Johnny returned to the sitting room. There he carefully folded his cap in two, placed it inside a brown paper bag and shoved it in the top drawer of his mirrored black dresser. His eyes lifted, and he stared at his face in the dusty mirror.

Reaching, he tenderly pushed what remained of his thick white hair back from the cracked, burned skin above his ears. Trembling, as he remembered the arsonist's Christmas present, he began to undo his wrinkled tie, wincing again as he gripped it with one hand and undid it with the other. As he pulled off the tie he said, "There was some crowd at chapel today, Maeve. Remember Mrs. Thompson, the one that married the Yank? Aye, her. Well, her son and his wife and the wains were all sittin' in the front seats, aye, near St. Anthony's statue. The front row has always been the McGreevy's, and ye shoulda seen the face on Mrs. McGreevy when she saw the Thompsons' sittin' there."

Just then the kettle began to whistle, and still cackling with laughter, Johnny returned to the scullery. After carefully dropping one spoonful of tea into the teapot, he shouted, "It's a pity ye weren't there! Father Carlin gave a fairly reasonable sermon today. He seems to be fitting in well. He seems very popular with the young ones."

Switching off the gas he remembered the fire. "I'll light the fire now, Maeve. Ah Maeve, I wish ye could have come to Mass with me. It's all changed now though—the young ones singin', guitars, a piano and all. Aye, it's different from my young days, alright—still the singin's very good."

He tilted the teapot carefully with his better hand, and his breath rasped through his wrinkled, dry, pursed lips as the teapot spat the brown liquid into the cracked white mug. Seconds later, as hot tea threatened to dribble over the edge of the mug, and trying to hold it steady, he walked slowly into the sitting room. His burned hands ached as he placed the hot mug on the dresser, starting a new ring to join the others on the dark varnished surface.

Reaching into his waistcoat pocket for his box of matches, he went over to the fireplace. As he bent on one knee, he grunted with pain as his vest slid up along the burns on his back. At the same time his knee cracked loudly. Moments later, he was pushing a lighted match at the firelighter. As it quickly caught, he stared into the flames, and suddenly he began to tremble. "Oh God," he gasped, remembering that terrible night—the night of the fire. "Oh God."

It was over a minute later before he rose to his feet again. He stared down at the fire for several seconds, still trembling, then returned to the dresser and carried his mug to the armchair. With an "Ahhh" he eased into it and took a quick sip of the warm beverage. Smacking his lips, he settled deeper into the chair.

"Now Maeve," he said. "What about this afternoon? What'll we do, eh? Go fer a walk?" He stared at the empty armchair opposite. The wood crackled in the fire, the flames struggling to reduce it to ashes as Johnny cupped his injured hands around the mug and took another sip. "Will we go fer a walk?"

Suddenly he sighed and turned away from the armchair and looked into the fire. The coal was beginning to catch, but the slow heat did nothing to dispel his depression. "Ah Maeve," he croaked. "How I miss ye. Why did they have to burn ye? They musta knew I had no one else." With his hands shaking he tried to take another sip of tea, but almost choking, he suddenly began to cry. As he bent forward, the tea dribbled over his bandaged hands, but he didn't feel the pain. It would come later. Moaning, he placed the mug on the linoleum to one side of the chair and cried loudly, "They musta knew I had no one else. Why did they have to take ye from me? Why? Why?" With his hands on his face he rocked back and forth, moaning as his tears found their way through his pale fingers, soaking into the tea sodden bandages.

After a few minutes he stopped crying, slid to his knees and crawled over to the armchair. Sniffing, he very gently brushed some white hairs into the middle of the smooth cushion saying quietly, "We'll go to the park fer a walk, eh? Aye, Maeve, ye'll like that. We'll head up after dinner."

At five past two, Johnny was approaching Kathleen Moore and Lizzie Morgan, who were standing at the corner of the street gossiping. The rain had stopped and a late burst of sunshine had raised the temperature slightly. The two woman nodded knowingly to each other as Johnny passed them, mumbling to himself.

"Poor oul crittur," whispered Kathleen.

"Aye, his head's away with it now, alright."

"Oul Johnny's gone through a lot. What were those young blaggarts thinkin' about when they tried to burn him out—and at Christmas, too? Do you know what one of them said when he was caught?"

"Naw, what?"

"That he was *bored*—bored, imagine! God Lizzie, when I was young I was never bored. But Lizzie, just imagine the horror of it—petrol bein' poured through his letterbox right on top of his oul dog, too. It's a good job one of his neighbors heard it screaming and saw the flames. The fire brigade was very quick to come. If it hadn't been for the firemen oul Johnny would have burned to death, too—and just because he was the only Catholic in the estate. But his Protestant neighbors proved what they were really like—imagine them rallying round to fix up his house? Pity they couldn't do much fer his oul dog," she nodded after the old man. "He'll miss it."

"Aye, they were inseparable them two," said Lizzie. "Except when he went to Mass, of course. Did ye know he tried to bring it into chapel one Sunday, but the priest made him take it home? God, Kathleen, that dog must have been a Quare age. When I was a wee girl I remember it was always with him."

"What kind of dog was it?"

"A bitch, I think."

"They say bitches live longer."

"Do they?"

"Aye."

27

DENISE LOVES MARK

They were gathered at the foot of the broad steps as usual. *One of them did it,* she thought, as she studied the girls through the narrow reinforced pane of the library door. She had just finished franking the new books and was getting ready to close.

She turned now to look at Miss Smythe, a retired schoolteacher who was leafing through a Jackie Collins novel. *A bit racy for her,* she thought. The old teacher always took her time to decide what her daily reading was going to be. Usually she settled for a Catherine Cookson or a Danielle Steele.

Mary sighed heavily. She was tired and angry—angry with the four girls outside. One of them had been responsible, all right; one of them was guilty. She had no doubt about that. She studied the tallest of the teenagers. *Was it her?* The red-haired girl had a cigarette dangling from her pouting lips. Maybe it was one of the two smaller girls who sat together on the low wall at the bottom of the steps. Perhaps it was the busty girl who was bent over tying the lace on her left high-heeled boot.

She studied the girl who was smoking and grit her teeth as her pouting lips dragged on the coffin nail. As she inhaled, her eyes narrowed into a crafty expression. *I hope the smoke burns the inside out of you,* thought Mary. Just then the girl looked up at the door. It was almost as if she had heard Mary's silent curse. Mary drew back. She didn't want them to see her. She felt guilty now at the thought of wishing the girl harm. But she was still angry.

Why did they do it? Why did SHE do it—the one called Denise? She wondered who Mark was; probably some scruffy, pimple-faced punk. She couldn't imagine Denise writing about any decent boy, a clean boy who would treat her with respect. She peeked through the pane at the girls again. Pouting lips suddenly laughed, a shrill, hateful sound that had Mary clenching her hands. A polite cough behind made her turn.

"Oh, Miss Smythe, I'm sorry." she said. "Ah, don't worry about keeping me back. I see you've chosen a Ruth Rendell. Her new one is due in soon. I'll put your name down for it. Yes, it is a nice evening."

Mary followed the old lady to the door, unbolted it and held it wide for her.

"Goodnight, Miss Smythe. Watch out for the steps." She glared at pouting lips when she laughed again. When Miss Smythe was at the bottom of the steps Mary bolted the door again and turned to tidy up before going home.

A few minutes later she reached under the counter for her handbag and the bottle of bleach, cleaning liquid and the cleaning cloths caught her eye. Suddenly her face was blazing with anger. Before she could stop herself, she rushed to the door, unbolted it, and pulled it open. She almost fell back such was the force of her action. She glared at the girls.

"Which one of you is, Denise?" she asked, trying to keep calm.

The girls looked at each other. With a smirk pouting lips, said, "There's no one here called, Denise. Sorry, Miss." She grinned at her companions.

I just bet you're sorry, thought Mary. Suddenly she surprised herself by saying, "There's a boy on the phone inside. He's looking for Denise." She studied the girls and said as she turned, "I'll tell him there's no one..."

"I'm Denise."

She swung around to look at pouting lips, but it had been the busty girl who had spoken.

"Come with me," said Mary.

The girl smiled at the others, and Mary grit her teeth as she climbed the steps. She held the door open for the girl. Pouting lips laughed again just as Mary closed the door and bolted it. The busty girl frowned as she looked at the locked door.

"Over here," snapped Mary.

The girl followed her to the counter. Suddenly Mary swung to face her. The girl was slightly taller than Mary who was finding it hard to restrain herself from hitting her.

"Where's the phone?" asked the girl looking around.

"There's no boy on the phone," snapped Mary.

The girl frowned. "But you said?"

"I told a lie to find out which of you was Denise, and let me tell you something, young lady! I spent an hour on Tuesday morning and an hour and a half this morning cleaning the words "Denise Loves Mark" from the Library door and steps."

The girl's face grew pale.

"Your name is written on almost every shop and building in this road." Nothing could stop Mary now. "You must have some ego to write your name all over the place. Do you know how much trouble you've caused? Do you know it's illegal?"

Mary got immense pleasure as the frightened girl stammered, "It... it wasn't me. I... I..."

Mary grit her teeth. The girl was not going to get off so lightly. "Oh, it was you all right. Don't try to deny it."

"On me ma's death it wasn't, Miss," whined the girl.

"Your mother, huh? I hope she's proud of you. Have you nothing better to do with your time? I'm sure whoever Mark is, he must think you're a right slut."

"But Miss, it wasn't me, honest," said the girl.

"It was. And let me tell you young lady, if I see your name on Library premises again, I'll report you to the police." She almost spat the words into the girl's face.

"But it wasn't..."

"Oh, get out of my sight. You're not worth talking to. Get out of my sight," snarled Mary.

The girl ran to the door. She tried the handle. Almost crying she said, "It's locked."

With a scowl on her face Mary hurried to the door, unbolted it, and pulled it open. She glared at the other girls as Denise jumped down the steps. They gathered around her. As Mary was about to close the door, she heard Denise shout, "I got the blame for you writing my name and Mark's all over the place!"

Mary closed the door. As she pulled the bolt into place she glanced at the girls. Pouting lips looked up at her and raised one hand, her middle finger pointing in an obscene gesture. Mary moved back out of sight. Her heart was pounding against her chest as she walked to the counter. Trembling, she reached with both hands, held onto the edge, and suddenly she was laughing, the tears running down her face, as she bent over the counter shaking hysterically.

Later, when she locked the library door behind her and walked down the steps, she saw the girls were gone. But on the low wall written in red lipstick she saw the words, "Oul Bitch." She smiled, and humming to herself she hurried up the road.

28

THE EMIGRANTS

She stood there, a tiny woman, distancing herself from them, watching uneasily, as they hugged and kissed, their loud cries of anguish echoing around the crowded Derry Quay. The drizzle falling on her face hid her own tears as she turned to look at the broiling river that rushed swiftly around the bend, and she cursed it. The River Foyle would soon be carrying her only son away from her.

The long ship bounced and lifted as the muddy water threatened to tear it from thick hemp ropes that held it to three squat wooden bollards. A bell rang. It was almost time.

She sighed heavily, her heartbeat quickening as she shuffled after her son and his wife to the bottom of the gangway.

Mary, her son's wife, tried to smile, but suddenly her contorting face erupted with tears bubbling from her deep-set dark eyes, and croaking unintelligibly she threw her thin arms around her mother-in-law's shoulders and sobbed into her soaking shawl. The old woman stiffened, unused to any kind of open display of emotion. Then it was over, and Mary still crying stumbled away up the gangway.

Now he looked down at his mother, his pale face smiling sadly. Awkwardly, he too reached to hug her gently at the same time, whispering through choking breaths, "Don't worry about Mary and me, Ma. Sure we'll be alright. As soon... as soon as I get work, I'll send ye some money."

She trembled in his strong arms as memories of his growing days and her own young life living along the upper Foyle valley came to her. All those happy, hard days would never return, just like her son. She would never see him again.

The ship's bell rang again, its heart-tugging peal followed by louder weeping and more frenzied hugging and kissing from the people around her.

"I'll hiv tay go, Ma," he rasped.

She forced a smile. "Aye, son, ye hiv tay go." Looking past him, she saw Mary, still crying, watching them from the deck.

The bell rang again, this time the ringing was accompanied by a high-pitched chant from the ship's cabin boy.

"All aboard fer Philadelphia! Ship sails in two minutes! All aboard that's goin' aboard!"

Bending, her son lifted his two cloth bags of belongings. He gulped as he looked at her again, and his dark eyes glistened as he whispered hoarsely, "I'd better git on board, Ma. They're gettin' ready tay sail." He gulped again, his big Adam's apple plunging up and down as he tried to choke back the tears, but suddenly he dropped his bags and reached to hold her for the last time. As she clutched to him, she could feel his heart thumping against her ear, and the memory of one particular late summer day came to her.

With her man, she had worked in the many potato fields that sloped down to the River Foyle. The weather had been kinder that year, the year she had given birth. She had been happy then, and her husband had been strong. They had both been strong and full of hope. She remembered that dinnertime after they had eaten some boiled potatoes, and she had fed her baby. The summer sounds and scents surrounded them as she lay with her husband by the high hedge near the river. She had been lying back with her eyes closed, a piece of grass protruding from her mouth, and he had gently tugged it out and kissed her. As she returned his kiss, she felt his warm tears on her cheek. The remembered words, "Thanks fer our son," still made her cry, as she relived that time in her mind often throughout the following years when her man's energy and drive waned as they lost hope and grew old before their time.

She sighed slowly as she felt her son release her, and suddenly with a cry, he grabbed his bags and ran up the gangway. She stood there for a few moments, her arms still outstretched.

The bell rang again.

"All aboard! All aboard fer Philadelphia, Amerikay!"

Philadelphia, she thought, as she moved back among the others. A name she had grown to hate, but a place that would welcome her son and his wife. Oh, they would do well out there, she had no doubt about that, and her prayers would protect them. Reaching for the ends of her shawl, she pulled it tightly around her. Her prayers had been wasted on her man. He had refused to come and see them off. His curt goodbye at the door had upset them all. But she could understand how he felt. He didn't want Eamon to go. He was angry, frustrated at losing him and so was she, but she couldn't say anything. At least her man was able to vent his feelings with anger.

But now, as one of the crewmen pulled in the starboard rope, she could feel the hot tears run freely down her face.

"Goodbye Ma. I'll write tay ye. Goodbye..."

Sniffing, her frail body heaved as she tried to hold her composure, and as the ship moved away from the quay, she was unaware that her own loud crying mingled with the others around her. She waved; Eamon and Mary waved; the people waved, and they all still waved, even as the ship rounded the bend and sailed away out of sight.

Soon she thought they would be at Moville; then Greencastle; then out and around the headland to the wide Atlantic Ocean. It would be a long hard voyage, but she knew they would be all right. After all, wasn't that what they had to go through? Wasn't all this laid out for them, and for her? She sighed heavily. Mary would have her day, too.

Gradually the people began to move away from the quay until she stood there alone, a wee lonely woman who had just said goodbye to her life. Stepping closer to the edge of the quay, she looked down at the swirling muddy pools that churned up from the bottom. My life is over, she thought. If only I had the courage to end it. She swayed, half hypnotized by the dark water. Suddenly, screaming loudly, a sea gull swooped in front of her, startling her, its piercing cry making her look after it as it flew down the river. The rain had stopped, and the black clouds that had hung above the Donegal Hills all morning were quickly breaking up. Shadows stretched down along the fields below them as the sun struggled to make it a day.

"Ah well," she sniffed tugging her shawl tighter around her and with a last look down the river she turned and walked away. *He'll be waitin' fer me.* He'll need me now more than ever. She sighed. And perhaps I need him.

29

THE LAST DANCE

She lived alone in her dilapidated cottage, forty meters up the lane from the main road. She had been living alone ever since her father had died on her twenty-eighth birthday, fifty years ago. It was a late summer's night, and she stood looking at herself in the flaking, black-framed mirror that hung above the warped wooden mantelpiece. *It's getting near the time,* she thought with a smile. Tightening her bunned gray hair with a plastic comb, she hummed her favorite tune—*their* tune—hers and Joes. Rose sighed deeply as she thought about him then, and that first time he asked her to dance with him.

Every Saturday night, even during the long bleak winters, the young men and women of Killiecastra would head for the Silver Slipper Ballroom. It was a ballroom for want of a better word; the old wooden building didn't have a sign to call it the Silver Slipper Ballroom. It was a hall. No one knew who had named it so, except that every summer the owner, George Cummings—a stout, saintly man—painted it the same dull silver color. For weeks until after the first heavy shower of rain the "Slipper" would reek of the smell of paint.

The Saturday night Joe asked Rose for a dance was a wet, stormy night, but as usual there was a big crowd at the "Slipper." And as usual, George was standing at the side of the bandstand watching out for any close dancing. Upon spotting a "sinful couple," he would jump lightly down onto the floor and nimbly dodge through the other dancers to the offending pair. A light tap on the male dancer's shoulder would be enough to separate them.

Rose stood near the lemonade table with May McNutt—a thin, plain girl who had asked Rose one Saturday night if she could stand with her. Rose was glad of May's company because her best friend and dancing companion had married in the spring and had gone to live in Killinchey. The few Saturday nights that she had stood alone, waiting to be asked for a dance, she had felt awkward and uneasy. She had almost made up her mind not to go to the dance at all...

Blinking in the dull light to see herself more clearly, Rose smoothed down her old dancing dress. It still fit, except around the waist where it hung slack. She smiled again as she remembered the suit Joe was wearing that night. It was a gray striped, double-breasted suit, and with his mop of curly greasy black hair, he looked like Rudolph Valentino when he smiled at her. Rose noticed Joe at previous dances, but he never asked her to dance. Once she caught him looking at her as he danced close to Maggie Moran, a flirty red haired girl, who died the following winter giving birth in Killiecastra graveyard.

Rose felt May stiffen as Joe approached them and she turned.

"May I have this dance, please?"

She smiled then. The other men never said please, when they asked her to dance. Still smiling, she nodded and took his extended hand. As they whirled about the dance floor to the popular dance tunes of the late 1930s, she trembled in his strong arms. The set of dances ended too soon, and she stood with Joe by the side of the floor, not knowing what to do. He didn't say thank you, and still stood by her side looking at the bandstand. It was then the bandleader announced it was the last dance of the evening and the music of a slow waltz, forever to be their song, soon filled the hall.

The next thing Rose remembered was George looming over them and whispering as he tapped Joe on the shoulder, "None o' that now. Behave yourselves." Shocked, she pulled away from Joe and with blazing faces they finished the last dance straight-armed. Later, Joe bought her and May a lemonade, and later still he walked Rose the three and a half miles home in the heavy rain.

She shivered now as the wind blew through the open half-door, and she turned to looked outside. *It's getting dark. He'll be here soon,* she thought. *I'd better light the lamp.* The ruby red glass oil lamp sat on the table by the door, and with twisted fingers she pumped it until the wick was soaked in oil. Going to the fireplace, she tore a page from one of a pile of old *Ireland's Own* magazines that lay there. With a shaking hand she held it to the dying turf fire. When it ignited, she quickly carried the burning paper to the lamp and lit it.

As the lamp glowed into life, she shook the paper out. Black pieces of charred paper floated to the floor as she carried the lamp over to the black dresser by the side of the bedroom door and set it down. As she stared down into the heart of the flame, her thoughts went to Joe again. They had announced their engagement that following summer and Rose smiled as she remembered that day, walking past the graveyard wall on the way back from Joe's house. The bucky roses were in full bloom and were bubbling over the gray stone wall. She remarked how lovely they were and Joe suddenly pulled her to him whispering before kissing her. "You're the loveliest rose of all."

Outside the echo of a barking dog from away down the valley brought her out of her reverie, and she turned and looked out of the open door. Shuffling to it, she took a long look out into the darkness. Standing there, she stared up at the starry sky, her eyes misting over as she thought how quickly that memorable summer with Joe had gone. Shivering, she remembered that windy winter's day on the way back with Joe from Maggie's funeral. It was then he told her he was going to war with some of the men from the town. She cried and begged him not to go. That spring she received his last letter.

The dog barked again, and with a heavy sigh she bolted out the night. *He'll be waiting,* she thought. *I'd better hurry.* Returning to the dresser she lifted the lamp. She smiled now, excited, the wrinkles unfolding from around her mouth and dark eyes. She began to hum and waltzed in a circle until she faced the bedroom door. Pushing it open, she held up the lamp and looked inside, then, still humming, she backed away from the room, her face glowing.

Joe, wearing his striped gray suit and with his black hair shining, walked towards her, one hand held out. "Rose, could I have this last dance, please?" Smiling, she nodded and placed the lamp on the table.

Outside, the light wind soughed, and music heard only by the night creatures came from the cottage as two silhouettes inside danced their last dance.

30

LIES

The boy threw his woolen bathing pants over the gate and climbed it. Steadying himself as the gate swayed back and forth, he dropped lightly to the dusty lane.

As he walked down the lane, a dog barked a warning. Cautiously, the boy approached the cottage gate. The lane ran on past the cottage and down to the edge of the river. The dog barked again, louder this time, and predictably the old man, pipe in his hand, came to the half-door.

"Quiet, girl!" he snapped. The dog immediately stopped barking. Its tail wagged furiously, and it pranced about in front of its master as he walked the eight paces to the small gate.

The boy smiled at him. "Hello, mister."

"Hello boy," said the old man, studying him. "Fer a swim?" He nodded to the bathing pants that were clutched tightly in the boy's hand.

"Aye."

"Well watch out. The big flood last week brought down some branches. There are a lot of them jammed just on the edge of the carry. Keep near the shallows by the carry gate and ye'll be alright."

Impatient to get down to the river, the boy wiped the sweat from his brow with his bathing pants, saying, "I'll do that. Thanks, mister."

He watched as the boy ran on down the lane, turned, and went back to the cottage. Disappearing into the semi-darkness, he sat down on a wooden stool by the fire. Puffing discontentedly on his pipe, he thought about the boy. What age would he be? About fifteen or less. It was hard to tell their ages these days. He would never have been allowed to go swimming near the carry when he was a boy, not by himself anyway.

In the silent coolness of the room the dog scratched, and occasionally snapped at a persistent fly that was intent on settling in its right ear. The old man studied his dog. *She's getting old.* He sighed. *Her and me both.* Taking a long drag on his briar, his thoughts went to the boy again.

A few minutes later, he rose from the stool and went to the open half-door and looked out. The familiar cacophony of late summer sounds filled his senses. Hens clucking as they strutted in the back-yard in their wire-netted prison, bees buzzing as their forever search for nectar carried them hovering among the fuchsia hedge, cows mooing in the back fields, and birds singing. High above in the sky, a long, white line darted north.

The dog waited, and barked excitedly as its master reached for his gnarled blackthorn walking stick that hung beside the door. Shoving his still lit pipe into his breast pocket, he then reached for his cap. The dog barked louder, bouncing and shaking its old white head as its master slipped back the bolt. In a flash, it was past him, running to the gate panting and barking, as it waited impatiently.

A minute later, the old man, preceded by his dog, was making his way down the lane. Soon he was among the high chestnut trees that bordered the river. He squinted through the thick trunked trees. *Where is he?* he thought. He scanned the calm, easy flowing deep river as it meandered towards the carry to tumble gently over to the lower water. The sound of a splash up river alerted him, and he moved on up the bank. "Ah, there he is," he said aloud, moving closer to the edge of the river. Standing beneath a chestnut tree, he watched, admiring the young swimmer's agility. The boy glided gracefully like an otter, sleek and swift his feet thrashing the water behind him into white foam as his sinewy arms pulled him forward.

The old man hurried towards a wide clearing where the sun shone so he could observe the stretch of water where the boy was swimming. Sitting on a rotting branch that had fallen the previous hard winter, he took out his pipe. His dog ran back and forth along the bank, barking loudly as it followed the boy up and down.

With boundless energy and great skill, the boy swam for another twenty minutes until finally, with a quick spurt, he swam to the carry. He lay a while panting in the lukewarm water, and with a shake of his head he stood up and splashed through the shallow water to the bank where the old man was sitting.

Shivering and with water dripping from his long hair, the boy threw himself down almost beside him. He lay there waiting for the sun to heat his shivering white body.

"Ye'll get pains in yer bones lettin' the water dry into ye like that, boy," exclaimed the old man.

"What odds," the boy said quickly. "Anyway, I'm warm now," he lied.

The dog moved to lick the dripping water from the boy's feet. With a kick at it the boy shouted, "Get away!"

"Here girl! Come here o' that. Here!"

With its head bowed, the dog slunk over to its master and sat with its head between its paws, eyes raised watching the boy.

"Yer a good swimmer, boy. Who learned ye?"

"Me Da. He was in the Merchant Navy."

"Merchant Navy, eh?"

"Aye me da traveled all over the world."

"All over the world, eh?"

"Aye." The old man digested this information.

"Where's yer father now?" he asked, his eyes resting on the boy's ribbed chest as it rose and fell.

"Dead," said the boy as a matter-of-factly.

"Dead?" The old man frowned.

"Aye, he was killed in an accident, in Egypt."

"An accident. I'm sorry."

"Doesn't matter. At least he enjoyed his life. He saw the world. That's what I'm going to do, see the world, travel." Raising his head and shading his eyes, he looked over at the old man. "Have you traveled much?"

"No, I've lived here all my life."

The boy studied him. "Have you never wanted to see the world?"

"No." The old man lied.

The boy lay down again, saying, "I wouldn't want to be stuck here all my life."

"I wasn't stuck here, boy," snapped the old man. "It was my own choice to live here."

The boy raised himself up again. "But you must have wanted to travel?" he asked.

"No, I've been fairly contented living here."

The boy stared at him a few moments and lay down again. They both listened to the low rumbling of the water splashing over the falls. The sound lulled them into a peaceful hypnotic trance.

Suddenly, "Thwack!" They both looked and were just in time to see the tail of a big fish disappear beneath the surface of the water. Immediately, the dog jumped to its feet and barking loudly it ran to the water's edge.

"That was a big 'un," the old man remarked.

The boy was now sitting up. Pointing, he shouted, "Look, there it is again!"

This time they saw the fish clearly as it left the water, its mouth agape as it snatched at a fly. With a plop it disappeared again. The ever increasing circles caused by the splash lapped towards the water's edge.

"I wish I had brought my fishing rod with me," the boy exclaimed.

"Ye fish then?"

"Naw, not really. I have a rod me da bought me, but I never learned how to fish. Me da died before he could teach me."

The old man frowned, and said, "I have a rod up at the cottage. If ye want ye could try it. I could teach ye. I don't use it much now. It's a good rod, light and springy."

"Naw," the boy said, turning to lie on his stomach. "It doesn't matter." He looked up at the old man and smiled. "Thanks anyway."

"If ye come tomorra," persisted the old man, "I'll bring the rod down and show ye how to use it. Maybe ye'll be here tomorra?" he asked hopefully.

"I might be. I dunno. If it's as nice as this, maybe. I'll be starting school soon so I won't get up here then."

The old man stared at the back of the boy's head for a few seconds, and he rose to his feet. His bones in his knees cracked, and he grunted. Leaning on his stick, he steadied himself as he said, "Maybe I'll see ye tomorra then?"

"Aye, maybe." The boy raised himself up on his arms and watched as the old man and his dog headed into the trees. He turned over on his back again.

Poking at the fire, the old man stared into it, his thoughts on the boy. Both halves of the door were bolted shut. It was dark, and the wind whistled through a crack in the door jamb. Outside, the rain ran down the window panes and through the thick ivy.

The boy will hardly be here tomorra, he thought dismally. He sighed heavily. Autumn was nearly here, and the long black winter stretched ahead. *No*, he thought, *I never wanted to travel.* He sighed again as he drew on his pipe. He had never wanted to see the world.

31

THE SAMURAI

Danny's eyes widened when he saw the sword. It lay on the table in the old man's sitting room. The blade glinted in the dull light as the old man pulled it from a sheath that was decorated with strange signs and symbols.

"It's a genuine Samurai sword, young fella," said the old man showing it to Danny, "not one of those tin replicas. I took it from a dead Japanese officer myself, during the second World War."

Danny studied the stooped white haired man. "Why are ye sellin' it?" he asked suspiciously. "'I mean it must... it must...'" He was going to say it must be worth more than twenty pounds, but he stopped.

The old man straightened. "Ah, sure it's no good to me now. The money's more use to me now than it hangin' on the wall. Annie never liked it anyway."

Danny frowned. "Annie?"

"Mrs. Doherty. My wife. She's dead."

"Aw aye," said Danny feeling stupid. "I'm sorry."

The old man glared at him. "Well," he snapped. "'Do ye want to buy it or not? I'll not take less for it. Twenty pounds is the price, and it's a bargain at that."

"Aye aye, I'm buyin' it all right," said Danny quickly and began to pull the money from both pockets of his blue jeans.

He had seen the sword for sale in the Derry Journal free sales list that Friday morning, and he had hurried to the address, praying that it was still there. Danny was a martial arts fanatic, and his bedroom was covered with posters and pictures of Bruce Lee, his favorite martial arts star. Now, as he put two five pound notes, six pound coins, and four pounds in small change on the table, he thought about the coins. The money belonged to his mother. It was money she had kept in a jar in the kitchen for emergencies, and that morning he had been tempted to take it. *It's not really stealin'* he had thought. *I'll pay her back. I'll be able to put it back before she realizes it's gone.*

"Twenty-pounds. It's all there," he said as he pushed the money across the table to the old man. As he did he looked at the sword.

It lay beside the sheath, and Danny was itching to touch it. Now he studied Mr. Doherty as he counted the money.

"Aye, it's all there," said the old man looking steadily at Danny. "Are ye sure ye can afford this?"

"Aye. I saved the money for my summer holidays, but I'd rather have the Samurai sword. I've always wanted one." Now he reached for the sword and slowly sheathed it. He was impatient to get home.

"Here," said Mr. Doherty suddenly. "Ye'd better wrap that up in some-thing' Ye can't be walkin' through the streets of Derry like that. I have an oul bag under the stairs I can give you."

Danny followed him out to the hall, clutching the sword. It seemed to vibrate in his hands, and he smiled excitedly. He was looking forward to strapping it on and posing in front of his bedroom mirror.

"Ah, here we are," said Mr. Doherty, shaking dust from a brown cloth bag and reaching for the sword.

"Thanks," said Danny, watching as the old man carefully wrapped it up.

A few seconds later, he followed Mr. Doherty to the front door. As Danny moved to go past, the old man stopped him and said, "Here, young fella. Here's a lucks penny."

Danny stared at the pound coin. "Naw... naw it's all right. Really..."

"Ah take it, and thanks, son."

Smiling, Danny took the coin. "Thanks," he said. *Now I only owe my ma three pounds*, he thought happily.

As he hurried down the street, his face was flushed with excitement. Twice he was tempted to unwrap the bag and look at the sheath and the black ornamented handle of the sword.

A few minutes later, he reached Spencer Road, and almost before he realized it, he was approaching the police barrier that blocked it. With a gasp, he slowed down. *Oh God, the barrier*, he thought. *I forgot about it. I should have gone the other way.* He slowed and was tempted to swing around and go back up the road, but it was too late. One of the two policemen who guarded the barrier stepped from the side of the hut and was staring at him. *Oh God*, thought Danny. *He's waitin' for me. If I'm caught with the sword I'm for it. I'll be arrested and taken to Castlereagh holding center. Oh God, oh God!* His bladder began to loosen as he still walked towards the policeman. Sweat trickled from his armpits and soaked into his shirt, and he almost dropped the sword when the policeman raised his rifle.

Oh God. Oh God. The pain of holding in his bladder almost made him stumble, and sweat bubbled through his hair and ran down his face stinging his eyes.

Suddenly, a horn sounded, and three land rovers roared to a halt at the barrier. The policeman hurried back to the hut to raise the barrier pole.

Danny's bladder eased considerably, and his step quickened as he almost broke into a run past the barrier. His heart was still pounding by the time he reached the bottom of the road, and a few seconds later he was walking across Craigavon Bridge.

On the way he met two of his school pals, Joe Smith and Sean Nichol.

"Yes, Danny. What brings you over to this side of the bridge?" asked Sean.

"This," said Danny, smiling excitedly as he unwrapped the sword.

The two boys stared at the sword, and one of them was about to reach for it when Danny pulled it away.

"Don't let the peelers catch ye with that thing," said Joe. "Yer not supposed to have anythin' with a blade on it over six inches long. That's the law."

"That's only for daggers, stupid. Swords don't count," snapped Sean.

"Aye they do," said Joe, looking at his watch. "Anyway, come on. We have to be over to the music shop before it closes." He looked at Danny. "See ye later, Danny."

"See ye," said Sean.

"Aye, see ye," said Danny, looking after them as they walked away.

"Swords don't count!" he heard Sean shout.

"How do you know?" snapped Joe.

"They don't, that's all."

"They do."

"Naw they don't..."

Frowning, Danny wrapped the sword up again. It was only when he began to walk on that he noticed the cars on the bridge slowing down. "Oh God. Oh God," he said aloud, gasping, as he saw that a checkpoint had been set up while he had been talking with his pals.

Twenty meters away, two land rovers blocked each side of the bridge and four policemen, two on each side, stood on the footpaths stopping people.

Ahead Danny saw the two policemen on the side he was walking on had stopped a girl and her boyfriend. One of the policemen was looking into the girl's handbag. The other policeman was looking towards Danny. There was no escape. Turning he looked back. The policeman would surely see him if he suddenly turned and went back the way he had come.

All of a sudden, his bladder began to scream. He stopped. Sweat bubbled out of every pore. Looking over the heavy iron railing that bordered the bridge, he saw the fast flowing water of the River Foyle below. Walking slower, he edged towards the railing, his eyes on the two policemen who had stopped a man and two boys who had passed Danny earlier.

Danny's hand loosened on the sword, and slowly he lowered it to one of the diagonal holes in the railing. Gently, he eased it through, and suddenly with a quick cough, he pushed and instantly stepped away from the railing. As he walked towards the policemen, he heard a light splash. The policemen looked down at the water for a couple of seconds, and the other policemen nodded for the boys to go. It was Danny's turn.

Thirty meters past the checkpoint, Danny stopped. Leaning his elbows on the railing, he stared down at the muddy water. Away on down the river, he thought he saw the brown bag that contained his sword, but it soon drifted away out of sight. He sighed. *I didn't deserve the sword anyway,* he thought. *It serves me right.* He sighed again as he turned and headed for home, his hand in his pockets. One hand held the lucks penny tightly. He still owed his mother three pounds.

32

VERMIN

The oldest rat in Derry took twenty-five minutes to crawl up the siege tunnel that ran under Shipquay Street. There, in the maze of rusting obsolete pipes, where part of the brick tunnel had collapsed, it stopped to rest. Its gray patchy body was heaving with the effort of the steep climb. Overhead, it could hear the dull rumble of the traffic going around the Diamond Square. With a sniff, it squinted at the pipes, and making up its mind, it dragged itself into the narrowest one and slithered through the slimy, stinking darkness.

On the way up the tunnel, it had been seen by hundreds of other rats who had stopped to gave way as it passed. After all, it was the wisest rat in Derry, and they knew where it was heading. They also knew something had to be wrong for it to leave the protection of its home, deep beneath the great Guildhall.

The rat headed on up until ten minutes later it was slipping into a huge sewer pipe under the courthouse. It scuffled along the cracked pipe for twenty meters towards a larger crack halfway up the pipe that oozed with a chemical, filmy substance. Squeezing through, it stopped again. The stump of its hind leg that it had bitten off many years ago in its attempt to get free from a man-trap, was aching. Breathing hard, it squinted up the narrow tunnel that ran alongside the sewer pipe, and seconds later it was off again. Three minutes into the darkness, it was coming to the wider siege tunnel. It stopped again, for it knew it just had to crawl along this for a few meters before it came to the great tunnel under St. Columb's Cathedral. Crawling over a few crumbling red bricks, it soon reached the tunnel. At the entrance, four huge rats moved out of its way as it waddled slowly inside. The rats stared after it and followed to where the other rats waited.

"We've been keepin' tabs on McCorkell's car. He's been doin' a line with Mary Doherty, and he calls fer her every Friday night, 8:00 on the dot. He's never late. We'll hijack it then."

The three men sat in the back of McClusky's pub discussing their strategy. They spoke out of the sides of their mouths, and their eyes never left the entrance to the lounge. Every customer who entered was given careful scrutiny.

Joe Conners had long black hair and a pale thin face. He wore a light green jacket and blue jeans. With his eyes fixed on the last customer who had just come in, he whispered, "Is it a big wan?"

"A big wan. Jesus, Joe, it's a thousand pounder," exclaimed the man beside him. His name was Michael Harkin. His brown leather blouson jacket, short crew cut, fair hair, Wrangler jeans and Italian shoes made him stand out from the other two. "Isn't that right, Jim?" He turned to the scowling cold-eyed man with red hair, beside him.

Jim Carlin, his eyes fixed on the barman, snarled out of the side of his mouth, "Keep yer bloody voice down, Harkin. That mouth of yers will get ye intay trouble wan of these days."

"Sorry, Jim. Sorry. I didn't think I was speakin' that loud."

"Leave all the thinkin' tay me, right," snapped Carlin. He scanned the lounge again as he whispered to Conners, "Harkin's right, Joe. It is a thousand pounder. Now both of ye listen up. Here's the plan. At 7:00, we'll meet at the top of Doherty's street. At 7:45, all three of us will head down tay Doherty's house. Joe, you and Harkin will knock on the door, take whoever answers the door and anyone else out to the kitchen. I'll wait outside fer McCorkell. When he comes, he'll knock. You, Harkin, will answer the door while Joe watches the others. I'll come up behind McCorkell, and we'll both take him out to the kitchen. I'll take the keys from him and go and pick up the Semtex. I'll drive to Shipquay Street, park his car and phone the Strand Road R.U.C. station. Josie Collins will pick me up at the Guildhall and drive me back to Doherty's. I'll blow the horn three times, and you two come out. We should be gone by the time the bomb goes off." He looked at Harkin and Joe. His eyes narrowed. "Have yees got all that?"

Joe looked blankly at Harkin. They both had puzzled expressions on their faces. With a heavy sigh Carlin rose to his feet. "Look, I'll get three more pints in and I'll go over it again."

Joe and Michael watched him go to the bar.

"Jesus, Mickey," whispered Joe. "A thousand pounder. It'll blow some hole in Shipquay Street."

"Yer not effin' kiddin', Joe. I hope nobody gets hurt." Harkin frowned and said, "Ach they'll have plenty of warnin'. Won't they?"

Just then Carlin returned with one of the beers.

"They'll have plenty of warnin', Jim, won't they?" asked Joe as he reached for the pint.

"Aye, fifteen minutes."

Conners and Harkin glanced at each other as Carlin returned to the bar. Harkin took a long drink from his glass. *Christ, fifteen minutes.*

The old rat hurried through the thousands of rats that were crowded into the tunnel. Strawberry colored droppings lay everywhere. In the far corner, a huge pile of it was covered in black fleas. Fleas jumped and crawled over all the rats as the wisest of them headed towards a pile of bricks that had fallen from the tunnel roof. The dead body of a rat lay decomposing under a brick on the edge of the rubble. The rats watched with alert black eyes as the old one dragged itself to the top of the rubble. Breathing hard, it slowly turned. It was a few seconds before its thoughts reached them and every rat within a fifty meter radius.

I have left my comfortable home to warn you to stay away from the steep tunnel. Something is going to happen soon, very soon. Something I can't explain. I fear it will be another one of the loud thuds that killed many of us a while back. The old rat paused to let this sink in. The squeaking of the rats watching him stopped as he continued. *"I won't be with you much longer. My time is nearly over.*

It stared at the rats below, and abruptly began to climb down from the rubble. *I am going now. Please heed my warning and spread it to the others. Keep away from the steep tunnel.* All the rats kept still as the old rat made its way through them. Soon it was at the entrance to the sewer pipe. Ten minutes later it had reached the top of the tunnel that ran down Shipquay Street.

Three quarters of an hour earlier, Mrs. Annie Doherty had answered the door. With a gasp, she stared at the two masked men. One of them held a gun.

"Inside Missus! Quick!" rasped Conners, looking into the hall behind her. Grabbing the shocked woman's arm he forced Annie in front of him along the hall.

Mary Doherty, her younger brother Kevin, and their father Paddy, were watching television when Mrs. Doherty was shoved roughly into the sitting room. Startled, Paddy rose to his feet. He glanced quickly at his pale-faced wife as Harkin shouted, "Now listen to me all of yees! No one will get hurt if yees do what we say."

"Wait a minute..." began Paddy. His face was almost as white as his wife's.

Pointing his gun at him, Conners snarled, "I would advise ye to do what we say, Doherty. Now all of yees, out tay the kitchen. NOW! All we're after is yer daughter's boy-friend's car. That's all." He glared at Mary. "He is comin' tonight, isn't he?"

"Aye... naw," said Mary, trembling as she walked with the others out to the hall. "Ye aren't goin' tay harm him, are ye? Ye wouldn't hurt him?" She began to cry.

"Enough of that blubberin'!" shouted Conners. "Out now! Out to the kitchen!"

In the kitchen, Annie's heart pounded as she filled the kettle. Harkin had told her to make a pot of tea. Conners stood with his gun on them while Harkin watched the hall door.

"When McCorkell knocks I want yees all tay be quiet. If any of yees so much as open yer cheepers..." Connors glared at Mary as he pointed the gun at her. "All we want is his car."

Now in silence, they all waited. The waiting seemed to take forever. Conners looked at the kitchen clock. It showed two minutes after 8:00.

"Is that clock right, missus?" he asked waving his revolver at it.

Annie dropped four tea bags into the teapot. "Aye," she snapped, glaring at him. "It's right."

The minutes ticked slowly by, but at five past 8:00 they heard a car stop outside, and a few seconds later they heard a knock. Six hearts pounded as Conners raised his gun. "Not a word," he whispered.

Harkin slipped along the hall. He pulled the door open. "Inside."

"What the...?" began Tommy McCorkell as he was pushed into the hall. Terrified, he stared at the two masked faces and froze.

"Out tay the kitchen. Quickly!" screamed Carlin, shoving his revolver hard into Tommy's ribs.

As soon as they came into the kitchen, Mary ran to her boyfriend.

"Yer car keys! Give them tay me!" hissed Carlin holding out his hand. Tommy gulped as he fumbled in his pocket. Carlin snatched them from him. Mary began to cry again, and her brother peed himself for the second time.

At the kitchen door, Carlin glared at the hostages. "You will be released in approximately twenty-five minutes. I suggest ye try to relax until then." He hurried to the front door, taking a quick look up and down the street, he ran for the car.

The old rat was a quarter of the way down the tunnel when it suddenly stopped. It shivered, and its whiskers began to quiver the way they had done all its life when it sensed danger. It looked about. It listened. *I'm safe here.* It began to move on down.

It was almost halfway down the tunnel when the bomb went off. The force of the enormous blast caused the thud in the tunnel to burst its eardrums, and the oldest rat in Derry was suddenly thrown onto its back. Squealing with fear, it tried to get up. It was then the bricks dislodged from the roof of the tunnel fell on it.

Ten minutes earlier the car pulled up outside Doherty's house. Carlin pressed the horn three times alerting Conners and Harkin. With tea dribbling from the wool at the mouth of his mask, Conners left down his cup and turned to the hostages. "Sorry tay have bothered ye missus," he said to Annie. "We'll be away now, and thanks fer the tay. Don't any of yees leave the kitchen for at least half an hour," he warned, waving his revolver.

With a quick look up and down the street, they ran for the car and seconds later, it was speeding up the street. Near the top of the street they whipped off their masks, and as they did they heard the explosion in Shipquay Street. As the car turned the corner at the top of the street, their shouts of joy echoed behind them.

Inside, Paddy looked at his wife and children and then at his daughter's boyfriend. Going over to the sink, he stared at the cups the two men had been drinking from. Suddenly, he grabbed the cups and flung them at the kitchen wall, smashing them to pieces. "Vermin!" he shouted, spittle splaying from his mouth. "That's what they are! Low, fuckin' vermin bastards!"

33

THE GUARDIAN OF THE WRECK

The collie waited, watching Paddy from beneath the oak table, its eyes turned upwards, and its black and white head resting easily on its dirty front paws. Its tail swished gently back and forth hitting the leg of the table with a dull, hypnotizing thud.

"Mornin' oul fella," he croaked, swallowing immediately. *What's the matter with me today?* he wondered. *I can hardly breathe, and it's so hot.*

Slipping out, the dog jumped to its feet and began licking greedily at its master's jaundiced, mottled hand.

Making his morning tea on the black stove proved a greater task than he thought, but at last he carried the steaming mug over to the table. Cupping his hands around the mug, he raised it to his lips, his thumb brushing against the several days' growth of white stubble on his chin. As he placed the mug back on the table he looked around. The dark, damp cottage walls seemed to close in on him. A few dusty photographs of his wife and family sat above the oak mantelpiece. Hanging bright and colorful beside them was a calendar.

Every year, ever since his one and only donation to the Nuns of Killieshandra, he had received a calendar from them. He squinted at it, and frowning, rose and took a close look at the date. *Holy Christ, is it my birthday?* He checked the date again. *Eighty-seven, I'm eighty-seven.* He sighed heavily and returned to the table shaking his head. *Where have all the years gone?*

The tea seemed to have helped him and feeling a lot stronger, he thought, *I'll go down.* Rising, he reached for his walking stick.

As he closed the wooden gate behind him, he glanced at the old cottage and turned to set off on the steep walk down the fuchsia-hedged road to Kinnagoe Bay. It had been a while since he had made the walk, and now familiar smells hit him as he slowly stumbled along the road.

Bees were already hovering hungrily among the scented hedges in their never-ending search for nectar. A magpie, with one of its beady eyes on the collie and the other on the juicy, dew-soaked worm lying on the edge of the hedge, landed in front of him. It was denied its meal for a while by the barking dog. Screeching, the bird lifted and flew out of reach of the attacking dog into the hedge, but its black wicked eyes never left the worm.

"One fer sorrow," muttered the old man as he walked on.

The road hadn't changed much since he had first taken his wife and family down it all those years ago. They had been the only family living in the glen then. Now several modern houses nestled on the steep slopes of it overlooking the picturesque bay. He remembered when he had brought his family to live at the cottage after his father had passed away.

The horse and cart had been loaded up with what little furniture they had and it took nearly three hours to make the ten-mile journey. The memory of that Saturday flit was as clear to him now sixty years later. How excited his son and daughter had been, and how strained and apprehensive his wife, Mary, had looked as she walked beside him behind the cart. She hadn't wanted to leave Greencastle, her hometown.

Suddenly a rabbit darted out from behind the ditch, its brown nose wrinkling with surprise, when it came face to face with the dog. With an amazed snarl, the collie tore after it into the hedge. The commotion snapped Paddy out of his reverie, and poking hard at the barking dog's rump with his stick, he shouted, "Here boy! Quit that! Here now."

He headed on, and shortly he was at the top of the winding path that led down to the beach. Pausing on the promontory, he leaned heavily on his stick, and shading his eyes, he gazed away out to the horizon. His eyesight hadn't faded much. He could still make out the misty outline of the islands off Scotland. Turning to his right, he looked along the near coastline, to the headland were the white waves crashed thunderously into the grey rocks tossing up a thick candy-floss of soup made of sea-weed and other flotsam the rough sea occasionally brought to the bay.

Kinnagoe Bay still looked much the same, as it had been when the survivors of the Spanish Armada ship, La Trinidad Valencera, had sailed into it. He had often tried to picture the scene on that stormy day as the great Galleon sank. He had learned about the history of the Armada at school, of course, and on cold winter nights he had often told his son and daughter of the sinking of the Valencera. Later, in the early seventies, he had enjoyed the duty of Guardian of the wreck of the Valencera.

Thirteen members of the City of Derry Sub-Aqua Club had found the galleon, and the Club had paid him a small remuneration to look after the wreck site in case any other divers tried to steal the cannon and other valuable artifacts that still lay beneath the clean clear waters of the bay. The BBC and some foreign television companies had filmed most of the salvage operations, and he had been featured in one particular documentary.

Perhaps it was this that had brought his son and his family all the way from America to visit him. It had been twenty years since he had last seen his son. He had been sixty-six then and the visit had disturbed him. He remembered studying his son with some astonishment, unable to take in the fact that this old man really was his son. He was dead now. A heart attack, the letter from his daughter-in-law had informed him. He didn't weep when he read it, for his son had been dead to him a long time. His daughter had married a Derry man, and she was living in the heart of the Bogside with her husband, and he had only met three of her adult sons. He had visited his daughter once, and it had disturbed him to see the change in her. It had been a long time since he had seen her. She had written a few times, but he had never replied.

He remembered sitting by the fire feeling a gnawing loneliness and depression a few nights after her wedding. He had missed his daughter then. They had been close, but now she, too, was gone. His wife had hugged him tight that night as he cried. He had cried for his son, too, and rocking in her arms, he made her promise never to leave him on his own.

"Ah well," he sighed as he stepped back onto the path again.

Barking, as if to say, "Can I go on?" the collie jumped around him.

"Alright boy!" he grunted. "Go on. Go on." He smiled as he watched his four-legged companion race speedily down the path past the car-park and onto the fine sandy beach where it began snapping at the waves, barking loudly as it frolicked excitedly at the water's edge.

Slowly, the old man picked his way along the narrowest part of the path using his stick more as the way to the beach grew steeper.

Halfway down, he stopped. His breathing had become much labored, and he felt hot again. Reaching up, he took off his battered cap, and wiping his sweating brow with the sleeve of his coat, he squinted up at the sun. Its full glare was hidden away in a hazy, white film of mist. *I shouldn't be that hot.* He stood, trying to catch his breath until he was breathing normally again.

A few minutes later he reached the quarry stonewall that separated the car park from the beach. Leaving his stick to one side, he leaned over the cemented top his stomach pressing against it. He watched, smiling, as the waves tried to catch his nimble-footed dog. *Mary would have loved this day.* No one about, just him and her. *What dog had they back then? It was the bitch, Lady. Aye Lady, that's what her name was. A lovely animal.*

Mary had died just over a year before the wreck had been found. The evening she died, calling for her son, he had cried, begging her to keep her promise not to leave him.

Every day for over a year after her death, he had gone down to the beach and walked for miles across the sand, up over the rocks and cliffs to the headland and back. Then the Valencera had been found.

He wiped his brow again. Reaching for his stick, he pushed away from the wall, stepped down from the car park onto the deep clinging sand, and headed along the beach, the collie snapping at the sand as it fell from his heels. Suddenly he stopped. Choking, he tried to catch his breath. His legs wobbled, unable to support his weight, and buckled causing his stick to dig deep into the sand as he fell on his face. As he did, he heard a bark, the sound sharp and unmistakable.

"Ladyeeee! Ladyeeee!" The voice, too, was unmistakable. It was hers, Mary's.

His head swam as he looked dazedly at his cap lying in front of him. Slowly, he raised his head and looked along the beach. It *was* his Mary. She was running across the sand towards him, with Lady barking by her side... and the waves stretched to carry him away.

34

MOVIE STARS

The three teenagers were grinning broadly as they approached the police barrier on Spencer Road.

"There's two new bastards on duty the day," whispered the tallest of them.

As if on cue they began to whistle, "The Sash Me Father Wore," nodding to each other when a small, blonde-haired Royal Ulster Constabulary constable stepped out from the barrier onto the footpath to block their way.

Constable McGowan scowled as he studied the grinning teenagers when they came nearer. *I'll give the Fenian bastards something to grin about.* The veins on each side of his pale, freckled face throbbed as the teenagers drew level. By then they were whistling louder. Each of them touched their forehead, walked around McGowan and headed on.

Startled that they hadn't stopped, McGowan made his move.

"Ahem, excuse me."

The teenagers, whistling louder than before, walked on.

"Excuse me!" shouted McGowan stumbling after them, his white hands and his even whiter knuckles gripping his rifle.

"Did you say somethin?" asked the smallest of the teenagers, turning to the one in the middle.

"Naw, I thought it was you."

"Excuse me!" said McGowan who was a step behind them. "Stop!"

Grinning, the teenagers stopped together and turning, they looked McGowan up and down.

"Who, us?" said the tallest of the teenagers.

McGowan grit his teeth as he left his rifle on the window sill of the house nearest to him. He pulled out his notebook. At the same time he nodded across the road to where his companion, Constable Joe King, was standing watching, his rifle at the ready.

"Yes, you," snapped McGowan glaring at the tall teenager who had long black hair and wore an imitation leather jacket and blue jeans.

"What's your name, address?" snapped McGowan.

The teenager looked at his companions and grinned. "Redford. Robert Redford."

McGowan studied Robert Redford. He wrote the name in his book. "Address?"

"Eh?"

"Your address," snapped the constable.

"Oh," said Robert Redford grinning at the other two. Then he looked across the street at King. He waved. "87, Strabane Old Road," he said. "Waterside, Londonderry." He stressed the word, Londonderry.

One of the other two giggled.

McGowan studied the tall teenager for a second or two and wrote down the address. "Stand over there," he grunted pointing to the wall of the house. He waited until Robert Redford was in position and turned to the second teenager, who had a black eye, brown hair, wore a short denim jacket and black jeans. "Your name?"

"Newman. Paul Newman," said the grinning teenager.

"Paul Newman," muttered McGowan writing the name in his book. *Paul Newman, eh. I'll Sundance kid you, you wee bastard.* "Address?"

"89, Strabane Old Road, Waterside, Londonderry," said Paul grinning at his pals.

Robert Redford sniggered.

"Londonderry," said McGowan slowly. He nodded to the smallest teenager. "Your name?"

"Martin Dean."

McGowan's upper lip curled as he studied the grinning teenager. Redford giggled again and Paul Newman waved to Joe King.

"Dean Martin," said McGowan as he wrote down the name.

"Naw," said the teenager.

"Eh? What do you mean naw?"

"My name's not Dean Martin. It's Martin Dean."

Redford and Newman giggled again.

"You just told me it was Dean Martin," snapped McGowan. He narrowed his eyes. "May I remind you, it's an offense to give an officer of the law your incorrect name."

"Is it? I didn't know that," said Martin. "But I didn't give ye an incorrect name. I told ye, my name is Martin Dean."

McGowan glared at him. "Martin Dean," he muttered. "Address?"

"24, Mountain View, Waterside, Londonderry."

McGowan's anger increased when he heard the other teenagers giggle. He glared at them. "Listen you, wee bastard," he said to Martin. "Do you see 'imbecile' stamped on my brow?"

Martin peered forward. "Naw. Maybe it got rubbed off."

Suddenly Robert Redford burst out laughing and Paul Newman began to giggle. Martin Dean, his face impassive, looked at McGowan—whose face had grown red with anger. He glanced across the road and nodded to King, who began to walk towards him.

"Joe, keep your eyes on these three stooges," snapped McGowan. "I'm going to do a body search on them. You, Redford," he snarled, "stand over here."

When Robert had joined Martin and Paul, McGowan snapped, "All of you face the wall and spread your legs apart. Now!"

On tip-toe, he reached up to run his stubby fingers along Redford's shoulders. As he did, Redford, ignoring him, turned to his companions. "Where we headed after?"

"Dunno Bobby," answered Newman. "The Bookies, I suppose."

"Then over fer a game of Snooker if we make a rise," said Martin.

"If we make a rise! Hey, easy on," exclaimed Robert as McGowan roughly thumped his hand up the inside of his left leg.

"I'll easy on you," snarled McGowan. "Now stand over there again. You're next, Newman," he snapped as he roughly pulled at Paul's jacket.

As he did Redford shouted to Joe King. "Are ye a good shot with that thing?"

"Fair enough," answered the constable coldly. "Good enough to put one in you if you don't behave yourself."

"Hey, is that a threat?" shouted Redford as he moved away from the wall. "Did yees hear that lads? The bastard threatened to shoot me. Did yees hear him?"

"Aye," said Paul, dropping his hands.

"You two shut it," snapped McGowan, and he began to search Martin.

When he was finished, he studied the smiling teenagers. "You three stooges think you're funny, do you?" he sneered. "Well I'll be checking your names and addresses and we'll see who's funny then."

"Big deal," hissed Robert, and his companions grinned.

"Aye, big deal, bastards," snarled McGowan taking a step towards Redford.

"Easy Phil," hissed King nodding to the security camera jutting out from above the Sangar. It was pointing straight at them.

"Hi, where ye goin' to hit me, then?" exclaimed Redford.

"I'll do more than hit you, you bastard," snapped McGowan, looking up at the camera again. "Now the three of you, get lost. If your names don't check out, you'll be sorry."

Grinning broadly, the teenagers began to walk past him. As they did, Robert Redford bumped against McGowan, almost knocking him off his feet.

"Sorry Constable," he said, following his companions.

Whistling "The Sash Me Father Wore," the movie stars headed on down Spencer Road.

35

ONE HALLOWEEN NIGHT IN DERRY

Anthony blinked at the ringed number on the calendar that hung above his bed. His grotesque, twisted mouth oozed saliva onto his broad chin as he smiled. His blood shot, good eye, narrowed again as he focused it on the month, his month, October, his day, the thirty-first. Halloween.

"Only a day to go," he grunted. His deep voice resounded around his bright bedroom. In the far corner of the room was a Sanyo television with a matching DVD player underneath it. All around the walls above his stack of DVDs hung pictures of his favorite movie stars, John Wayne, Jack Nicholson, Humphrey Bogart, and John Hurt. A big poster of *The Elephant Man* almost covered the opposite wall.

"Only a day to go," he sang now, his hump rising and falling as he danced clumsily around the room until he lost his balance, staggered against his bed, bounced off it and fell onto the floor.

His bedroom door opened a few seconds later.

"Did you knock, love?"

It was his mother. He smiled as he studied her. She looked very beautiful, even if her dark eyes were sad. She was wearing a long blue frilled dress and her black, grey-flecked hair hung in a pageboy style around her pale face. He licked his lips to allow his words to form more clearly.

"Naw, Mammy. I was just excited that's all. I was thinking about tomorrow night."

His mother smiled.

Her even, white teeth always made him think, why couldn't I have been born with nice teeth at least?

"Will you be okay tonight, Anthony?" she asked. "Daddy and I won't be back until after midnight."

He nodded. "I have the DVD Daddy got me, *The Witches of Eastwick*, Jack Nicholson."

"One of your favorites," said his mother as she walked over to his bed. "How many times have you watched it now?"

"Oh I don't know." He watched as she tucked in his blanket. "Mammy," he asked, "what's a Nuts Ball? I overheard Daddy and you talking about it."

She smoothed his blanket flat and straightened. "It's the dance organized by the Derry Chamber of Commerce. Your daddy and I were invited to it." She smiled. "He'll be up to see you in a minute."

Anthony stiffened, his frown twisting his face into an even more grotesque shape. His daddy didn't like coming into his room. But he smiled when his mother held out her arms to him. With a slurp, making the saliva disappear into his mouth, he shuffled towards her, his misshapen bare feet dragging across the thick carpet. He hugged her carefully, his enormous twisted hands clutching gently at her narrow shoulders. He had broken her shoulder two years ago in his enthusiasm to hold her. He had been horrified and still remembered the sound of the crack and his mother's scream of pain. His father had been angry.

"Your night's tomorrow night, love," she whispered, and he quivered. "Now I must hurry and get ready." She rose, and he moved his bulk out of her way to allow her to get past to the door where she turned. After blowing him a kiss, she whispered, "I'll call in when we get back."

He smiled, unable to stop the trickle of saliva that had been building up, from running onto the front of his Tee shirt. "Have a nice night, Mammy."

"I will. Thanks love." She opened the door.

"Mammy?" She turned. "You look lovely."

She winked at him and left the room. Quickly, he hurried to the door, and placing his best ear against it, he listened for her long soft sigh. A few seconds later, he heard the fourth stair from the top creak as she went downstairs. Remembering that his daddy would be up shortly, he switched on the television to wait. His hands clenched, and his heart began to pound until a long two minutes later his father knocked and came into his room.

He turned away as his daddy said, "We'll be going now, Anthony. Have you everything you need?"

"Yes, Daddy," he mumbled, turning to look at his tall, grey haired father who was wearing a black suit, white shirt and a black bow tie. Now it was his father who looked away. He stood by the door fumbling with the balsa wood Messerschmidt fighter plane he had made for his son and hung from the ceiling. "Good. Good. Well, I'll see you later, then."

"Goodnight, Daddy. Have a nice time."

"Yes... goodnight... ah," his father mumbled and quickly left the room.

Tears welled up in his eyes. *Why can't Daddy talk to me the way Mammy does? Why can't he look at me? Why doesn't he hug me?* He sniffed again, unable to stop, a single tear trickling down his face. He looked at the DVD lying on top of the television and sighed. Taking it out of its protective box, he fumbled with it for a few seconds to get the DVD into the correct position before slotting it into the machine. Pressing play, he waited.

Downstairs the front door slammed and he knew his parents had gone out. In a moment he had scrambled onto his bed to wait to be entertained.

The sharp click of his television set being switched off woke him, and he smiled when he saw his mother. He snuggled deeper into his bed as she bent closer, and he sighed when he felt her soft lips kiss his swollen left cheek. Seconds later, after she had left the room, the last thought he had as he drifted off to sleep was *Tonight's my night.*

Anthony pushed gently through the Derry Halloween revelers to the front of the car park near the Guildhall Square. In front of the crowd, at the edge of the fast flowing River Foyle, a scaffold had been erected. Three men standing on a platform out in the river got ready to start the fireworks and waterworks spectacular and shortly, with his eyes wide with excitement, Anthony watched as the first skyrocket soared into the air, streaming colored sparkling lights behind it. Now another rocket shot upwards and with a loud crack exploded out over the river. "Ohhs!" and "Ahhs!" came from the crowd as purple and red lights floated down to the muddy river. Now another man pulled a lever, and the waterworks spectacular began. Multi-colored sprays of water flew into the air, and the sky became a magic flashing color of light.

Anthony stood near two girls who were dressed as witches. They wore low-cut revealing short dresses, black knee-length high-heeled boots and black pointed hats. He moved closer to them and stared into the sky as more skyrockets cracked above him.

Suddenly one of the girls grabbed his shoulder. "Ohhh, look at that one!" she gasped, pointing to a stream of blue lights bursting into the sky. "Isn't it lovely?" He nodded and smiled at her. She smiled back, and for a second his heart stopped, but she didn't cower away from him. His attention was drawn to the scaffold as a man put a light to three Catherine wheels. The revolving bright fireworks whizzed around and around throwing off different colored smokes and lights and the crowd cheered louder. As the Catherine Wheels spun, Anthony looked back. Thousands of Derryians, many dressed in out-landish costumes and wearing rubber and papier-mâché masks were enjoying the festivities.

Over to his left, he saw someone dressed as the terrifying Grim Reaper, wearing a long white sheet and a skull mask. The Reaper carried a cardboard scythe with a bent pointed end. Other girls were dressed as witches and several young men were disguised as women, their overdone makeup, making them look even more terrifying than one young man who was made up to look like Frankenstein's monster.

The fireworks display lasted almost an hour, but to Anthony it only seemed a few minutes. With loud claps and cheers the crowd began to leave the car park and head towards Guildhall Square where John Anderson and his Big Band had already begun their first number.

"One, two, three o'clock, four o'clock rock..." The pulsating music quickly drew the crowd and the squeals and roars of the young people made him feel even more excited as he joined them.

High above, the old Guildhall Clock looked down on all the madness.

In the middle of the Guildhall Square, near where Anthony was stand-ing, four youths dressed as Nazis, wearing replica uniforms and Swastika armbands, began to dance with some girls. Very soon the square was filled with jiving and dancing couples. A girl with a false moustache, dressed like a gangster and wearing an oversize man's suit, a Dick Tracy hat and holding a toy machine gun stood on her own watching her two girlfriends. They were similarly dressed and were laughing and dancing with two of the Nazis.

With a grunt, Anthony pushed towards her. "Would you like to dance?" he asked, quickly licking the saliva from his lower lip.

"Aye surely, c'mon," replied the girl giving him a cheeky smile.

Gently, he pulled her by the hand into the dancing throng. The music beat in tune to his bouncing hump as he did an awkward jive with the girl.

"What's yer name?"

"Eh?" he shouted holding his hand up to his misshapen good ear.

"Yer name? What is it?"

"Quasimodo," he replied with a saliva-accompanied grin.

"Ha, ha, ha, that's a good wan. And I'm Esmeralda." The girl laughed, her eyes flashing eerily, as the bright lights from a line of different colored bulbs that surrounded the square reflected from them. With a grunt, he too began to laugh, his hump quivering like a jelly.

He was enjoying himself, but all too soon the dance was over, and he watched the girl join her friends. He smiled sadly as he saw the girls disappear into the crowd. With a grunt, he looked up at the clock. It was 11:25. *It's nearly over.* Pushing gently into the crowd, he made his way over to Shipquay Gate. A minute later, he was climbing the steps up to the Derry Walls. He ambled over to where a huge black siege cannon sat pointing towards the Guildhall. Nimbly, he climbed onto it and easily pulled himself along the barrel where he sat astride it, his short legs dangling on each side. He stayed there for almost a half hour, looking down at the people hurrying out of the square. It was beginning to rain.

Five minutes later, only a few people remained in the square, and with a heavy sigh, he climbed down and made his way back to Shipquay Gate. As he slowly headed up the steep Shipquay Street, he heard the Guildhall Clock strike the hour of midnight. Halloween was over.

Fifteen minutes later he reached his house. Looking around to make sure no one could see him, he rang the doorbell.

His mother appeared almost at once. "Did you enjoy your night, love?" she asked, smiling as she moved aside to let him in.

"Yes, Mammy. I had a great time."

His mother raised her eyes.

He knew she wanted to hear all about it. "Mammy, I'm tired now. But I'll tell you all about it tomorrow."

At the bottom of the stairs, he turned. "Night night, Mammy." He hurried up to his bedroom to dream of next year and Halloween, when he could be normal again.

36

THE OLD SCHOOLHOUSE RESTAURANT

The sun burned down on the left hand side of Spencer Road as Johnny Conaghan leaned against the warm white wall that fronted the new Credit Union Building. "Whew," he whistled through his parched lips. "It's hot!" His head swam and bubbles of sweat glistened on his white brow in the early morning sun.

Raising his head, he looked up the road. Thirty yards further on, he could see the metal summer seat at the top of Lower Fountain Hill. The seat faced up the steep Fountain Hill that ran adjacent to Spencer Road. Taking a deep breath, Johnny pushed away from the wall and tottered unsteadily towards the seat, gripping his walking stick tighter to steady himself.

Two minutes later, he reached it, and with his knee bones cracking loudly sat down. Taking another few deep breaths, he waited until the dizziness subsided. With his back rigid, he still held onto his blackthorn stick that he had planked directly between his boney knees. He looked around. Spencer Road was deserted except for a dog that had taken up its usual vigil, outside the gate at Finlay's butcher shop.

A sign swinging in the light breeze above the footpath at the bottom of Fountain Hill caught Johnny's eye. "The Old Schoolhouse Restaurant," he muttered. The new restaurant was an extension to the Coachman's Pub. It had been converted from Derry's first national school that had been used in recent times as a Blacksmith's forge and a dwelling for an old Waterside family called the Elliot's.

A restaurant? Is that what's become of my oul school? I wonder what Foley would have had to say if he saw the oul school now? Johnny's narrow shoulders shook as he laughed quietly at the thought. A traffic warden had just come up the steps that led to lower Fountain Hill and was passing Johnny when he noticed him laughing. He smiled at the old man and gave him a nod. But Johnny wasn't even aware that the warden was there, for his mind was years away, back to when he was a pupil at the school.

"Now boys," the stout, black-haired teacher, Mr. Foley said. "On Monday the School Inspector, Mr. Fogarty, will be paying us a visit."

The boys' groans echoed around the small packed classroom.

"Now now, boys, there's nothing to be worried about. Mr. Fogarty won't ask you anything you haven't been taught already." He grinned as he looked around the boys. "I know you won't let me down."

The boys half nodded.

"You won't, will you?" the teacher said his smile replaced by his most menacing scowl.

"No, sir!" chorused the boys.

Foley's smile reappeared. "Good, good. Now let us begin our spelling lesson. Get out your slates."

The clatter of the desk-lids opening and the slates being banged down on them was deafening, and Foley grimaced. He watched as each boy raised a piece of chalk.

"Right. We'll begin with a fairly hard word today. I want you to spell the word 'perspiration.'"

As the rest of the boys thought about the word, and some of them began a tentative stab at their slates, Foley saw Johnny quickly write down the word. Johnny looked up, and Foley smiled at him. Johnny was his best pupil at English, and if the teacher had been a betting man he would have bet his life that Johnny had spelled perspiration correctly.

Later, when the lesson was over, he reminded the boys about the inspector's visit.

The dreaded day came. Some of the boys wore shoes, boys from well off families wore clean shirts. The teacher wore a tweed sports jacket and grey trousers. His thick hair was plastered flat and parted in the middle.

The inspector was due at ten and the hour from nine dragged by. Foley could see his pupils were nervous and their nervousness began to get to him. Tugging at his shirt collar he occasionally glanced at the classroom door. The boys fidgeted as they recited their tables. At five past ten, Mr. Fogarty knocked and entered.

Quietly, as rehearsed, the boys stood up. Foley's pale face broke into a nervous smile as Fogarty, who was wearing a black suit and carried a small leather briefcase, walked towards him.

Turning to the boys, Foley said, "Boys. Say good morning to Mr. Fogarty."

"Good morning, Mr. Fogarty," chorused the boys.

The thin faced, gimlet-eyed inspector looked around the class. "Good morning, boys," he said. He turned to their teacher. "I'd like to begin right away, if you don't mind. I have to visit St. Eugene's before twelve."

"Right, James Cross," said the teacher to a small stout boy nearest to him.

In single file, Jimmy Cross led the rest of the boys around the edge of the classroom, and moments later they were standing, heads erect, waiting.

Fogarty smiled, his smile making the boys feel more nervous as he walked slowly down the middle row of desks and sat on top of one. "Now," he said. "Let's see how good you are at arithmetic." Pointing suddenly at Cross, he said, "Boy, multiply ten by twelve."

Jimmy licked his lips. He was shocked at being asked first, but he thought quickly about the sum. "A hunnerd and twenny," he said quickly.

"A hundred and twenty," said Fogarty. "Correct." Pointing at another boy in front of him, he said, "You boy, multiply fourteen by three."

"Who me?" asked Mickey Shields, a tall, gangling bare-footed boy with red hair.

"Yes you, with the red hair."

"What was the sum, sir?" asked Mickey.

Fogarty sighed. Foley grit his teeth and tugged at his shirt collar. "Multiply fourteen by three," repeated the inspector.

Mickey thought about the answer for a few seconds. "Forty two, sir," he said, smiling and looking at Foley who smiled back at him.

After ten more correct answers the inspector said, "Well, you certainly know your sums. Now let us see how good you are at spelling."

Johnny smiled. He was glad arithmetic was over. Arithmetic was the only thing he was weak on.

Now pointing to Jim Carlin a pimple faced, blonde-haired boy, Fogarty said, "You boy, spell the word 'clean.'"

"Clean. C-L-E-A-N," said Jim smiling.

Pointing to Tommy Nichol, a tall, reed thin boy with a squint in his eye, Fogarty said, "You boy, spell 'unclean.'"

Tommy frowned as his hand went to his mouth, and he began to chew on his right forefinger nail. "Un...clean," he muttered.

Johnny and the rest of the boys held their breaths. Foley licked his dry lips. Then...

"Oh, unclean," said Tommy brightly. "U-N-C-L-E-A-N, unclean."

The breath being expelled from the boys hissed around the room. Foley coughed and wiped his lips.

Johnny looked at him and smiled.

"You boy, spell 'cleanse.'"

Johnny was still smiling at his teacher unaware that Fogarty had asked him to spell the word cleanse.

"Did you hear me, boy?" asked Fogarty angrily.

The boy beside Johnny nudged him, and it was only then that he realized the inspector was speaking to him.

"I asked you to spell the word 'cleanse.'"

Johnny gaped at Fogarty. His mind had gone blank. He tried to say the word, but his mouth had dried up. Gulping, he glanced at his teacher. Foley's eyes were wide as he nodded for Johnny to spell the word. This only made Johnny worse, and he shook his head as he tried to think. The inspector's eyes burned into him. The whole class was looking at Johnny. A boy beside the broad radiator at the bottom of the classroom giggled nervously, but no one looked at him. Foley's eyes widened even further as he stared at Johnny, the best speller in his class. It wasn't a particularly hard word, and Foley knew nearly all the boys could spell it. He was astonished that Johnny couldn't.

"Very well then," said Fogarty breaking the long silence. "Spell 'cleaning.'"

Johnny gulped, but managed to say, "C... cleaning..."

"Yes, boy. Cleaning. Cleaning," snapped the inspector. As Johnny's mind cleared, Fogarty swung to a boy at the bottom of the room. "You boy, spell, cleaning."

After that the rest of the inspector's questions were a blur to Johnny.

At 11:00 Fogarty left after praising the boys and their teacher. When he was gone the boys returned to their desks. Smiling Foley said, "Boys I think as a reward you can all go home early for your dinner. But be back here at 1:00 again!" he added, shouting above the sound of the cheering boys.

Johnny was the last to get up to leave. He was still numbed by his failure to spell cleanse. Foley's head was bent as he read the inspector's signed report. At the door Johnny stopped. Then before he could stop himself he blurted out, "C-L-E-A-N-S-E. Cleanse!"

Raising his head Foley stared at him. He smiled. "Yes John. I knew you could spell it. Now run along."

Smiling, Johnny closed the door. With a loud, "Yippee!" he ran down the steps, turned left and raced up Fountain Hill.

Maggie Collins carrying two heavy bags of groceries just happened to be passing when Johnny slid sideways off the seat and hit his head hard on the footpath. Shocked, the thin woman dropped her bags and bent to help him. Dazed and dying, Johnny stared at her as she raised his head.

"C-L-E-A-N-S-E." he whispered.

"What?" asked Maggie.

"Cleanse," said Johnny smiling, his face grotesquely twisted as blood bubbled from his mouth, for now he was back in the classroom again, and the inspector was asking him to spell cleanse. The boys and Mr. Foley were cheering as Johnny slowly spelled the word correctly. Johnny looked at the inspector and smiled for he too was cheering.

In the ambulance, before he died, Johnny spelled cleanse for the last time.

37

THE OUL HAND

The ruddy-faced man clad in the Aran pullover held out a tanned, calloused hand to Maureen. "Mind yer step there, missus!" The strange touch of him made her flinch, but she gripped his hand tightly. She flinched again as he tugged gently reaching for the crook of her elbow, and she allowed him to lead her down the wet wooden steps into the deep hollow of the bobbing boat.

The engine was already ticking over its, "put! put! put!" echoing across the dark Lough Derg as Maureen stumbled across to the stern of the cumbersome craft.

The rain was getting heavier. Shaking the wrinkles from her plastic coat before she sat down, Maureen pulled it on. As she tightened the belt around her slim waist and sat on the worn wooden makeshift seat, she glanced around at the rest of the pilgrims.

They aren't too many, not like the oul days. She looked across the broad boat at a young man with long greasy unkempt hair who had a denim-covered arm around his freckle-faced red-haired companion. They smiled at Maureen who gave them a quick smile back and quickly turned away, her eyes darting to three giggling girls who sat near her. Beside the teenagers sat an old couple. The grey-haired woman's arm was linked tightly on her husband's. In her other hand she held a rosary.

All of a sudden Maureen felt panicky as she swung to look at the redhaired girl again. Her own hair was red, not as red as it used to be, but red all the same. Wasn't there something about a boat sinking in Lough Derg many years ago, a curse, a boat with two red haired women on board?

A loud laugh made her turn back to the three girls, and her mind was once more at ease as she saw one of them had red hair, too.

"Right!" bellowed the captain as he swung hard on the spoked wheel.

A ferret-faced youth beside him quickly reeled in the looped mooring rope and carefully coiled it away beneath his Wellington boots. The youth sniffed loudly and wiped at his nose with the sleeve of his navy polo-neck before turning to look towards the island as the boat slowly moved away from the pier.

Maureen stared down at the deep water as it rippled quietly past, listening to the murmur of the Hail Mary's coming from the old couple. Somehow she felt irritated, and for a second or two she forgot why she was making the pilgrimage.

How many times have I made the trip to St. Patrick's Purgatory? God, it must be at least twenty-five. Let's see, I'm forty-two, and I'll be forty-three in August' She sighed. She had been seventeen when she had first visited Lough Derg with Jim.

Jim. Her whole life back then had been Jim. She had loved him. When he was twenty-one he had gone to America. She had never heard from him again. There had been other boyfriends, but no one had ever been able to match up to Jim. She had never married.

Another loud peel of giggling snapped her from her thoughts. One of the girls was leaning over the side of the boat and splashing water up at her two companions. Some drops of water hit Maureen in the face. Her lips tightened and she glared at the girl.

Giggling louder the girls ignored her and with a snort Maureen turned away from them and looked towards the island. *God, was I ever like that?* Too sensible, that's what Jim had said she was, the night he told her he was going to America. She had wanted to go with him, but there was her sick mother.

Jim's last words to her as the boat carried him away were, "I'll write ye when I get a job. I'll send fer ye."

How long she had waited for his first letter, but it never came. It was over a year before she realized she would never hear from him again. Two years later, her mother died. She remembered now how embarrassed and hurt she had been after she had visited Jim's parents to ask for his address. She had been determined to go to America to be with him.

Jim's mother had smiled and listened quietly, glancing occasionally at her husband as Maureen told her of her plans. Later Maureen had been so angry with Jim's mother for not telling her sooner that Jim was married with a "lovely wee baby girl."

That evening she had cried until she thought she would never stop. For days after she was in a trance. Even at Mass she thought everyone knew, knew how foolish she had been, how stupid. That year she had visited Lough Derg twice. Somehow doing the pilgrimage seemed to help her, help her forget.

As the boat drew nearer Maureen could make out the Pilgrims on the island already doing their penance. With their heads bowed and bare-footed, they stumbled their painful way over the sharp stones at the base of a tall wooden cross overlooking the slipway. The high church towered above them, the grey stone building, somber, cold and unwelcoming.

Two minutes later, a raucous blast from a brass horn fixed to the side of the boat announced to the passengers and the people on the island the boat had arrived.

Cutting the engine, the captain steered carefully towards the pier as the youth, with one hand holding the looped rope clambered nimbly along the edge, then leaped onto the pier. Moments later the boat bobbed gently to a halt.

A group of smiling people were waiting patiently on the pier for Maureen and the others to disembark. Minutes later the happy pilgrims were aboard.

Maureen stood watching as the boat carried them back to the mainland. *I wonder how long it will be before they forget.* With a sigh, she turned, skipping lightly up the slippery steps, eager to begin her penance.

38

WHO WAS THAT MAN?

I know you are not going to believe my story, but I'll tell it to you anyway and you can make up your own mind whether it is true or not. It happened last summer, the Derry August bank holiday, in fact, when my wife and I were staying with her brother and his wife in their holiday bungalow in Magheroarty, County Donegal.

The bungalow overlooked the pier and the long beach that stretched to Falcarragh. Beyond was the pointed promontory of the foreboding Horn Head. The bungalow was nestled halfway up the valley and behind it were sparsely populated hills dotted with a few quaint, whitewashed thatched cottages and many wall-steads. It was the wall-steads—the rain and wind battered remains of former homes—that interested me. It was on that first day of my holiday weekend that I rose early with a mixture of excitement and guilt, looking forward to two hours of treasure hunting.

"You're not bringing that thing. You'll ruin the weekend for us all."

I could still hear my wife's voice the evening we packed our weekend case. My promise had been that I would rise early, metal detect for two hours, and then put it back in the suitcase for the rest of the day.

Anyway, as I was saying, it was a beautiful, sunny summer's morning, and at 7:45 I checked the battery power on the display unit of my detector, and by 8:00 I was already moving through the winding dirt paths to the higher hills. One hour later, away up in the bee-buzzing, fuchsia-scented hills, I was happily engrossed in searching around the garden area of a wall-stead. I had a fairly successful hour, finding five old Irish pennies, one pre-decimal Irish shilling, and a small ring of indeterminate value.

After twenty minutes, I finished the garden and switched off my detector. It was almost 9:30. *I'll need to be getting back soon.* Scanning the hills further up, a little to my left, I spotted a tiny-whitewashed cottage. In a field just below the cottage, an old white horse was busy chewing on the long grass. *Maybe they'll allow me to detect around their cottage?* Quickly I set off up the narrow overgrown path to it. Three minutes later, I knocked on the door. The top half swung open a few moments later and a tall, tanned, white haired man wearing a cowboy hat greeted me with a friendly smile.

"Hi there. Top of the morning to yuh," he said with an American accent.

I took in his appearance as I asked his permission to metal detect around his cottage. The hat he wore was white. On his feet, he wore knee-length black leather cowboy boots. A checked shirt, blue jeans and a small scarf around his neck made up the rest of his attire. His dull blue eyes flickered over me, then taking a pair of horn-rimmed glasses from his shirt pocket he put them on. Looking down at my detector he said, "A metal detector, yuh say. What exactly does it do, pard?"

Smiling I explained. "It detects anything metal that has been buried or lost in the ground."

"Yuh don't say." Turning his head he called out, "Hey Tonto! Come here a minute tuh see this."

Tonto? I laughed to myself. But when I saw the old man with shoulder length gray hair, a tobacco colored face and wearing buckskins and moccasins appear from another room I almost choked.

"Guy here says he would like tuh detect around the cottage, says the thing will detect any metal lost in the ground."

The old Indian smiled, his leathery features crinkling into even more wrinkles as he said, "We could have used machine in old days."

"We sure could have, Kemosabay."

Kemosabay, I laughed to myself again. *This must be the old fella's faithful companion.* My thoughts were interrupted by the taller man.

"Could we watch, pard?"

"Sure," I said smiling, "Just a minute until I set the controls." Taking a coin from my pocket I placed it on the grass in front of the window of the cottage, and then I set the dials on my detector discriminator. When I was satisfied it was in the correct mode I began to sweep the detector over the grass. Almost at once, I received a signal. Bending I pushed my trowel into the earth, making three incisions. Then carefully lifting back the sod I unearthed a tiny spoon.

"Waal I'll be hornswoggled, Tonto. Did yuh see that?"

"Me think this good way to spend time," said Tonto.

"It sure would, old friend."

I caught the smile between them but drove a question out of my mind as I carried on. Ten minutes later, I had finished the front of the cottage. Straightening, I asked the taller man, "Would it be alright if I detected around the back of your cottage?"

Just then, a loud neigh from the white horse drew both men's attention.

"Look like Silver, him still hungry, Lone Ranger."

"Silver? Lone Ranger?" I questioned, but neither of the old men answered me. I watched as Tonto opened the gate and ran quickly down the field, his movements belying his age. I turned to the other man and saw that he, too, was watching Tonto. He had a broad smile on his face. Turning back, I saw Tonto swing lightly onto the old horse's back and with light kicks prodded him into a gallop. With a loud neigh, the horse stopped beside the gate, snorting excitedly.

"Ahhh Silver, old boy. How are yuh today, eh, eh, boy?" the older man whispered as Tonto dropped to the ground and ran to the back of the cottage. Seconds later, he returned with a basket of potatoes and a peeled yellow turnip. I watched for a few minutes as the two old men fussed around the big horse, then the impatient buzzing of my detector reminded me. I looked at my watch. It was 10:00 already.

"Would you mind if I did a quick bit of detecting around the back?" I asked. "I have to go soon."

Without turning around the tall man said, "Sure. Yuh just go right ahead."

I studied the two men for a few seconds then hurried around the back. Soon I was giving the back garden a quick going over but my thoughts were on my wife. I had promised her two hours and it was way past that now. I was about to switch off my detector when it give a loud beep. I bent to the ground quickly and began to dig furiously at the earth. Then I saw it. Gasping, I straightened up and stared at what I had found.

Suddenly, a noise behind me made me shove it quickly into my pocket.

"Any luck, friend?" It was the tall man.

"No, nothing." I lied.

His eyes fixed on me, then fell to the disturbed earth at my feet. He smiled. "Waal, keep trying. Yuh never know what yuh'll find. Say look, why don't yuh stay for some vittles. Tonto's just gone tuh fix some."

I looked at my watch. It was ten past ten. It would be past 10:30 by the time I got back. "No thanks," I replied. "I really must get back." I stared at him, trying to picture him as I remembered. "But maybe I could come up tomorrow?"

"Sure pard. Any time yuh want. Yuh'll be most welcome." He smiled again.

When I reached the bottom of the field, I stopped and waved. The tall man was patting Silver's neck. He waved back. I stared for a few moments longer, then slipped my hand into my pocket to feel for the thing I had found. I shook my head. *It couldn't be.*

Seconds later, I was heading down through the maze of paths and grass-covered roads to the valley below. They were all waiting for me when I returned.

"Two hours, two hours—you promised," my wife hissed at me. "Now we're too late for the boat for Tory."

I tried to explain but it was no use. The others glared at me, trying hard to disguise their annoyance.

Later when I had my wife on her own, I told her what had happened. To substantiate my story I showed her the silver bullet I had found. She gave me one of her "Are you getting senile?" looks, then completely ignored me for the rest of the day.

The next morning I was up early and quickly headed in the direction of the cottage. By now, I suppose you'll have guessed I never found it. I never found the two old men and the white horse again.

But, I still have the silver bullet. You can see it any time you like.

39

BACK IN BRIT'

The shop doorbell pinged, alerting the shopkeeper. Squinting over his gold-framed glasses, he looked up to see who had come into his shop. It was Christmas Eve and most of his customers had called early in the morning to pick up the sporting goods they had laid by, and apart from that he hadn't been particularly busy.

Now he studied the young man with short black hair who had just entered. He wore a light blue tee shirt under a blue denim jacket. His blue jeans were tattered and on his feet he wore heavy black leather boots. Looking through his shop window, the shopkeeper saw three other young men outside, similarly dressed. One of them was smoking, and occasionally they glanced up and down the grey, wet Derry Street. Soldiers, he thought, his attention drawn again to the young man in his shop.

Moving along a row of double-lined, one-piece wetsuits hanging limply from a long, shiny rail, the young soldier stopped and gently squeezed the neoprene material of one of the suits, then turned to the shopkeeper.

"Have you any kayaks, mate?"

"Kayaks? Oh, canoes. Yes, I have the new range of Perception can...er, kayaks upstairs. Would you like to see them?"

"Sure, mate."

The shopkeeper removed his glasses and put them beside the sports brochure he had been reading, then rose from his chair and walked quickly to the door. He turned a sign that read, "Back In Five Minutes," locked the door, then walked to the bottom of the stairs.

"Do you canoe?" he asked, looking into the soldier's brown eyes.

"Not 'ere mate, back in Brit'. We can't 'ere."

The shopkeeper looked sympathetically at the young man, not knowing what to say to him... but he wanted to say something. Instead, he said quietly, "If you'd care to follow me."

Slowly he climbed the stairs, leading the young man up to a long, narrow room that was above the main part of the shop. Here, canoes of all types lay in rows on the floor. Whistling appreciatively, the soldier dropped to his knees beside a sixteen-foot Canadian Kayak. Slapping the sides of it, he looked up at the shopkeeper.

"Polyethylene; roto-molded plastic," the shopkeeper said. "That's what all the best canoes are made from these days."

"When I go 'ome, I'll have to get me one of these."

"Home? Where's home?"

For a few moments the young man stared at him, saying nothing. The shopkeeper tensed.

"London," said the young soldier with a smile.

The shopkeeper relaxed.

"Plenty of good kayaking there," the soldier continued. "Me and me dad used to kayak a lot. We 'ad a Canadian. It was made of fiber glass. We took it out on the river near 'ome. Two years ago. It was a great summer. We camped a lot, too." A thoughtful expression clouded his face. Then his voice grew cold. "Dad died. I joined up soon after." The young man frowned and looked steadily at the shopkeeper, realizing he had said too much.

The shopkeeper looked away, then to change the subject he pointed to a pile of different types of paddles that lay in a heap by the long window. "That's what's left of the new range of Schlegel paddles I got in for Christmas."

Straightening, the soldier studied them, then he crossed the room and bent down to pick up a right-handed, curved paddle. Stepping away from the window, he stood with his legs slightly apart and then rocked to get his balance. Feeling the weight of the paddle, he slipped it evenly through his hands. Suddenly he snorted a few times and began to paddle. Left, right, left, right, the yellow fiberglass blades of the paddle became a flashing blur that had the shopkeeper growing dizzy as he watched. Suddenly, with a final, vigorously loud snort, the whirling blades stopped and breathing easily the soldier replaced the paddle. "Nice paddle that, mate," he said.

"Well you certainly know how to handle one," the shopkeeper said admiringly.

"I told you, mate. I did a lot of kayaking back 'ome."

"Are you going home for the Christmas weekend?"

"No, mate. End of February."

The shopkeeper gave him another sympathetic look.

"Anyway, mate," the soldier said. "Thanks for showing me your kayaks."

Following him downstairs to the front door, the shopkeeper opened it. The bell pinged again.

"Cheers, mate."

"Yes, ah...cheers."

Pressing his face against the door, the shopkeeper stared up the street after the soldiers. Then stepping back, he sighed, shook his head then he returned to his sports brochure.

It had turned out to be busy day after all and he was tired. The rain had poured down all afternoon and he was glad to close his shop for the long Christmas weekend. After setting the alarm, he hurried outside and as the rain battered against his back, he locked the front door, pulled down the steel shutters and locked them.

Driving home he smiled as he thought about the three-day holiday with nothing to do but sit in the comfort of his own home with his family and relax. Licking his lips, he thought about the fine dinner that would be ready and laid out for him on the table by the roaring fire when he got home.

What's that up ahead? he thought suddenly, snapping out of his reverie as he noticed the traffic slowing down. With his wipers working overtime, he peered closer to the windshield as he tried to see more clearly through the heavy rain. Not a check-point? he groaned as he pulled in behind a Volkswagen and waited until it was his turn.

Winding down his window, he stared out at the streaked, blackened face of a soldier.

"Would you mind getting out of your car and opening your boot, sir?"

Cursing silently, the shopkeeper switched off the engine. He pulled the collar of his tweed coat up around his neck and stepped out into the downpour.

Two soldiers, their faces blackened, one carrying a rifle and the other a flashlight, walked with him to the back of the car, their heavy boots splashing through the puddles. When they reached the trunk of the car, the shopkeeper fumbled with his keys in the rain, but eventually inserted the key in the lock and pulled it open. One of the soldiers stood beside him while the other searched inside, pulling out a canvas tool bag so he could shine his light into it. Holding the bag in one hand, the soldier then shone his flashlight all around the inside of the trunk, until satisfied, he replaced the bag inside. He switched off his light and straightened.

"OK, mate. You can go ahead."

As the shopkeeper banged the hood of his trunk closed, both soldiers walked to the front of the car. The shopkeeper, who was soaking wet by now, hurried after them to the heat of his car. As he quickly sat down and belted up, he heard one of the soldiers shout, "Cheers, mate!"

He looked out the window and saw one of them wave him on.

Minutes later he was backing up his driveway. Switching off the engine, he paused before getting out. In the rearview mirror he could see the flickering shadows from the flames in the fireplace and the small Christmas tree standing by the window. He smiled as he walked to his front door, and turning the key he pushed the door open and stepped inside.

He was home.

40

PICASSO, WARHOL & A WIG

Eamon "Docs" Doherty, the barman at the Rockin' Chair pub, was cleaning the same beer glass for the sixth time as he strained to listen to the banter from the table across the room. His pale face almost shone in the dull light. A thin strand of hair was plastered across his head, starting at the top of his left ear and extending to his other ear in a vain attempt to cover his equally pale and balding head.

"Picasso was no painter," Dillon was saying.

"What?"

"Yer man, Picasso—the Italian guy, with the baldy head."

McGinn shook his head and raised his grey, bushy eyebrows at the other three men sitting at the table with him. Four half-empty pints of beer sat in front of each man. "What do ye mean, Picasso was no painter?" McGinn sneered. "Wise up, Dilso! *Picasso was no painter!* Huh!"

"That's what I said," exclaimed the thin-faced Dillon. "He was a con artist."

"Dilso, Picasso was not a con artist. His paintin's sell fer millions. How does that make him a con artist? And fer your information, Pablo Picasso was Spanish, not Italian."

"Italian or Spanish—whatever! He was a European con artist! Imagine paying a million smackers fer a paintin' with three eyes in it and bits of legs and stuff attached to it. That's what I call a con job!"

"Dilso," said Terry Moran, who sat beside him. "Picasso, the *Spanish* artist, was one of the most talented, celebrated artists of the twentieth century."

"Talented? Celebrated? Me arse! Ye don't need talent to paint shit like that."

Dillon looked at Paddy Stewart, who sat beside McGinn. "Your daughter could paint better."

Paddy Stewart frowned, trying to figure out whether Dillon had just insulted his seventeen-year-old daughter, who had Down's syndrome, or if he was praising her.

"And what about Warhol?" asked McGinn, after taking a drink of his beer, bringing what was left in his glass equal to the other three. "I suppose ye'll say he was a con artist as well?"

"Who?"

"Warhol."

"Who the hell is Warhol? Is he anything to Paddy Warhole from Deanery Street?"

McGinn shook his head in exasperation. "See, Dilso, yer thick."

"I am not," snapped Dillon, looking at the others to see if they agreed with him." Who is this Warhole guy, then?" he asked in a subdued voice.

"Andy Warhol was only one of the best known of the twentieth century artists."

"Aye, well I never heard of him."

"Have you ever seen a paintin' or a print of Marilyn?"

"Marilyn... Monroe?" Dillon frowned. "I... I think so. I dunno..."

"The one where she is painted a different color? There are about twelve Marilyn's on the paintin'?" said Stewart.

"I've seen that one," said Moran. "Did Andy Warhol do that?"

"Aye, and ye must have seen his Campbell's Soup paintin'?" said McGinn.

"What?" exclaimed Dillon. "Soup? He painted soup? That's some artistry that, paintin' soup. Hah!"

"Not the soup, thicko," snapped McGinn. "The cans! He painted the cans. Warhol's paintin's of soup cans were very popular in the sixties."

"He painted Coke cans and Coke bottles too, didn't he?" said Moran.

"Coke cans? Who the hell would want paintin's of Coke cans hangin' in their hall?" said Dillon.

"Millions of people, especially if they were painted by Andy Warhol," said McGinn.

"Well I wouldn't—no matter how much they were worth."

The four men took long sips of their remaining beer. Over at the bar, Docs was smiling. McGinn, Dillon, Moran and Stewart had been coming to the

Rockin' Chair bar ever since he could remember, and he always enjoyed their banter. Yesterday afternoon they had argued and discussed John F. Kennedy's relationship with his wife and Marilyn Monroe. These discussions—and the arguments that usually followed—were almost always about some documentary that had been on the television the night before.

Docs glanced at the clock. It was quarter to two. It would soon be time for the first race. The four men never missed the first race.

"He was gay, wasn't he?" said Moran.

"What?" the others chimed in as everyone looked at Moran.

"Yer man, Warhol. He was gay."

McGinn glanced at the other two. "Aye, I... I think so." He looked at Moran. Terry was the only one of the four who was single.

"What about it?" asked Dillon, then took a quick sip of beer.

"They say gays are talented... artistic," replied Moran.

"Do they?" said McGinn.

"Hitler was a painter, wasn't he?" said Dillon. "*He* wasn't gay. Dear Lord!" he gasped. "Maybe he was! He had a funny walk, didn't he?"

"What do ye mean, he had a funny walk?" exclaimed Moran. "All gays haven't funny walks."

"That's quite correct," said Stewart. "If ye could tell a gay by the way he walked then everyone would know who they were."

They all looked at Moran.

"You've got a funny walk, Morany," said Dillon.

"I have not," snapped Moran rising to his feet.

"He has, hasn't he?" said Dillon to the other two.

"Wise up, Dilso," snapped McGinn. "He's only windin' ye up, Morny."

"I... I had an accident when I was a teenager. That's why I walk the way I do," exclaimed Moran.

"Aw, aye, that's what you say," said Dillon, nudging Stewart in the ribs.

"The Duke could have been gay," said Stewart.

Dillon stared at him. "The Duke? The Duke of Edinburgh?"

"Wise up! The Duke—John Wayne, my favorite actor. Ye must have seen the way he walked? Take a look at the last scenes in the movie, *The Searchers*."

"I saw that movie," said McGinn. "Brilliant. What about the last scenes?"

"The scene when he walks away from the ranch house door with his arse swinging about like a hula girl's."

"Stewarty, yer not trying to tell me John Wayne, the Duke, was gay?" exclaimed Dillon. "You'll be tellin' me next that Randolph Scott was gay!"

"Er... I think you'll find that he was, Dilso."

McGinn frowned. "But yer right, Stewarty, the Duke could have been gay. He definitely had a funny walk..."

"Not everyone with a funny walk is gay," shouted Moran suddenly.

"Another pint, lads?" shouted Docs. "The first race will be starting soon."

Dillon glanced at the big clock behind him. "Aye, we've time fer another." He looked at the others. "Whose round is it?" They all looked at him.

"I think it's yers," said McGinn.

"Maybe we should wait until after the race," said Dillon quickly.

"Aye, and by then ye'll either be skint or ye'll have forgotten it's yer round," snapped McGinn.

"Naw, I won't. Ah the hell with it, Docs! Pull them. I couldn't stand the yammin' if I didn't buy me round."

"Harp all round," said Docs, pulling the first pint.

"The Pope could be gay," said Dillon after draining his glass.

"The Pope?" Everyone stared at Dillon as Docs reached to pull the second pint.

"You've never seen the Pope walkin', have ye?" said Dillon. "I'm just saying he could be. Maybe that's why ye don't see him walkin'."

"Wise up," snapped Moran.

"Well, he could be."

"Not logical," said McGinn. "They'd hardly elect a gay Pope."

"Why not?" said Moran reaching to drain his glass.

"They wouldn't, that's all," said McGinn. "And goin' by yer logic, Dilso, that could mean Stephen Hawkings is gay. You've never seen him walkin', have ye?"

"He can't walk, can he," snapped Dillon with a frown.

McGinn shook his head and blew an exasperated breath. "Look, all this talk about gays is boring. Let's get back to Picasso and Warhol."

"I'm bored with them two," snapped Dillon.

"Well it was you who started it all, comin' out with shit like, 'Picasso's a con artist.'"

"He was."

"How was he? It wasn't Picasso who sold his art, it was his agent. It wasn't Picasso who had his paintin's hung in the Louvre and museums all over the world, it was his agent. Picasso's art is there because people like it, because Picasso and Warhol were talented geniuses."

Everyone looked at Dillon to see what comeback he would have. Just then Docs came over with the drinks. After Dillon had paid, everyone took a long drink.

"I could be a talented painter too," said Dillon. "And maybe I don't know it."

"What do ye mean?" asked McGinn looking around the table to see if he had the same amount of beer in his glass as the others.

"Well, McGinn, ye have to admit, anyone could paint like Picasso. A four-year-old could do better. My wee niece, Patricia, painted a house at school the other day and if you had shown that paintin' to me and said that Picasso painted it, I wouldn't have argued with ye."

"Yer niece?" said Stewart.

"Aye, Patricia."

"Patricia Picasso," laughed McGinn. The others giggled. Everyone took a drink.

"That was his best movie. He should have won an Oscar fer it."

"What?" Everyone looked at Stewart.

"*The Searchers*. That was his best western, his best movie."

Back behind the bar, Docs leaned in closer. He knew Stewart was a movie buff.

"I liked *The Quiet Man*," said Moran.

"*The Quiet Man* was shit," snapped Dillon. "Irish shit. Sure Ireland was never that way, the way it was depicted in the movie."

"The movie was shot mostly in America," said Stewart.

"Was it?"

"Aye."

"I liked the Duke better in his earlier movies," said McGinn. "When he got older he didn't look right."

"What do ye mean? He won an Oscar fer his portrayal of Rooster Cogburn," said Stewart. "Fill yer hand, ye son of a bitch," mimicked Dillon.

"Naw," said McGinn. "It was the wig he wore. No hair looked like yon." He nodded to the bar. "Can ye imagine Docs wearing a wig like John Wayne's? Sure he wouldn't look right."

Dillon giggled, causing the others to giggle as well. Docs growled and rubbed harder on the glass. "Hey Docs, why don't ye get a wig?" laughed Dillon. "Ye never know—ye might look like the Duke."

McGinn and the others and three men at the far end of the bar room laughed.

"Dillon," growled Docs, leaving down the beer glass. "If ye want barred, just keep it up."

"Sorry... sorry," said Dillon. "Keep yer hair on."

Everyone in the bar laughed louder. Suddenly the glass slipped from Doc's hands and smashed on the barroom floor. At the same time, McGinn rose to his feet.

"Christ, look at the time! The first race will be startin'." He made for the door. "Docs, keep our beer there. We'll be back shortly."

Without another word the men hurried out of the door.

Docs glanced around. The three men at the far end of the bar room were leaving by the side door. When they were gone, Docs began to clean up the broken bits of the beer glass.

After he had dumped the broken glass into a plastic container beneath the bar, he came out from behind the counter and walked towards the table Dillon and others had been sitting at. Looking at the door, he picked up Dillon's beer, hawked back and let the green phlegm drop slowly into the glass. Smiling, he looked at the door and replaced Dillon's beer glass on the table.

"I'll keep me damn hair on, all right," he muttered as he returned to the bar.

41

The Reluctant Volunteer

The few hairs on Joseph Doherty's head whipped at his gaunt face as he bent to open the steel shutters that covered the front of his news agent shop window. Every day, seven days a week—ever since he had had the shutters installed at the height of the Troubles in 1972—he had opened them. As the well-oiled shutters noisily slid into position above his head, Joseph checked his window. Satisfied that everything was in order, he grabbed the first of two bundles of daily newspapers, pushed open the shop door and went inside, automatically turning the blue Visa "Closed" sign around to show a faded "Open." With a grunt, he returned to the front door and bent over, pulling the heaviest bundle of newspapers and magazines inside.

Reaching for a pair of scissors that hung on a piece of cord by the cash register, he cut the cord holding the newspapers together. Ten minutes later he had all the daily papers carefully arranged in neat rows on the counter. As he finished, he stared at the headlines on one of them. With a heavy sigh he walked around to the window and looked up and down the street. There weren't many people about, but it was early yet. He felt apprehensive.

Earlier that morning he had listened to the reports on the radio about the one-day strike against the Anglo Irish Agreement. He had been in two minds about what to do, but in the end he decided to open his shop. He didn't support the strike, and besides, his customers would be looking for their newspapers. He couldn't let them down. Anyway, what would he have done with himself all day? He had no hobbies. His little news agent stand had become his whole life since his wife died.

Around eleven o'clock, after he had finished putting the *Woman's Monthly* magazines in their racks, he heard the doorbell ring. Turning around, he saw Paddy McCullough come diving into the shop, his usually tanned face quite pale as he croaked through dry lips, "Jesus, Joe! I was nearly caught there. They're comin'. They're comin' down the street…"

"What? Who?" asked Joseph, looking towards the window.

Before he could question Paddy further, he heard the heavy *thump, thump, thump* of leather boots drumming into the street, moving closer. A crowd of about two hundred men and youths were marching in full formation down the dull and wet Derry Street. Most of the men wore green combat jackets; many of them had their faces covered up to their eyes in red, white and blue scarves. At the head of the marchers, about twenty heavily armed R.U.C. men marched on each side of the footpath, while another thirty or so policemen came behind them, followed at last by three noisy, grey land-rovers.

Joseph and McCullough stood transfixed with fear as the marchers came closer. Just as the marchers were passing his shop, the hair on the back of Joseph's neck stood out and his heart pounded with fear when he saw a tall, masked, burly man point at the shop with a short wooden baton. Two men beside him immediately left their ranks and ran to the shop door.

"Jesus Joe, they're comin' in," gasped McCullough, quickly moving towards the back of the shop. The doorbell pinged sharply as the two men, with their faces covered, entered. One of them, his eyes glinting like a trapped ferret, stood by the door while the other man walked to the counter. He studied Paddy for a couple of seconds and then turned to Joseph. "You the owner?" he snapped in a broad country accent.

"Aye," stammered Joseph, glancing quickly at McCullough.

In a daze he felt the man roughly grab his hand and put a piece of paper into it. Staring down at the leaflet, Joseph saw two men's photographs. One was the somber looking Ian Paisley, and the other, a grim-faced James Molyneaux. Above their photographs were the words, ULSTER SAYS NO! printed in large blue letters. Raising his head, Joseph gave the man a sickly smile and muttered, "Thanks son."

"Aye thanks!" the man suddenly screamed, his eyes wild with hatred. "We'll remember you didn't close, ye bastard, ye!" With a snarl he swung around and strode to the door that was being held open by the other man. They both turned and glared back at Joseph and Paddy then hurried away after the other marchers.

Trembling, Joseph heard Paddy say, "Whew. Thank goodness that was all."

Joseph stared again at the leaflet. The photographs were a shimmering blur as his hand shook. Then the door bell rang again.

"Any problems?" asked a round faced, leather coated policeman, his bulky body half in and half out of the door. He smiled.

"Problems?" whispered Joseph. "No, no problems, officer. They just shouted somethin' and left."

The policeman laughed. "I didn't think they came in fer the papers." He looked at Paddy, his smile vanishing as he said, "Well if ye have any trouble just report it to the station."

"Yes... yes, I'll do that officer. Thanks," said Joseph.

As the policeman hurried away after the marchers, McCullough went to the window and with his face pressed up against it, he looked up and down the street. "I'm gettin' tay hell out of here, Joe." He opened the door then turned before leaving. "You'd be better tay close, ye know?"

"Close?" Joseph stared at him. "Aye, aye, maybe I will."

"Well see ye the morra, Joe," said Paddy. Looking up the street, he hurried away.

Joseph's legs trembled as he walked slowly to the window. He pressed his face against the pane and tried to see how far away the marchers were. Sighing heavily, he reached for the Visa sign and turned it to "Closed."

Half an hour later the marchers, now led by two of Derry's Councilors, marched back up the street. The shutters covering the newsagent's shop front told them they had another reluctant volunteer.

42

THE AWAKENING

The rings on the disturbed calmness of the water grew bigger and bigger as the fish disappeared into the murky deep. Although he had been fishing, the trout rising from the water somehow disturbed him. It had interrupted the tranquility he had been lost in, remembering the first time he had been here with Rosie.

⁘

They were children then, as well as neighbors, living in the small village of Drumahoe.

"Me mammy will tan me if I get me new shoes wet, Tommy. Will you carry them for me?" Rosie's curly auburn hair bobbed about on her tiny head as she undid her shoes.

"Oh alright," he grumbled. "I'll tie them together by the laces and hang them around my neck. They'll not get wet there. Come on, hurry up and get them off."

Shortly, with his own and Rosie's shoes hanging around his neck, he was entering the shallow clear water. Gingerly stepping on the submerged flat rocks, he began to wade across the narrow stream to the far side.

"Wait for me, Tommy!" cried Rosie.

With a heavy sigh, he reluctantly stopped mid-stream to wait for her.

Rosie stumbled towards him, her freckled face flushed with the effort as she tried to keep from falling into the water.

"Oh come on, Rosie. You're very slow. Hurry up."

Her face was blazing when she reached him. "I'm really sorry, Tommy," she whispered.

He could still see her face and her bright green eyes looking up at him.

Suddenly a huge mosquito landed on his arm and got ready to pierce his skin, bringing him back to the present. Quickly he brushed the insect away and began to reel in his line. A few seconds later, he was wading back to the river bank. Clambering up it, he threw his rod beside his tackle bag and pulled out his flask. Soon he was eating the whole-meal bread sandwiches his wife had made for him. That memory of his young days had disturbed him somehow. The peacefulness of the day was gone.

"A relaxing day fishing," he had said to his wife that morning. He sighed and lay back, watching the water easing slowly towards the carry to tumble gently to the lower level below. *Retired*, he thought. *I'm retired, put out to pasture, thirty years working and now, now, nothing.*

"Good luck, Tommy. Enjoy your retirement. You've earned it," the Water Board manager had said, shaking his hand for the first and last time as he handed him the check.

He remembered that evening. How excited his wife had been. She was full of plans of the things they would do. Places to see, trips they would go on. But that had been last month and here he was, discontented and uneasy. A trout leaped from the water again as if to say, "Here I am; try and catch me."

"Ach, it's no use," said Tommy aloud. Two minutes later, he had gathered up his fishing tackle and was quickly walking away from the river and up the daisy covered fields to the main road where his car was parked.

He drove about two miles until he came to the Cozy Inn, the pub he had spent some time in these past few days.

"Any luck, Tommy?" the barman asked, pulling him a pint of his usual.

"Naw, far too bright, Paddy. Too bright."

"Aye, it's a lovely day, alright, but too bright for the fishing. Still Tommy, I envy you. You've all the time in the world now, now that you're retired."

God, thought Tommy. *He envies me. I'd swap my retirement for his job any day.* He sipped slowly at his beer, his eyes fixed on the row of glasses behind Paddy, not really wanting any conversation.

"Ah, come on, Da. Let's go home. Mammy will be waiting. Come on..."

Tommy blinked to see more clearly in the semi-darkness of the lounge. In the small snug at the far end of the bar a tall, unshaven man was drinking. A girl about ten years old was tugging on his arm.

"Houl on a minute, will ye. I'll be goin' in a minute. Be quiet now."

"Ah please, Da," the little girl whispered tearfully, lowering her voice when she noticed that Tommy was watching them.

Tommy studied the little girl's pitiful appearance. Her thin face peeking from her unkempt hair reminded him of an urchin in one of Charles Dickens novels.

"Da, Mammy will be crying if ye drink any more. Please don't drink any more. Please."

"Oh for God's sake girl, will ye be quiet? I told ye I'll be goin' in a minute." He glared at his daughter and took a quick drink from the whiskey glass.

Tommy turned away. Paddy caught his eye. "McLaughlin's got a drinking problem," he whispered. "His wife would crack up if she knew he was in here."

"Paddy! Give us another half, would ye?"

"Ah, please Da, no more. You promised."

Paddy hesitated and said, "I think you've had enough, McLaughlin."

McLaughlin glared at him. But holding out his glass he said, "Just one more, Paddy."

Paddy glared back at him. "I said you've had enough. Go home."

"Please, Da, let's go home. Please..."

Cursing loudly, McLaughlin slammed the glass down on the counter, stumbled out of the snug and into the bright sunlight.

"Wait for me, Da. Wait for me."

"Poor wee mite," said Paddy as he cleaned a glass. "It can't be much of a life for her or her mother. I bet when the little 'un grows up she'll be away. And who could blame her?"

"Aye," said Tommy thoughtfully. "Who could blame her? You have to give children a lot of your time." He thought now about his own daughter, who lived in America with her husband and three children. He had not had much time for her when she had been growing up. He had always been impatient, always in a hurry, never listening to her. Then one day she was gone.

"Another pint, Tommy?"

Looking at his empty glass and then at Paddy, Tommy said nothing as a grin slowly brightened his face. "No thanks, Paddy, I just don't have time." Without another word to the puzzled barman, he left.

Fifteen minutes later he was home. As he came into the sitting room his wife came out of the kitchen her apron still wet from washing the kitchen floor. "You're back early, Tommy. Did you catch anything?" She studied his flushed face, and frowning, she asked, "What's wrong?"

"Wrong, love?" Tommy smiled. "Nothing's wrong. In fact everything is right. You and I are taking a long holiday. We're going to America to see Rose and our grandchildren."

His wife studied his happy face. She sniffed as the tears filled her green eyes. "What brought all this on?" she asked smiling.

"Never mind, love. Come with me now into Derry. We'll need to book our flight."

"Now? But I'm not ready. I've still the floor to mop..."

"Ah, never mind the floor. Hurry up. I'll get my checkbook. You get your coat on. Hurry up." Quickly he rushed upstairs.

Two minutes later his waders changed for a pair of brown brogues, he came back downstairs. "Come on, love. What's keeping you? Hurry up." Opening the front door, he walked quickly to the car.

"Wait for me, Tommy! Wait for me!"

With a smile he stopped, turned, and walked back to the house. Closing the front door behind him he shouted, "I'll wait for you, Rosie! Take your time, I'll wait for you."

THE END

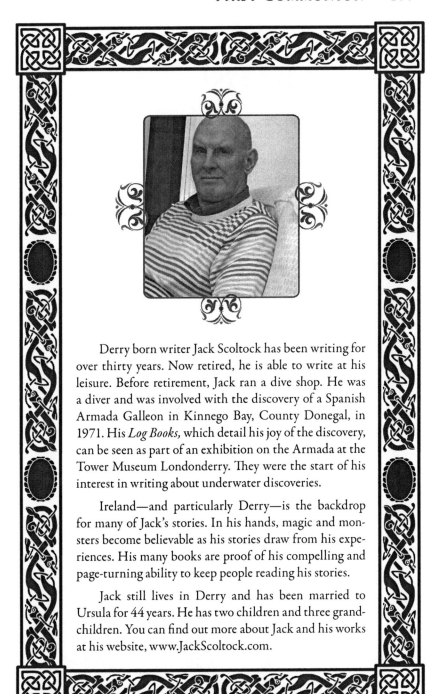

Derry born writer Jack Scoltock has been writing for over thirty years. Now retired, he is able to write at his leisure. Before retirement, Jack ran a dive shop. He was a diver and was involved with the discovery of a Spanish Armada Galleon in Kinnego Bay, County Donegal, in 1971. His *Log Books,* which detail his joy of the discovery, can be seen as part of an exhibition on the Armada at the Tower Museum Londonderry. They were the start of his interest in writing about underwater discoveries.

Ireland—and particularly Derry—is the backdrop for many of Jack's stories. In his hands, magic and monsters become believable as his stories draw from his experiences. His many books are proof of his compelling and page-turning ability to keep people reading his stories.

Jack still lives in Derry and has been married to Ursula for 44 years. He has two children and three grandchildren. You can find out more about Jack and his works at his website, www.JackScoltock.com.

ABOUT
BARKING RAIN
PRESS

Did you know that six media conglomerates publish eighty percent of the books in the United States? As the publishing industry continues to contract, opportunities for emerging and mid-career authors are drying up. Who will write the literature of the twenty-first century if just a handful of profit-focused corporations are left to decide who—and what—is worthy of publication?

Barking Rain Press is dedicated to the creation and promotion of thoughtful and imaginative contemporary literature, which we believe is essential to a vital and diverse culture. As a nonprofit organization, Barking Rain Press is an independent publisher that seeks to cultivate relationships with new and mid-career writers over time, to be thorough in the editorial process, and to make the publishing process an experience that will add to an author's development—and ultimately enhance our literary heritage.

In selecting new titles for publication, Barking Rain Press considers authors at all points in their careers. Our goal is to support the development of emerging and mid-career authors—not just single books—as we know from experience that a writer's audience is cultivated over the course of several books.

Support for these efforts comes primarily from the sale of our publications; we also hope to attract grant funding and private donations. Whether you are a reader or a writer, we invite you to take a stand for independent publishing and become more involved with Barking Rain Press. With your support, we can make sure that talented writers thrive, and that their books reach the hands of spirited, curious readers. Find out more at our website.

WWW.BARKINGRAINPRESS.ORG

Barking Rain Press

CPSIA information can be obtained at www.ICGtesting.com
Printed in the USA
LVOW101701030512

280236LV00004B/69/P

9 781935 460329